KANSAS

RUTHLESS KINGS
ATLANTIC CITY

BOOK TWO

K.L. SAVAGE

ISBN: 978-1-952500-41-1

LIBRARY OF CONGRESS CONTROL: 2021903494

PHOTOGRAPHY BY WANDER AGUIAR PHOTOGRAPHY
COVER MODEL: CLAYTON W
COVER DESIGN: LORI JACKSON DESIGN
EDITING BY: INFINITE WELL
FORMATTING: CHAMPAGNE BOOK DESIGN

FIRST EDITION PRINT 2021

READING ORDER

To all of those that can't seem to catch a breather and are busting their asses working from home, taking care of the family, working away from home, and still taking care of the family in these crazy times.

It's crazy out there. We aren't in Kansas anymore, folks.

And we hope this book brings you an escape from the harsh reality of the world we are living in today.

AUTHOR'S NOTE

I can't believe it's been a year since the light bulb went off in my head, and I had the random idea that I wanted to do this. As always, I shared my idea with my bestie, and we started hashing everything out. It was a random idea with tons of what-ifs and unknown variables but just like every other time Lynn said, "Let's go for it. Let's make it happen. All you can do is try."

Things might not be how we envisioned this when we started but the one thing that never changes is her support and her drive to help make our books the best they can be. I can't tell you how many times she goes without sleep working on something, so I don't have to. With the seed already planted, I called The Instigator, and I said, "Sooo feel free to say no but Lynn and I discussed this, and I think we can, but would you consider writing this MC book with me. Before you decide you should know I don't really have money for this and it's going to be a while before you see any money so just think about it."

Of course, she didn't even think about it she said, "I don't care, I trust you. If you think we have a shot at this, I'm in. I don't care about the money. I just want to be a part of it." Knowing how hard we all had it at that point in time, I couldn't believe she said yes, but she did. And for a long time, she was killing herself working full time and staying up all hours trying to keep up. Now let's get to my mom. If you knew our history, you'd think I had a death wish asking for anything. But pretty much like I did with The Instigator I said sooo mom, and I laid it all out for her, and she didn't even have to think about it. She handed over her credit cards and her perfect credit score and said, "I know you can do this, and it's going to pay off in the long run." It's been rough at times and even then, she just says it's gonna pay off.

Then there's my stepdad, he is the best. I'm pretty sure he talks about our books more than we do. I can't tell you how many times he'd say you need to write a book. Our books might not be what he had in mind, but he doesn't care. He still reads them. He is still one of our biggest supporters and will still pull all-nighters working on our stuff. Why? Because this is my baby. This is a random thought, a dream I had for me and my bestie and The Instigator.

Since it's our one year anniversary, I thought it was only fitting I shared with you how K.L. Savage started and tell some of the most important people in my life thanks for all they do because I know I don't say it enough.

Kansas

PROLOGUE

Sixteen years old,
Tulsa, Oklahoma.

I ALWAYS HEARD MY POPS SAY THAT IN ORDER TO GET RESPECT, YOU have to give it. I think that's the biggest load of shit I've ever heard.

Trust and respect are what people offer when they can't be trusted or respected. Everyone who says they aren't like that are nothing but liars.

And let's face it.

Everyone lies.

I'm only sixteen. I shouldn't be so damn cynical, but I am. My instincts have always been chalked up to being young, naïve, and paranoid, but I know better. It's how I know not to respect or trust my Pops. It's been that way forever. My hatred for him goes back years. I can't remember a time where I didn't look at him and wish he were dead.

There is something... off.

I don't know what it is. I don't know if maybe I'm just the piece of shit who has the problem, but my gut says my Pops is a liar. How is he lying or why? I can't say. I don't have an answer, but I know for the last few years, my mom has been depressed.

All she does is take a dozen different pills every day, and I think it has everything to do with him. Mom knows something, and if she doesn't, she feels it the same way I do.

"Man, that's the eighth strike in a row. What the hell is going on with you? You never don't swing the bat," my best friend Nigel shouts at me from the pitcher's mound. His arms are spread to the side, the ball in his throwing hand and the glove in the other.

I kick the dirt and swing the bat back up until it's lying on my shoulder. "Sorry. I have a lot on my mind." Nigel and I always come to the local baseball field every day after school to get in a little extra practice before the season starts.

"You okay?" he asks, jogging to me. His cleats kick red dust in the air, and when he stops in front of me, he has sweat dripping down his face. "What's going on, Amos? You know you can talk to me."

"It's nothing new."

"Your dad again?"

I nod, grinding my teeth back and forth. "You know I can't remember a weekend where he stayed with us. It's always been me and Mom. She isn't doing great. She's barely conscious half the time, man. I think she knows something is going on, and I want to find out what it is. I want to know where he goes on the weekends," I say, slamming the bat against my cleat to knock off the dirt.

"You don't think he goes to work like he says?"

I snort and squint my eyes toward the sky. "Not for a damn second. Every weekend he has a work trip? No. I don't believe it, and you know what? My mom deserves more than what she has right now. She deserves more than sleeping her life away because she's so damn miserable."

Nigel's hands fall to his hips and he spits onto the ground. "So let's find out where he goes."

"Really? You'd go with me?"

"Yeah, man. Let's lay this to rest. Let's see what the ass-hole is up to."

I shake my head and grab his arm when he starts to walk away. "I can't have you go with me. I don't know what I'll do to him if I find out it's something bad."

"I won't let you do anything stupid," Nigel tells me, clutching my shoulder with his hand. "Best friends, remember? Plus, I never liked your dad either."

"I don't know many who can see through his fake exterior. He thinks he has everyone fooled, but I know he is a damn snake, Nigel." I wrap my hand around the bat a little tighter, wishing my dad was in front of me right now.

"Listen, you sure you want to go down this road? He is your dad."

"I don't care. When people are bad for you, especially family, I believe in cutting them out of your life, because toxin kills. And Mom is soaking up all his toxic bullshit. I'm done with it. I need to know."

Nigel digs into his red duffel bag and holds up his keys.

"Well, I just got my license, so how about we follow him and see where he goes?"

A wicked grin stretches my lips. "You must be the smartest person I know."

"I get that more than you think." He stuffs his keys in his pocket and throws his bag over his shoulder as we leave the dugout.

Everyone thinks Oklahoma is this dry piece of useless land, and I suppose the majority of it kind of is. Tulsa isn't like that though. It's the big city to go to. We have green grass here, and only every now and then does a tumbleweed cross the baseball field.

I like it here for the most part. It isn't a place where everyone knows everyone, but big enough where everyone knows someone, who then eventually knows someone else. It's a constant chain of "Oh, you know Bobby? Me too. He's my brother's friend's aunt's sister's ex-husband."

It's a whole lot of bullshit and a whole lot of gossip, but it's home.

At least, I thought it was.

Right now, it feels very temporary, like the rug is about to come out from under my feet. I'm tired of feeling that way.

"I'm going to go home, shower, and change. What time does your dad usually leave?" Nigel asks as he unlocks his bike from the fence.

Yeah, I never bother doing that. My bike isn't new like Nigel's.

"Seven," I reply, swinging my leg over my bicycle.

He glances at his watch and nods. "Okay, that gives us a few hours. You go home and do what you need to do. I'll tell my parents I'm spending the night with you. You tell yours you're spending the night with me. We both pack a bag because we have no idea where we will end up being when we follow him."

"Yeah, you're right. Okay, sounds good." We slap our palms together, then our fists, and then point finger guns at each other. It's our secret handshake. He pushes off the ground and begins to pedal when I call out for him, "Hey, Nigel?"

He hits his breaks so hard the tires skid. "Yeah?"

"Thank you."

He grins. "Brothers, remember?" Nigel pushes off the road, and his bike sways from left to right with every circle of the pedals to make the bike go faster.

I slide my bat into my bag and hook it around my shoulders, then take off on my bike in the opposite direction Nigel went. We live a ten-minute bike ride from one another, but the baseball field is right between us, so it never takes long to get home.

Thinking about what we are going to do has me nervous. What if my dad catches us? What do we do then? And what if I'm wrong? What if I learn he isn't the problem, but I am?

I jump over the curb and land on both wheels, zooming by a stray cat that's staring me down as if I'm its breakfast.

The familiar song of an ice cream truck almost has me turning around to go get an ice cream sandwich, but I decide against it, since we don't have that much time between now and when my dad leaves.

The sun beams down against the top of my shoulders, warming my skin, but as soon as I take the next right down the street, the heat is blocked by trees. The chain against my bike spins as I coast down the road, passing green garbage bins at the end of every driveway.

Until we get to where I live, of course.

I'm the only one who takes out the trash, does the laundry, dishes, mows the lawn, pays the bills and whatever else. Mom is incapable right now, and my dad works late and leaves on the weekends. So it's up to me to be the man of the house because my dad does not count.

"Damn it, I missed trash day," I grumble to myself.

I sigh when I see the overflowing trashcan while everyone else's is empty. Dropping my bike in the middle of the yard, I step over the dead bushes and onto the walkway. Every step gets heavier the closer I get to the front door. My mom's favorite garden gnome, Jack she named him, is looking a bit grungy with dirt.

I pick him up and stare at the faded green door. "Looks like it's just you and me," I say to him, knowing I'm insane for talking to a gnome. I turn the gold knob, and the door creaks open as if I'm entering a haunted house. The living room is dark, the TV isn't on, but I know they are home because both cars are in the driveway.

Pops' briefcase is on the coffee table, the latches undone, and I'm tempted to open it and look inside, but I hear footsteps coming down the hall.

I beeline to the kitchen and pass the stack of dishes I need to go through, then bite the inside of my cheek as that rage inside me begins to build. I place Jack in the sink, flip the faucet on, and douse him in soap. I scrub him, grinding my teeth together when I remember Jack only exists because Pops got it for her.

She loves the damn thing.

"Amos, hey. I didn't think I'd be seeing you tonight. Lucky me," Pops says from behind me, messing up my hair from behind with his hand. "How was practice with Nigel?"

"Good." I breathe in and out, wanting nothing more than to turn around and smash Jack against the side of my Pops' head. "We always make the team, so I'm not worried."

"I'm just proud of you for going out there and practicing like you do. Takes dedication. I can't wait to go to your games. They are my favorite part of my week."

He talks like that, and I feel guilty. My Pops isn't a deadbeat. That's what makes this entire situation harder than it is, because I feel like it's all in my head. He never misses a game. He's always there cheering me on. He tells me he is proud of me every day. He says he loves me. He doesn't hit me, talk down to me, or anything negative.

He's the perfect father, minus how he's never home on the weekends until my games begin. It really just makes me more curious.

"Yeah, I think I'll be starting this year too. My batting average is good."

"That's great, Amos. Hey, maybe next time when you and Nigel go to the baseball field, I'll tag along. I want to see what you're up to." He grips my shoulder and gives me a slight shake. "So damn proud of you." He kisses the back of my head.

I cringe away, like I do from any affection. "Pops, stop."

"Okay, okay. Just wanted to let you know I love you," he says.

Great. Now I feel guilty again. "Are you still leaving tonight?"

He sighs, and I know that fake regretful sound from anywhere. "Sorry, Amos. You know if I keep working hard like I am, I'll get that promotion, and we can finally have what we need."

"I know. It's been a while. When is the promotion going to happen?" I ask, wondering how long he thinks he can feed me the same line of bullshit. It's been years.

"Soon. I really think it will happen soon."

"Great. Can't wait to have you home more," I lie. Turning off the water, I dry Jack off and set him to the side to dry. "I need to go hop in the shower. I'm going to go check on Mom."

"She's wasting away. There's nothing you can do for her," he says to my back once I begin to leave the room.

I pause, the familiar shivers of the discomfort I feel about him tingling my spine. "She's sick. She isn't wasting away. She needs help."

"You'll see, son. She wants us to take care of her when she's a grown woman and needs to learn to take care of herself. I don't mean this in a bad way." He walks around me and grips my biceps with his hands. He smiles, and his hazel eyes crinkle on the side as he stares at me. I know I'm looking straight at the devil. I know I am. I just need to prove it. "Go on. Go shower. Soon, you'll see how much I'll be able to better your life without her in it."

I shrug out of his hold and push by him with my shoulder. I'm only sixteen, but I'm already taller than he is, so I tilt my chin to my chest and stare down at him. "I don't want a life without her in it. She is my mom. I'm not giving up on her because you think it's the easiest thing to do." My feet pound down the hallway, and I kick the bathroom door open, then slam it shut.

I've always known he hates Mom, but it isn't very often he is outspoken about it.

I sigh. I can't contemplate too much about what he said, but I don't like how he said 'soon.' What's that mean?

I'll find out soon.

I turn the shower on, take off my cleats, and then go check on Mom since it takes a minute for the water to get warm. The TV sounds from the living room, and it ticks me off how he makes himself at home.

Tiptoeing along the carpet, I push open her bedroom door and peek my head inside. She's laying on her side underneath the floral patterned quilt she made before she got depressed. The curtains are black to keep all the light from the windows out. I can tell by the material on her shoulders that she is wearing her favorite robe. Her hair is wet, which means she showered today.

That's good.

I walk up to her and brush her hair out of her face. She looks so tired all the damn time, and I wish I could fix it for her. "I'm going to figure this out, Mom. I swear you'll be happy again one day." I bend down and kiss her forehead. "I love you." When emotion starts to sting my eyes, I stand and head toward the door, closing it behind me so she can rest.

I stand in the middle of the hallway and look at the pictures hanging half-assed on the walls. Some are crooked, some of the glass is broken, but the ones of me in my baseball uniform are always perfect.

I don't know if we have ever been a happy family, now that I see the proof lining the walls. If someone loves something, they take care of it.

The proof is in my Pop's actions and words when it comes to my Mom, and then the house being let go and run into the ground. I'm only sixteen. I don't know how to do half the stuff that needs to be done around the house.

This house is full of deceit, and I'm going to air it out.

I open the bathroom door, and steam hits me in the face. Undressing, I toss my clothes on the old, cracked-tiled floor. The house was made in the seventies and it still looks that way. Baby blue sink, baby blue tile, and the shower?

Nope, not baby blue.

They must have run out of the color because it's puke green instead. Whatever. I don't care. As long as the water is on and I can bathe, I don't care where I have to shower. After washing my hair and body, I step out of the stall, dry myself off, and wrap the towel around my waist. I toss my clothes down the laundry chute and head out the door. My room is right across the hall.

And it's bare bones. Bed. Dresser. Closet. TV with a PS2. I don't like clutter. The fewer belongings a man has, the less can be taken away from him.

I shuck off my towel, get dressed, and pack a bag like Nigel said.

The doorbell rings, and it's around six at night. Right on time.

"Nigel is here!" Dad shouts so I can hear him from my room.

"Cool, just send him back!" I yell in return.

A knock at the door sounds, and Nigel is there, standing right next to Pops. Nigel has a tight smile on his face, and Pops is happier than a clam. I run my fingers through my damp hair and flip on the PS2 to act like we are going to be gaming all night.

"What's up, Pops?"

"Just wanted to see my two favorite people before I leave. Are you staying the entire weekend, Nigel?"

"Ah, you know how it is, Mr. Taylor, Amos and I always jump back and forth. We never know where to settle."

"Good. It's good to have a friendship like that." He checks his watch, and Nigel and I share a knowing look. "Alright, I need to get ready. You guys be good this weekend. I don't want to get a call from the cops," he laughs.

He laughs at his own joke every time, because every single time he leaves, he says the same damn joke.

"You know you won't," I say.

I sit on the bed and hand Nigel the extra remote.

"I know. I'm lucky you're so responsible." He knocks on the doorframe and leaves, entering the room across from mom's.

Yeah, they don't even sleep in the same bedroom.

Red flag number 562.

"Bag packed?" Nigel whispers.

"Yep."

"Okay, I'm going to act like Ashlyn is inviting us to a party. We are going to leave before your dad and stay in the car, then tail him," he informs.

"You talk like you've done this before."

"I watch a lot of crime documentaries." He climbs on my bed and opens the window. "Let's toss our bags in the bushes so he doesn't see us leave with them."

"You are way too good at this." I throw him my bag and he catches it with one hand, then tosses it outside along with his. "Ready?"

No. "Yeah, let's go." My stomach is turning, and I feel like I'm about to puss out. I can't. I need to do this.

We pretend to laugh and enter the living room from the hallway to see Pops locking his suitcase tight.

"Hey, thought you two were staying in?" he asks, lifting a brow.

I think what I hate most about him is how much we look alike. Same dark hair and hazel eyes. Luckily, I got my height from my mom's side. Other than that, that's the only difference.

"Ashlyn invited us to Rizzo's Pizzeria. We were going to stay in, but pizza sounds good," I explain, pretending to text Ashlyn back. "I told her we were on our way. It's cool, right?" My nerves are still on edge. I'm worried he won't believe me.

"Yeah, of course. Just be safe, okay?"

"Obviously." The door creaks when I open it, and cold air whips around me. I can finally breathe easier when I'm not being suffocated by the house I've grown up in. I just want to be an average teenager. Nigel has his damn license, and I should too, but I'm too busy doing what the adults need to be doing. I don't have an adult to teach me how to drive or take me to take the driver's test. And the last time I remember being able to be a kid was when I was ten.

The good ol' days when I could run in mud puddles and play outside in the rain.

Now when it rains, it pours.

The dead bushes scrape against my ankle as we trudge over to the side of the house to get to the bags.

A sharp pain suddenly pricks my leg, making me hiss. "Ow, mother fu—" I growl, slapping my calf. Damn mosquitos.

"Stop being a baby. Come on. I parked over here." He points three driveways down to the left side of the road.

"A fucking minivan?" I tilt my head back to my shoulders and stare at the stars before we cross the street in a fast jog.

"Hey, be thankful my parents even gave me this car, okay? Plus, this thing is sweet, and it has more punch than you think.

12

Get in or get left behind." He opens the driver's side door and gets in. The engine cranks, and I swear a wheeze escapes from under the hood.

I look around to make sure no one can see me and get in, suddenly feeling like a soccer mom. "Dude—"

"If you don't have anything nice to say about my new wheels, you can walk trying to follow your dad."

"Yes ma'am," I tease him.

"Ass."

He turns on the radio to a classic rock station and AC/DC comes on, then turns on the a/c when it becomes too stuffy.

Good thing I showered.

"Hey, there he goes," Nigel points, placing the soccer mom van into drive when my Pops pulls out of the driveway.

"Well, what are you waiting for? Go!"

"I can't yet. I have to follow a few car lengths back, so he doesn't catch the tail."

"The tail? You really watch too much TV."

"You're welcome," he scoffs, finally pressing his foot to the gas.

The streetlights illuminate the inside of the cab with each one we pass. We are covered in yellow light, then dark, light, then dark, until we are finally on the freeway chasing my Pops' taillights.

My leg begins to shake when we lose sight of him dodging in front of another car. Nigel is quick, flickering his blinker on as he dips in the left lane. "There he is," he points to the right of us with his eyes, dipping his chin. "We stay like this and it looks less suspicious."

"Alright." I prop my head in my hand and stare at my Pops' car. He has a damn sticker on the back that says, 'My kid

13

is on the honor roll' from last year. I know he says he is proud of me, but I don't believe him.

"Don't sound too excited. Can you not admit you have adrenaline coursing through your veins, right now? I'm freaking out on the inside. I've never done anything like this before."

"I'm not excited," I mutter, turning my eyes away from my Pops' car. "I don't know what I'm about to run into. I don't know if I'm crazy or if I just hate my dad for no good reason."

"Considering we just passed the state line into Kansas, I'm starting to wonder if maybe your reasons are valid."

"He could work in Kansas," I argue.

"Kansas?" he scoffs. "No one works in Kansas. It's... well... Kansas."

I can't seem to find humor in the situation when we follow my Pops into Wichita, Kansas two and a half hours later.

"That wasn't nearly as long as I hoped. I wanted us to go clear across country, do odd jobs to pay for gas and food. Bet it would be the best road trip we ever had."

"This isn't a damn vacation, Nigel! This is serious. My life could change at any moment with whatever we find."

A beat passes between us before he clears his throat. "You're right. I'm sorry."

Exhaling, I rub my eyes, wishing we never followed my Pops to begin with. "I'm sorry. I shouldn't have snapped. I'm just..."

"...Scared?"

I hate being afraid. "Yeah, I'm scared. What kind of shit is that? I can't stand the man. Why should I be afraid?"

"Truth always hurts, Amos. No matter how you find out. This is going to change your life forever, like you said."

We take the same turn as my father does, down an old abandoned-looking road, where houses are few and far between.

"This is not a work trip," I whisper, tears in my voice that I can't hide.

"You don't know that. Don't jump to..." his reassurance trails off when my Pops pulls into a driveway. Nigel places the van in park across the street, and I have a clear view of my Pops getting out of his car with a bouquet of roses in his hands.

The house is quaint with a white picket fence. The lawn is mowed. The grass is green. The mailbox isn't broken. It's the house I've wanted for us for years.

Nigel's window is rolled down, so when the white-painted front door opens and light spills out, two young kids run out with smiles on their faces.

"Daddy!" they squeal at the same time, and the sound of their childish voices steals the strength and breath right out of my lungs. "Daddy, Daddy!"

The little girl has pigtails that sway as she jumps into my Pops' arms and he squeezes her tight.

"Oh, I missed you my little munchkin." Pops places a big kiss on her cheek.

"I missed you too, Daddy," she says in her cute little girl voice that makes me hate her.

"Dad!" an older kid, a boy, around eight, greets him and gives him a big hug.

"Ah, look at you. I swear, you've grown..." Pops pauses as he checks out his kid, analyzes him.

I finish the sentence for him as a tear runs down my cheek and we speak in unison, "You've grown like a weed."

A woman younger than my mom is at the doorway and she's pregnant. Very pregnant. Her stomach is round, like she's about to pop.

I feel sick. I've been kicked in the stomach.

"Hey sweetie," she says to him.

Pops wraps an arm around her and kisses her deeply, the way he used to kiss Mom. They walk inside, the little girl on his hip, and he hands the roses to his girlfriend? Wife? I don't know what she is. They close the door and turn off the porch light.

"Fuck," Nigel whispers, then rolls up the window with the crank on the side of the door.

"He has an entire other family. That's where he fucking goes every weekend! This is where he comes? Are you kidding me?" I kick the dash underboard underneath my feet, then punch the seat between my legs and roar at the top of my lungs. "Fuck him. I knew it, Nigel! I knew it. That fucking bastard. I'm going to kill him."

Nigel pulls me in for a hug, and I try to push away. I don't need comfort. I'm fine. I don't need him. Mom won't need him. We will be okay.

"Let me go. Let me go!" I fight Nigel more, but he holds on tight, and I punch him in the arm weakly. "Let me go," I sob pathetically for a man I fucking detest.

Why? Why am I wasting my breath on him?

Because deep down, I wanted to be wrong about him.

"He has another family, Nigel. He has everything I've wanted for me and Mom. The house, the siblings, the perfect fucking yard. They have everything! He has given them everything." I kick the dash again, and the hate I felt toward Pops before is nothing like it is now. "We need to get home. I need to pack his stuff and set it on the lawn. No way in hell can my mom stay with him. We are done."

"Let's go, then. I'll help you pack up his shit and burn it," Nigel says, letting go of my shoulders, then slamming the van into drive. "I am so sorry, Amos."

The van begins to move, and I stare out the window, staring at the same sky I'll be looking at when I get to Oklahoma. "I hate Kansas," I rasp, wiping my cheek on my shoulder. I'm going to give myself this one free pass to break, to be mad, to cry, but when I get home, I refuse to shed another tear for that man.

Is this what he meant by soon? Was he going to leave Mom and expect me to come with him here? I would never choose to be with him.

"Me too, Amos. Me too."

I remain silent for the entire two-and-a-half-hour ride back home to Tulsa. I still can't believe what I witnessed. I have half-siblings.

Siblings I have no want or need in knowing ever. My heart at this moment turns to steel. I only let a few more tears fall before I decide that man has never been worth a single breath I've ever wasted on him. My instincts told me he was a fucking dirtbag. I hated him for a reason. I wasn't crazy. Something wasn't wrong with me.

I knew.

When we pull up to the house, I can't help but laugh. The driveway is cracked, the grass is overgrown, the garage door doesn't work, and there is a leak in the roof.

Yet he has a white picket fence in Kansas.

"Rotten bastard," I spit, opening the passenger side door, then slamming it shut.

Nigel does the same, following close behind me. I unlock the front door, and we enter the house. The keys jingle as he tosses them on the counter.

"Amos?" my mom shouts to make sure it's me.

"It's me, Mom. Go back to sleep. I love you." I lock the door behind me, and an idea strikes. "I'm changing the locks this weekend. I won't be playing baseball either, because I'll need to get a job. My Mom will need me. Things are going to change around here."

"Just tell me what you want me to do," Nigel says.

"I just want you to stop me from killing him when he comes home Sunday."

"I can do that."

I'm not going to tell him he is wrong. I don't think anyone is going to be able to stop me.

It's Sunday, and I haven't slept a wink. All of Pop's shit is packed and on the lawn. I'm taping up the last box when my Mom finally enters the room. It isn't often she's up and walking around, but when she is, I always see the side of her I miss.

She gasps. "What are you doing?"

My eyes slide over to Nigel, who did his best to stay awake but passed out about two hours ago. I'm not going to wake him. "Packing up his shit." I tear the tape from the roll and close the box. "Mom—" I stand up, then grab a bin I set aside of all his fucking secrets he dared to keep here in this house.

"Nigel and I followed him Friday. He went to Kansas. He has a whole new family. Did you know that? Another woman, kids, the works. That's where he goes on the weekend." I pick up a photo from the bin. "This is of his daughter." I place the baby picture in her hand. "This is of his son, who plays basketball, by the way. Look at the trophy. Oh, let's not forget this gem." I hand her the wedding photo of him and that other woman. "His wife. He kept this here! Right here. We deserve more than him," I say to her, trying not to cry again when I see her silently sob as she looks at the pictures.

"I knew there was someone else. I assumed, but... What are we going to do, Amos?" she wails, which wakes Nigel up from his sleep.

I catch her in my arms when her knees give out. She clutches onto my shirt and cries like I cried to Nigel.

"Mom? Look at me. I need you to look and listen." I push her away and cup her face. "I am going to take care of this. We only need each other. I want you to go in there and take your sleeping pill. I want you to go back to bed. I'll make sure he doesn't come back."

"I can't. You can't handle this alone, Amos."

"I have Nigel. You've been through enough with him. I need to know you're on my side, Mom."

She nods, staring at the wedding photo of Pops and his 'wife'.

"You're prettier," I say, tucking a piece of hair behind her ear.

She places the photo in the bin and tugs the belt of her robe tighter. "I'm not going to bed. I'm going to look good when he comes home, and we can tell him to fuck off together."

I smile, surprised by her words. "You better hurry, then. He will be home soon."

"Right. Okay." She sniffles and spins around, the ends of her robe fanning out. She hurries across the hall into her room and closes the door.

An hour later when she comes out, she's not the same woman. She's wearing a dress. Her brown hair is combed and parted, shining like silk. She has makeup on, and her blue eyes are brighter than ever.

"Damn, Mrs. Taylor. You look hot," Nigel whistles.

"No, don't," I warn him, giving him a look that could kill.

"Why thank you, Nigel." She gives him a small curtsey, and Nigel winks at me.

A car door closes outside, and we all hold our breaths.

It's him.

My anger, my exhaustion, my pain, they energize me as I march to the front door.

"What the fuck?" my father curses on the other side. "What's all my stuff doing out here?"

When I hear his voice, his confusion, I snap. I swing the door open and yank him inside by his shirt. I shove him against the door.

"You dare put your hands on me?" he growls, shoving me back. "What has gotten into you?"

I throw the first punch and split his lip on the first try. Mom is screaming for me when she comes into the living room.

"How about you go ask your new family?" I throw another punch, my fist connecting with his jaw. "How about you go to your new son, daughter, and wife!"

His eyes turn into large circles, and his face pales when he realizes he is caught.

"Yeah, I saw you. Nigel and I followed you Friday. I saw you greet your family. I saw you treat them better than you ever treated us. So yeah, your shit is packed, and you can get out."

"No, no. Amos, Linda, they were a mistake—"

"They didn't look like a mistake Friday." I punch him in the face again and then do something I never thought I'd do.

I whip out the gold-plated gun he kept from his grandfather that I found under his bed and point it to him.

"Amos!" my Mom screams.

"Amos put down the gun." Nigel steps in front of Mom to protect her. "This isn't like you. You don't want to do this."

But I do. I really fucking do.

Pops trembles, and his voice shakes. "What... What are you doing?"

I have no idea what I'm doing. All I see is him getting out of the car and holding roses for another woman, greeting kids, being happy with another family. "All you have done is made us miserable. I saw through your façade."

I shove the gun against his cheek and place my finger on the trigger. "You sorry piece of shit. You're the reason for Mom being depressed. You're the reason this house isn't a home. Go to your other family."

"I love you and your mothe—" he stops speaking when I glide the gun down his jaw.

I cock the heavy weapon, and a tear threatens to leave my eye, but I made a promise to myself. "I want to kill you for what you did, but instead, I'm going to tell you to get the fuck out of this house. We never want to see you again. If you come back, I will kill you. Do you understand? If you come near Mom or me, I'll blow your brains out."

I push the barrel against his lips. "Get. Out. You aren't in fucking Kansas anymore," I sneer.

Like a coward, he runs out the door, and I tuck the gun in my waistband, locking the door behind him.

"We are going to move," my mom says. "Away from here. I know someone in Jersey. They will help us."

Nigel's face falls, and the last thing I want to do is to leave my best friend, but my Mom deserves this chance at a new life.

I hate my Pops more than I ever have, and if I never go to Kansas again, it will be too damn soon.

CHAPTER ONE

Present Day

"**B**3!" THE BINGO ANNOUNCER CALLS OUT INTO THE MEGAPHONE. I want to bang my head against the wall. I don't give a flying fuck about bingo, but Prez has made me keep an eye on Homer when he goes out since he's so damn old. We don't want him keeling over any time soon. Boomer is paranoid Homer is going to slip and fall and break a hip.

Personally, I think Homer is going to outlive all of us. He'll go to some remote island with all of his weed and just smoke and drink and play bingo until his dying day.

"N38!"

I place a red chip on the number and glance to my left to

see Homer playing four cards and two have N38 on them. I only have the one card. There's no way I'm going to win, not that I care. I want to go home to the clubhouse. My mind is a jumbled mess. All I keep thinking about is the woman I carried off the boat and her two sisters.

I think they are sisters. They all look alike, so they have to be. She's beautiful. A man like me doesn't deserve to look at her or think of her, but I'm also the kind of man that will make sure a woman is safe.

No matter what it costs me, I will give everything I have to bring security to a woman in need. I don't care if it kills me.

I blame my heroics on my Mom. Ever since what happened with my Pops, I take what happens to women personally.

And if a man says he doesn't take it personally, he isn't a fucking man. We men wouldn't be anywhere in this world without women. We aren't shit. They are the ones that run the world, and we just fucking live in it. It's hilarious to see men pretend otherwise.

"You fucking idiot. You have bingo." Homer nudges my arm, which causes my elbow to slip against the counter. My chin slips out of my hand, and I almost fall out of my chair.

I stare at my card, oblivious to what the hell he is talking about. Newsflash, I've never played bingo, and I don't know what I'm looking at. "What? Where?"

"Are you stupid? Did your mother drop you on your head as a child?" he asks, jutting his pointy chin out at me.

Probably more than once.

"You little shit. You have bingo twice. Look, each number she's called out, you've put a stamp on. You have an X on

24

your card. Hit your buzzer, you idgit," Homer gripes, "and yell bingo."

I grumble and hit my buzzer like he said to do. With less enthusiasm and in a monotone voice, I speak up, "Bingo."

"What?" half of the elderly people say in unison.

"I need to turn my hearing aid up." One woman fiddles with the aid in her ear while the announcer walks over to me. Slow as a sloth, since he is using a walker.

My god, I'm going to age fifteen years just by the time he gets to me.

"What'd ya say, sonny?" his voice wobbles from old age.

"I said I have bingo. Two times. Bingo," I yell, sounding out the words so he can understand me.

"He's hard of hearing, not stupid, Kansas," Homer bitches while taking a swig of coke.

They don't have alcohol here at the bingo hall, so I'm drinking a damn root beer. Apparently, a lot of these old folks are on medication and they aren't allowed to drink alcohol because of it.

"Well, everyone we have a winner! A double bingo. What a rarity!"

I don't know what I expect, but I sure as hell don't expect dirty looks. One guy motions his finger across his throat while mean mugging me. A woman across from him slams her fist into her palm, her messy, pink-painted lips curling in rage at me.

This is getting out of hand.

"You won the grand prize today, sonny!"

Oh, yeah. Can't wait. It's probably an oxygen mask.

"You lucky sonofabitch. You better take me somewhere nice." Homer slaps the back of my head, and I curl away, rubbing the spot he hit.

The announcer hobbles over to the gray counter where the prizes are, like stuffed animals, coupons, and balloons, but he comes back with an envelope instead.

Fuck me.

It's a bunch of coupons. I know it.

I'll send some to my Mom. She'll have a use for them.

"You won a free dinner at Johnny's steakhouse and five hundred dollars! That's what you get from a double bingo."

"No shit?" Huh. Maybe there's something to this bingo playing after all.

"No shit, Sonny. Well, that's it for the night. I'll see everyone on Friday."

There are sounds of disapproval and a few hard stares again, so I tuck the envelope inside my cut pocket. I don't trust any of these old people. I bet they would hit me with their canes or run me over with their wheelchairs to get their hands on this prize.

"Ulysses, have a good night. Don't forget to take your heart pills. We don't need a scare like last time," Homer warns his friend, the announcer guy.

I wasn't here last time. I switched with Satyr because of the woman I carried from the boat. I stayed with her as she slept and kept an eye on her sisters. It's only been a few days, and they are awake, but they won't talk to anyone.

"Eh, I got my pacemaker to keep my heart going. I'll be fine," Ulysses taps his chest.

"If you die, I'm not coming to your funeral," Homer says, sliding off his barstool.

"I don't want you there anyway." Ulysses waves his hand at Homer and shuffles his feet as he leaves while using his walker to keep his balance.

"Always was an ass."

"Homer, be nice. Good god, would it kill you?"

His eyes seem bigger through his new prescription glasses as he glares at me. "What? I've known Ulysses since I was a young buck in my prime. He liked my Betsy. Kept asking her out even after we were married."

"Want me to go take his walker?" I crack my knuckles, not liking Ulysses so much now. A man should respect when a woman is taken, and when he doesn't, it usually means he has no respect for anything. Not even himself.

"Eh, another time. I'm tired. Take me home."

"Yes, Ms. Daisy," I tease him and open the door for Homer.

He pulls out a joint and lights it as soon as we are outside. It doesn't matter where we are. He finds a way to smoke. He says it's for his glaucoma, but we all know better.

Fucker doesn't even have glaucoma.

The wind chill wraps around us, and the clouds filling the sky threaten to add more snow to the few feet we already have from the previous storm. One thing about Jersey that I have never gotten used to is winter lasts forever.

We step off the sidewalk onto the parking lot and Homer slips on a patch of black ice. I'm quick, catching him right under his arms. My heart is pounding, and my skin is sweating. Our worst fear almost came true. This is why he always has someone with him. He might be old and ornery, but this club wouldn't exist without him.

He's kind of the glue that holds us together. I'll never say that out loud.

Ever.

But it's the truth.

"You okay, Homer?" I set him on his feet, and he jerks away from me, catching himself on the hood of the car.

"I'm fine. You guys need to stop treating me like I'm going to break. I'm tougher than I look."

"I know, Homer. We just care." I open the passenger side door and get ready to lift his tiny self into the truck.

"Homer, wait!"

A woman's voice has me turning my head, and Homer hides behind the door that's opened. Not that it actually hides him. His legs show.

"Homer, I brought you something." The lady stops in front of the door, and she has a bright smile on her face. She has big blue eyes that pop with her long silver hair. She's wearing skinny jeans, black biker boots, a green shirt, and a bright pink marshmallow jacket.

"Aren't you going to greet the nice lady, Homer?" I cast my eyes toward him, and he is running his hands on either side of his head to fix his hair.

For the first time since I've known the man, when he looks at me, the tough exterior is gone. He's terrified to talk to her, but he swallows and steps out from the door. The woman grins, her eyes lighting up like those damn fireworks Boomer loves so much.

"Elise," Homer finally speaks. He leans in and gives her a quick hug that's awkward, yet adorable. "How are you?"

I give them some privacy by stepping a few feet away, but close enough to where I can still hear them. I kick the snow on the sidewalk, waiting for this torturous moment for Homer to be over so I can give him shit for it.

"I'm good. I didn't do that great at bingo, and I'm sad I didn't get to talk to you much this time around. I'm happy I caught you before you left," Elise says.

My smile fades when I think of how much effort Elise is putting in. She's giving all the signals, but I don't think Homer will ever move on from Betsy. No matter how much we all wish Homer would date, we all agree no woman can stand against the memory of Betsy.

"I brought you your favorite." She hands him a baggy of more weed. "I know how much you like the Mile-High flavor."

"Thanks, Elise. I...I really appreciate that. Thanks for thinking of me."

"I always think of you, Homer."

Aw, damn. That hit me right in the heart.

"I was thinking," she begins to say, and my eyes round in fear because I know she's about to shoot her damn shot. She's going to get turned down. Her cute fragile, elderly heart might stop beating, and she'll die.

"Hey, Homer! Sorry to interrupt, Boomer just texted." He didn't. I'm lying. "He needs us back right now." I hurry to the driver's side to act like it's an emergency. "Now, Homer. Now!"

"Okay, okay. Elise, I'm sorry. I have to go. I'll see you Friday for bingo, okay?"

The disappointment and understanding blooms across her face, and it makes me feel like a real shit bag for lying, but I'm thinking of her.

"Sure, Homer. I get it. Be safe. I hope everything is okay." She waves, crosses her arms over her chest to keep herself warm, and begins to walk to her car across the lot.

Homer grabs the gray-plastic handle on the roof and groans as he hauls his ancient bones into the truck. He slams the door just as Elise drives off behind us in her green Prius.

"Thanks, Kansas."

"Honestly, I didn't do it for you. I did it for her. Elise is beautiful, and she likes you. She was about to ask you out, and you were going to break her heart. I couldn't see that happen. Just tell her you aren't interested, Homer. Stop taking her fucking weed and using her." I slam the truck in reverse, a bit irritated. "And you know what, I don't have a problem taking an older woman out. I might ask her to go to this steakhouse with me." I turn the wheel as I back out of the spot, the tires crunching along a thin sheet of ice and bits of snow on the pavement.

"No."

"No? Sorry to break it to you, Homer, but 'no' isn't enough. I think Elise deserves better than the cold shoulder you've been giving her. She loses hundreds of dollars giving you all that green for free. You're being a bastard," I tell him honestly, curling my hands around the wheel tighter.

As I said, I'm protective of women.

"I like her, okay!" he yells at me. "Is that what you want to know? I like her, damn it. I don't know what the hell to do about it." He has tears in his voice as he stares at the windshield. "I haven't been with anyone since Betsy. I feel guilty. It's why haven't done a thing about it. I took vows, Kansas. That should mean something."

"Ah, Homer, Betsy would want you to be happy."

"I don't deserve to be. Not after how she died."

"Homer, yes you do. What happened to Betsy wasn't your fault. It was the old chapter. They killed her, not you. And I can bet anything that Betsy would say the same thing. Don't spend the rest of your days alone, Homer."

"I'm not alone. I have the club."

I sigh as I turn the wheel, taking a left down the street where the clubhouse is. "You know that's not what I mean."

There's a difference between being with friends and then crawling into bed alone.

In the old Atlantic City chapter, before I got strung up in the barn and whipped within an inch of my life, there were only a few times where I hooked up with cut sluts. Everyone has an itch they always need to scratch and that's why the club whores exist, but the club started bringing in young girls, kidnapping them, drugging them, that's when I stopped messing around.

Even with the whores.

And the old Prez didn't like that.

When he strung me up, all those nights I hung there wishing I were with someone I loved instead. So yeah, I'm not the biker that fucks biker bitches anymore.

I want my own woman. I want someone to curl up to at night.

And I want to be the little fucking spoon sometimes. I want to feel her arms wrapped around me too.

With all the effort I give to make others feel safe, I want to feel safe too.

I might be a big badass biker with tattoos, but my heart hasn't turned to steel, no matter how many times I tell myself it has.

It's soft.

I pull into the parking lot of the clubhouse and park. The bikes are still in the garage since it's so snowy. Boomer doesn't mind when we ride in winter, but he has a rule of 'no bikes' when there is ice and snow on the ground.

"Come on, Homer. Let's go see what everyone else is doing." I slide out of the truck, close the door, then run around to the other side to help Homer out. He opens his door, and I pick him up and set him on the ground. I'm too nervous for him to

31

jump out. What if he breaks an ankle? "I had fun at bingo," I add, remembering the hard-earned cash in my pocket.

"You aren't going to want to come next Friday. People hold grudges. They need space."

I stuff my hands in my coat pocket and kick another mound of snow. I have a habit of doing that. I can't help it. It's just there, looking so... kickable.

"I feel like I'm getting dumped."

"Just give the bingo hall some time. They'll come around."

Homer stomps his boots when we get inside the breezeway, knocking the snow off from each one.

I do the same and chuckle. "Whatever you say, Homer." I head inside the main room, Homer hot on my heels, and the heater blasts me in the face. The tip of my nose defrosts, and I shuck off my coat, hanging it on my given hook on the wall. Each hook has our names above it, which was Scarlett's idea.

It's home. She's made it feel like home for all of us. And the teddy bear she placed in each of our rooms wearing leather jackets? Each individual one has our names hand-sewn on the front left side. I keep the bear on top of my dresser so I can see it every day. I love that damn thing. Other than my Mom, I've never met another woman so selfless.

I bypass everyone and head toward the bathroom, check my hair, and put on some extra deodorant before I go see the woman from the boat.

I don't know what it is about her, but she makes me want to be better.

Just looking at her, she makes me want to be Amos again.

And as much as that scares me, I welcome it. Because I turned into the one thing I hated most: Kansas.

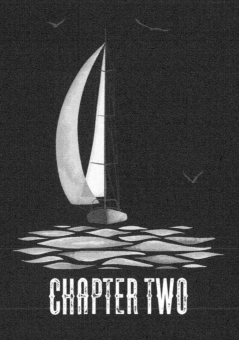

CHAPTER TWO

Violet

WAVES CRASH AGAINST THE SIDE OF THE SAILBOAT, ROCKING IT violently. The snow whips across my face, stinging my eyes and cheeks. It's freezing, and the storm is stronger than Dad anticipated. My hair is wet, and my clothes are sticking to my body from the waves crashing over us.

"Dad! We have to turn around," I yell over the roar of the ocean and the hiss of the snow bulleting against the sailboat. "The storm is only going to get worse!"

I hope he can hear me over the howl of the wind. I scream when the halyard, the rope that pulls up the mainsail, snaps. The sailboat groans and takes a sharp turn right into a strong wave. I have to hold my breath as we wade through the water.

The sailboat manages to make it out of the wave, drenching us in freezing water. Ice has started to form on the rails. The temperature is dropping. My teeth chatter as I hold onto the rail. I'm hunched over, staring off into the gray abyss of the sea. The clouds get darker, rolling together to form a mass of fury. Thunder rolls above, rolling with the same tenacity as the ocean.

I've heard of thundersnow. People don't think it's a real thing, but it is. It's just like a rainstorm, only instead of rain, it's a downpour of snow and thunder, sometimes lightning.

"Mom!" I cry out for her as I watch her stagger across the boat to get to me.

"Get in the cabin with your sisters right now!" she yells, her hip slamming against the side of the boat when it rocks again. We are going to keep going in circles since one of the sails isn't working now.

I shake my head, then wipe my hand down my face to clear the snow from my lashes. "I'm not leaving you."

"You need to be with your sisters—"

She's silenced by a strike of lightning that hits the mast. A giant crack spreads down the beam. And then it snaps in half at the same time the boat dips.

Water crashes against our feet and the mast swings, threatening to hit us. We dive to the floor. Mom looks over my shoulder to check on Dad behind the helm. We hold onto each other's hands, her skin as cold as the snow in the air. She has a deep cut on her forehead that's bleeding red drops down her face.

"Please," she begs, squeezing my hand. "Go to your sisters. Make sure they have their life vests on." She raises her voice so I can hear her over the cacophony of waves. Her blonde hair sticks to her face, hanging in thick curly strands.

"Hold on!" Dad yells at the top of his lungs.

I tilt my head up to see black swells of water on either side of us. "Mom, hold on!" I grasp her hand and the rail at the same time to keep us in the boat.

Her nails dig into my skin, and I bow my head right to block my face from the water. We rock, dipping down into a quick valley the sea naturally creates. Two shadows engross us in a cold cloak, and there is a quick moment of silence.

Peace.

And then the peace is broken when the waves swallow us. I scream, but it's muffled by a flow of water entering my mouth. I choke and gag, tasting the fish and salt of the sea. The sailboat twists and turns, rolling all the way to its side until I slip off the boat.

My mom's hand slips away from mine, and I don't have a full second to think about it because I'm about to lose the grip on the rail. Half my body struggles against the current in the water while trying to pull myself onto the boat again.

I can't hold on.

Screams from my left have me turning my head, and that's when I see my mom drifting further away.

"Mom!" I wail, but I know she can't hear me. "Mom!" But the next time I blink, she's gone. All I see are the violent, moving hills.

"I got you." Dad grips me by the forearm and lifts me back onto the boat. Pins and needles tingle through my entire body. I'm frozen to the core, but it doesn't numb the pain of losing Mom. "It took Mom. It took Mom!" I scream.

Dad grips my arms, his eyes swollen and red from losing Mom. "I need you to go to your sisters." Thunder rolls above us and fat snowflakes pour in white blankets on top of us.

The sailboat rocks again and it has the mast swinging around behind Dad. "Get down!" I shout and fall to the ground, trying to tug him down where I am, but it's too late.

The mast swings and hits him right in the back of the head.
I watch as his body topples over the boat and—

"Wake up, Springs. Wake up!" a deep voice cuts through my dream.

I snap my eyes open, but all I see are angry waves and snow. I scream and fight against the heavy mass over me.

"Springs. Hey, it's okay. You're safe. You're safe."

I sob as arms wrap around me, and my cheek is pressed against a warm, broad chest. I clutch onto his arms, holding onto him for dear life as if I'm about to fall out of the boat all over again.

"Shhh, you're alright. I got you, Springs. I got you." He pets the top of my head, and he just holds me while I cry. "You were having a bad dream. I have you now. It's okay."

I don't know who this man is, but I know he is here to wake me up from every bad dream I've had over the last few days, which have been a complete blur, since all I've been doing is sleeping.

"They're gone." I bury my nose against his chest and inhale. His scent settles in my bones and the familiar comfort I find in rain radiates from him. He smells like the air during a storm. Wicked and powerful, yet needed. "They died."

"Who died, Springs? Talk to me," he croons softly.

I can't speak. I can't breathe. Everything hurts. My body, my heart, my mind, everything aches. Tears won't stop flowing. My mind is racing with sadness and disbelief. The overwhelming emotion of grief hits me hard, just like the storm hit us in the sea.

"Pulse!" the man shouts next to me when my heart rate monitor begins to race. "Pulse! Something is wrong. Get in here." The handsome stranger stands from the edge of the

36

bed, the mattress dipping from his absence. I reach for his wrist and grip onto it like I did the rail on the sailboat.

Hold. On. For. Dear. Life.

"I ain't going to leave you, Springs." His free hand cups the side of my face. "But you're breathing awfully fast, and it's worrying me."

Heavy boots bang against the floor, reminding me of the thunder that scared my sisters while we were sailing.

"Hey—" his thumb brushes across my jawline, and when his eyes meet mine, the panic begins to fade. He has eyes the color of moss, and thick lips that look soft. He's got a bit of scruff on his face from not shaving for a day. It's the first time I've gotten a real good look at him, and he might just be the most handsome man I've ever seen.

Even through my disarray, his voluminous eyelashes framing his hazel eyes have a calming effect settling in me. My sights fall to his chest, and I watch it rise and fall, the faded vintage Duran Duran shirt stretching to accommodate the muscle.

"—You're going to be okay." He looks to the right just as something sticks me in my arm.

I jump and crane my neck up to see a familiar face. The doctor, I think. He seems nice. He always has a smile on his face and kind eyes. He has long hair, like Fabio from those romance novels. I giggle.

"There we go," he says, helping me to lie back down. He checks the monitor as the beeping slows, then gives me a genuine smile. "That's where I like to see your heartrate. You feel better?"

I nod, feeling loopy and lightheaded like I'm floating.

"How many times are you going to have to drug her?

Every time she wakes up?" the guy that visits me every day asks Fabio.

I move my eyes to the romance model and wait for him to answer.

"If she wakes up with anxiety like that, then yes. She needs to relax. She's been through a lot. Hell, her body temperature is finally stable after beating hypothermia. She deserves the damn drugs."

"Will she always have anxiety?"

The question has me darting my eyes back over to the handsome stranger.

"It's possible, Kansas."

I slide my eyes back over to Fabio.

"How are her sisters?"

I'm getting dizzy looking at each man, but I want to know if my sisters are okay, so I focus on my new friend.

"They are resting. They woke up in a fit of nightmares too. Health wise, they are better than our Jane Doe here."

But then I can't help it, I have to look away from Fabio as *he* speaks.

"You ever going to tell us your name, Springs?"

I jump over to the stranger that's been watching over me like a biker guardian angel. Well, he didn't do that great of a job. Helloooo, where was he on the boat? I'm going to have to ask to speak to his guardian angel manager. I'd like to make a complaint.

"You're cute. Boop." I hit the tip of his nose with my finger. He blinks at me for a second, stunned, and I do it again. "Boop." I tap him again. His nose crinkles, and Fabio laughs at him.

"Don't laugh at him, Fabio."

"Fabio! Oh man," the biker savior chuckles, slapping his knee as he falls into a fit of laughter. "I can't wait for the guys to hear that."

"Fifty bucks, it stays in this room, Kansas."

"A hundred, Fabio."

"Deal."

"You don't look like Kansas. Kansas is really... state-shaped," I mutter, and he smiles brightly, showing all of his straight white teeth. "If I had to pick a state, I'd say Texas."

He scoots a little closer to me and tugs on one of my curls. "Why's that, Springs?"

"I don't know. It's big." I spread my arms wide and smack Fabio in the stomach. "Oh, sorry."

"You're forgiven," Fabio inserts another needle in my IV, playfully grinning. "I love how people think when they are all dopey."

I ignore him and focus on Kansas. "You're big. This big." I keep my arms spread until an itch on the tip of my nose has me reaching my finger to my nose and scratching it.

"Well, that's impressive. Thank you for thinking so," he says.

"You're welcome," I slur again, as if I've had a few too many to drink. "I don't want to sleep."

"You need to, Springs."

I know the drugs they give me will win. I'm feeling heavier by the minute. I fight to keep my eyes open, but I'm only fighting the inevitable. "Don't want to see them," I mumble, then turn to my side facing the man who thinks he is a state. I'll never understand that.

"Who?" he asks, tucking a piece of hair behind my ear.

"My parents." A tear flows down my cheek, but the heart rate monitor stays the same. "They died on the boat. I see them when I sleep." I yawn. "I don't want to sleep."

Kansas scoots closer to me and takes my hand. His palms are warm against my cold fingertips, and I sigh in relief when he slides his other one over the top. "I'm sorry to hear that, Springs."

"Me too, state man. Me too." He goes to pull away from me, but I entwine my fingers with his to stop him.

"What is it?" he asks kindly, a bit of a contradiction with how he looks.

"Don't go. I don't want to be alone." The thought of being alone scares me more than the nightmares right now. I don't know if it's hit me just how much me and my sister's lives have changed yet. I want to believe we will be okay. I want to believe I'm able to take care of a sixteen and seventeen-year-old. It's up to me.

I'm only twenty-two. I don't know how to be ready to take care of them, but they need me. We are all we have now. We have to stick together.

"I won't go anywhere. I'm going to stick right here." He points to the chair directly next to the bed. "I won't be far. I never am."

I want to ask why. Why is he here? Why does he care? Why is it him, and not someone else like Fabio? He's the doctor, shouldn't he be the one staying?

He tugs on my hand again, but I won't let go. "I promise, I'll be right here."

"I'll go," Fabio says, writing something down in the chart before placing it at the end of the bed. "Just let me know if I'm needed."

"Bye Fabio. Thanks for the drugs." I scratch my cheek against the pillow, so I don't have to remove my hand from Kansas's.

He chuckles and sighs. "I'm never going to hear the end of it."

"Don't forget, you owe me a hundred bucks, Pulse."

"I'll go to the ATM in the main room. Don't get your thong in a twist, Kansas."

I laugh so hard I snort. "A thong—" I snort again, "—in a twist."

"She's so fucking high. I need me some of that."

"Patients only, Kansas," Fabio informs as he leaves, keeping the door open behind him.

"Ha-ha. Sucks to be you." I stick my tongue out at Kansas. I don't know how it's possible to feel playful, tired, and sad all at once, but I do. Kansas makes it easy.

"I know a man that can cut that out if you aren't careful."

I suck my tongue back into my mouth and widen my eyes.

"Don't worry. He's in Vegas. He can't get you here." He tries to sit down again, but I stop him. "You need another blanket?"

I shake my head. "Lie next to me."

"I don't think that's a good idea. You need your space."

"I trust you," I mumble.

"You shouldn't."

"I know." I can't deny the fight to sleep, so I close my eyes and scoot over to make room for his massive body.

The bed dips and creaks and his boots scuff against the end of the bed. He doesn't wrap his arms around me, he doesn't hold my hand, he just lies flat on his back with his hands behind his head, staring up at the ceiling. It gives me the perfect view of his tattoos along the entirety of his neck. They are a geometric design, heavy with blank ink and swirls. He swallows, which forces his Adam's apple to bob and the circles that form around it move.

I know I have no reason to be close to him, but right now, he's the only person I know and feel comfortable around. I wiggle my body closer to his and press my head into the nook of his arm. I shouldn't think like this, but it's a perfect fit. I lay my cheek on the side of his chest and the warmth radiating from his skin through his clothes makes me warmer, like I'm sitting in front of a fire with a blanket wrapped around me.

The scent of rain hits me again, mingled with his leather vest, and I clutch onto it, fisting the material as hard as I can as emotion hits me out of nowhere again.

I cry and my tears fall to his shirt. He is unknowingly drying my tears.

One of his arms wraps around me, his palm rubbing up and down my arm. He doesn't say anything, he just traces his fingers up and down my arm, a slight caress that has me relaxing into his side. The tears slow, but the pain remains.

"It doesn't seem like it now, but you'll be okay. It just takes time." His chest vibrates when he speaks, and I cuddle harder into him. I like how he sounds. He has one of those deep voices that people listen to and can't get enough of while listening to a book being read. He could talk me right to sleep and I would have no objections.

The vibrations begin again, but this time he isn't talking.

He's humming while drifting his hand up and down my arm. I can't believe a man like this is trying to get me to relax by singing me to sleep. Just like his talking voice, his hum is deep and smooth, a natural baritone that has me sinking further into darkness.

I hate that our boat crashed to shore, but out of all the shores we crashed into, I'm glad it was this one. Me and my sisters might not have been so lucky if someone else found us.

Wrapping an arm around his waist, I hold on tight to his safety. His humming grows more distant, his touch turns into a feather, and the strength of his heart beats against my ear.

I never thought a touch from a stranger would feel so familiar. I've never met this man before in my life, but something about him has me trusting him more than I should.

I might have crashed onto his shore, but right now, he's the one crashing into me.

Kansas

UNITED STATES

CHAPTER THREE

I WAKE UP IN THE MIDDLE OF THE NIGHT TO THE SOUND OF whimpering. For a second, I don't know where I am, but then I hear a soft beep of a monitor and realize I'm with Springs. I glance down, and my nose gets buried in the bush of her unruly, wild, curly hair. I've never seen hair like this before. It's how I came up with the name Springs. Each strand of hair looks like a tightly wound coil or spring.

Since I don't know her name, I've been calling her Springs.

She quiets down and settles against me again, and I do something weird, something I've never done before, and I'm glad she's asleep for it.

I inhale the scent of her hair, and my eyes roll to the back of my head when I smell peaches. I have to hold back a groan and many, many other things that are not appropriate right now.

I'm such an ass.

She rolls away from me, and blood rushes through my arm. Static tingles my fingers, and I slide my arm out from under her and then fix the sheet as it slides down her shoulders. She has a small tattoo right under her collarbone, simple, delicate, and sophisticated. It's a simple flower, a rose. The line work is thin, which gives it a feminine, elegant appearance. I want to lean down and kiss it so badly, but it's selfish thinking, considering everything she's been through. I shouldn't want her like I do. I have no right.

There are a few things I tell myself to stay away from.

Love.

And hate.

I like to be balanced. Being right in the middle means nothing can go wrong. There are no expectations to be met. No promises can be broken. No disappointment can be felt. No love can be lost.

I live life in the middle for the most part. Personally, I think it's worked out pretty well, minus being whipped and strung up like a pig for standing up for what I believe in.

Keeping my desires close to my heart saves me, even if what I want suffocates me every day.

Even though I want love, even though I want more, and I don't want to slide between the legs of a club whore, I'm scared.

What if I'm just like my father? What if what I have isn't enough, and I'll want another life, another family? What if his bad blood runs through my veins, and I'm just this piece of shit human being? Maybe I try too hard to be a decent man because inside I know just how rotten I am.

My stomach growls, yanking me out of my pity party. I rub my hands over my face and look at the time. It's four in the morning. No wonder I'm hungry. I missed dinner, and that means she did too.

I sit up and swing my legs over the bed as I stretch my neck left, then right, getting the cricks out. My boots hit the floor with a soft thud, and I look over my shoulder to make sure I didn't wake her. Her curly hair looks like a huge cotton ball on the pillow. Her body is covered by the sheet and all I see are those curly coils. I chuckle to myself and fight the urge to reach up and run my fingers through her hair.

The heat kicks on and warm air drifts over me, since the vent is above my head. Pressing my hands against my thighs, I stand. The room is different from Doc's in Vegas. Where he has a basement full of hospital beds, Boomer designated a part of the motel for medical rooms. He wanted people to have their own space as they healed.

There's a painting of Atlantic City hanging to the left on the wall and a lamp on the nightstand next to her bed. A recliner is settled in the corner and there is a bathroom attached. Even though it isn't a hospital, it somehow manages to still smell like one.

Drives me nuts.

I give Springs one last look to make sure she's alright, and she is sound asleep. I head out the door, keeping it open so I can hear her just in case, and walk down the hall. There are a few pictures up, not many since the club is still growing. Scarlett always carries a polaroid around so she can take pictures whenever she wants. She ends up making a collage and framing them. We have three so far.

And then there's one of just Wolf and Abigale.

46

Before she died.

I rub the ache in my chest. She was my friend.

And poor Wolf, he has been fucking devastated. As he should. Abigale was the love of his life. I barely see him. He never comes out of his room, and when he does, it's to grab another bottle of vodka. He's drowning his pain, and Prez says to let him do it to heal, but I don't know if Wolf is healing.

I think he might be dying.

I press a kiss to my fingers and tap Abigale's picture before pushing an industrial size door open that leads into the main room. No one is in here. It's quiet. The middle of the night kind of quiet. I can't hear the waves outside like usual, but I can see the snow building against the window, right around the corners, and the middle is frozen with a sheet of ice.

When I get to the kitchen, which is off to the side of the main room, I flip on the light. Stainless steel appliances shine, and the kitchen island has a bowl of fruit on it along with a few bananas.

I don't feel like cooking. I'm too damn tired.

"You're up early."

I turn to look over my shoulder to see Satyr coming through the front door.

"Me? What the hell are you doing up?" I open the pantry and grab a box of Captain Crunch. My all-time favorite cereal.

"I can't sleep." He plops on the couch and snags the remote from the coffee table. "So I heard you had yourself a little sleepover."

The cereal pops as I pour the milk into the bowl. "It wasn't like that. She wanted me there because she felt safe."

"You're interested."

I open the farmhouse chic fucking drawers that Scarlett loves so much, grab a spoon, and slam it shut with my hip. I stuff my mouth full, so I don't have to talk to him.

"Man, you're in there every day. You wait for her to talk to you. To say something, but nothing is ever said, yet you continue to go in there."

I lift a shoulder, not wanting to make a big deal about it.

"You like her. Admit it."

"I don't even know her name. I don't know enough about her to like her." It isn't wrong, but I can't say I'm not drawn to her. I am. It's powerful enough to make me want to get to know her. It's strong enough for me to push my fears to the side and try to have something that I can consider mine. "I want to get to know her if the opportunity presents itself, but I don't know if it will. She's been through so much. Her fucking parents died on that boat. The last thing she needs is me lusting after her."

"You like her. You want to kiss her. You want to hug her. You want fuck her. You want to hold her." He snaps his fingers and dances to the song he is singing. "You want to wine her. You want to dine her. You want—"

I shut him up by throwing an orange at him and it hits him right in the head.

"Ow, what was that for?" he rubs his forehead and bends down to pick the fruit up off the floor, then begins to peel it.

"Shut up," I chuckle as I chew.

"I'm just saying, you meet a good girl, why not?"

Plenty of reasons, but I'm not going to list any.

Because I know at the end of the day, I'm going to ignore all of them. Everything Satyr said was true. I do want all those things with her, and despite every reason I shouldn't, I really hope this feeling of being drawn to her plays out how I want it to.

I drink the milk out of the bowl and wash it out in the sink, staring at a sign Scarlett made that says, 'You mess it up, You clean it up.' It's in pretty cursive and is tilted against the turquoise backsplash she wanted.

Whatever she wants, she gets. Boomer makes sure of it.

I open up the dishwasher and put my bowl inside, along with my spoon like a good little boy. Scarlett does not and will not clean up after us.

If we leave a mess, Boomer will threaten to throw cherry bombs at us.

No, thank you.

A scream coming from the medical wing has me forgetting about the open dishwasher. I don't bother closing the door. Without a second thought, I dash out of the kitchen, Satyr right behind me. I slam open the door and sprint down the hall and into her room.

She's sitting up in the bed, tears streaming down her face.

"Springs, hey, I'm here. What's going on? Are you okay?" I squat down beside the bed and look up at her, so I don't seem so intimidating.

"I woke up and thought I was in the boat," she explains, wiping her cheek on the shirt she's wearing.

My shirt.

Something else that's been driving me crazy. Scarlett asked for big t-shirts and sweatpants from us when we got the girls inside from the cold, since they were soaked. Springs ended up wearing my things, and damn it, she looks so beautiful in them.

"The mast hit my dad in the back of the head." She shows us with a hand gesture. "But..." her lip begins to tremble "I couldn't hold onto him. I tried, I really tried, but he fell off the boat when the next wave hit. Mom had already been taken by the storm. It was just me and my sisters. I can't get their faces out of my head."

This is the most she's ever talked, so I don't say a word. I just let her vent. I do get up and sit on the edge of the mattress again. I take her hand in mine and her fingertips are like ice. I place my other hand on top to warm them up.

"I'm going to go check on her sisters. I'll be back with an update," Satyr tells me.

I give him a quick nod, and he exits the room, closing the door behind him to give us privacy.

I flip on the lamp so I can see her clearly, and what I see steals my breath. Her big, round eyes stare at me wide open for the first time instead of drooping shut. They almost look cartoonish, because not only are they large, but the color is unlike anything I've ever seen before. So blue, but I swear there is a hint of violet in there to give them a purple hue. They are so unique.

"I tried. My mom and I were holding on to the rails, but the waves hit, and the sailboat flipped to the side, and we slide off the side. I held on, but my mom couldn't. She drifted away. My dad... he was right there in front of me. Right there. Talking. And then he wasn't."

Her pain has me remembering that now isn't the time to admire how beautifully different she is. Not when she's in pain.

"I tried," she sobs. "I tried so hard to not let them go, but it didn't matter." Her shoulders shake, and I pull her against

50

me as she cries again. She's done this a lot for the last few days, for good reason. It's never easy to witness someone you love dying, and she had it happen twice in a matter of minutes. "I don't know how we survived."

I draw small circles against her lower back and lean my head against hers, my face getting lost in the forest of her hair. "You almost didn't," I say to her.

She pulls away from me, but I keep my hand on the dip of her back, not wanting to let go just yet. Her brows furrow and a cute crease forms in the middle. Her eyebrows are full, shapely, and thick, yet perfectly groomed. "What do you mean?"

"I carried you from the boat while Arrow and Teeth carried your sisters in. All of you were unconscious, dehydrated, malnourished, and hypothermic. You still aren't in the best condition. Pulse wants to see more kidney output from you."

"Kidney..." her cheeks turn a bright shade. "He wants more pee?"

"Yeah, you're still dehydrated so he's pushing fluids in you like crazy."

The door opens, and Springs lets out a relieved breath. I don't see why she's embarrassed. Kidney function is important.

"Your sisters are doing well. They are sleeping, so I didn't wake them," Satyr informs. "I'm going to head off to bed too. I'm glad you're feeling better, uh..."

"Violet," she says.

"Violet," Satyr finishes his sentence. "Have a goodnight."

He shuts the door behind him, leaving me alone with Springs.

Or should I say, Violet? A beautiful name for a stunning woman.

51

"I'm glad they are doing okay. I'd like to see them tomorrow if I could."

"Anything you want. Prez will want to talk with you though."

"Prez…" she sounds confused. "I don't know what that means."

"Prez is the man in charge of the club, the President. There are a few things he wants to ask you, but until then just rest."

"So this is a biker club?" she asks, suddenly scared.

I twirl a finger around one of her curls, tug it down, and watch it bounce in place. "Yeah, Springs. It is, but you're safe here. It's the safest place you can be. I promise." I don't want her to think she and her sisters are in danger. "We're the good guys."

"I believe you. I don't know you, but something tells me to trust you."

There's that word again. Trust.

I've done nothing to earn it, and she's giving it to me freely.

"I'll do everything I can to make sure you can trust me."

"You've been kind. You saved me. You've stayed with me when you didn't have to. If that isn't reason, then I don't know what is."

I scratch the back of my head and give a crooked smile. "You got me there."

She sniffles and wipes her cheeks with the blankets, then gives a genuine smile. "Jeez, look at me. I'm a mess." More tears escape from the corners of her eyes. She lifts her lashes toward the ceiling. "I'm sorry."

"Don't apologize. You've been through a lot."

"I'm… uh…" The tip of her nose is red, and her lashes are wet. I want nothing more than to reach out and touch her skin, make her feel better, but again, I have no right. "I'm Violet." She sticks out her hand, giving me a watery grin. "We haven't been properly introduced."

"I suppose we haven't. I'm Kansas." I slip my hand in hers and we stare at each other longer than what's deemed normal. I don't want to look away.

"Kansas."

I like how she says it. I've never liked it before, but the way she says my name brings hope to it.

"Yeah, you know, the state man. You think I need to be called Texas cause I'm—" I spread my arms out as far as I can, "—this big."

She buries her face in her hands and shakes her head. "Oh, no. Oh, god. I remember bits and pieces of that conversation. I'm so sorry."

I laugh, leaning back on my hands. "Ah, it's alright. You were all doped up on whatever Pulse gives you." I snap my fingers when I remember an important detail. "You know him as Fabio."

"Stop," she groans, flopping back onto the bed. She hisses in pain and the playful moment is over.

"What is it? What's wrong, Violet?"

"My head. It's killing me." Her eyes are pinched shut, and she rolls to her side.

"Let me see."

She jerks away from me when my hands touch her head.

"I'll be gentle, I promise."

I wait for her to give the go-ahead and finally she nods. She reaches across the bed and holds the edge of it while I dig

53

through the jungle of her hair. Holy hell, this woman has the thickest, curliest hair I've ever seen.

A dirty thought pops into my head, and I imagine gripping onto the curls while she's on her knees and taking me down her throat.

She groans when I touch the part of her head that's bothering her, and my cock stops perking up when I hear her pain.

I'm a bastard.

"I see what the problem is." She has a few stitches in her head. She must have taken a tumble on the boat too and can't remember. I didn't know, or I would have taken better care of her. "You need more pain killers. I'll get Pulse."

"No, I'm fine. I don't want anything that makes me loopy."

"You still need him to look at it and to give you something better than the Advil I have in my medicine cabinet," I tell her. "Try to stay off the left side of your head."

"It's my favorite side to lie on."

"No it's not. When I was lying in bed, you were on your right side all cuddled up against me," I tease her again, and she rolls until her face is buried in the pillow.

"I'm going to sleep," she mumbles against the down feathers.

"You got it. I'll go." I get up and her hand snags around my wrist again, stopping me from going anywhere.

"Stay with me."

I stare at where she's touching me and close my eyes, trying not to think too hard about it. It means nothing. It's a simple touch. She just wants to feel safe.

"Please," she whispers, and the sweet sound of her voice has me opening my eyes.

Like I could say no to violet eyes.

I pull my arm from her grip and shrug off my cut, so I

don't sleep in it again. Unlacing my boots, I kick them off and set them under the bed. I walk around to the other side and lie down. The plastic over the top of the mattress crinkles as she turns to her right side and cuddles against my side, which makes me smirk.

"Hush. I still prefer my left side. It just hurts right now." Her head is against my chest again, and this time I wrap my arm around her to hold her close. She still sniffles, somehow managing to keep a good attitude when she's crying and heartbroken. It's obvious she's strong.

Much stronger than she gives herself credit for, I bet.

"Why do you call me Springs?" she asks in a sleepy tone that's followed by a yawn.

"'Cause you have the curliest damn hair I've ever seen."

She doesn't say anything. Her silence has me glancing down to see her eyes closed and her chest rising and falling in even beats. She's fallen asleep.

Her nickname will be my secret, or she'll figure out what it means on her own.

I don't know what it is about this woman, but I'd be lying to myself if I said I don't want to know everything about her. Just being here, lying next to her, holding her, I feel like I've done it a hundred times.

My stomach is in knots with the excitement of meeting someone new and having those butterflies or whatever the fuck they are called, flying around are making me feel like a teenager.

And I'm not a liar.

With one look, those violet eyes thawed my stone-cold heart. I'm so fucking screwed.

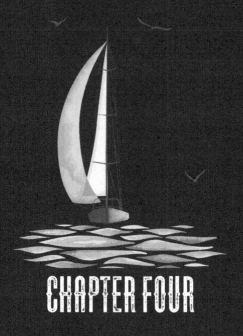

CHAPTER FOUR

Violet

I HOLD MY SISTERS FOR THE FIRST TIME IN DAYS. I HAVE EACH ARM wrapped around them while their heads are against my shoulders. "I'm so glad you're okay." I kiss the top of Victoria's head, then Veronica, and they cry. I don't have any more tears in me, but my eyes burn with the need to weep. I know I can't. I have to stay strong for them. They have to see everything is okay, even if I have no idea if it is and how it will be.

"Are they really dead?" Victoria leans back and wipes her arm across her. She looks so tired, with bags under her eyes and a small cut across her cheek.

"They can't be." Veronica pulls away and crosses her arms

across her chest. "They can't," she whispers in denial. "Where are we? Can we go home? Will Mom and Dad be waiting for us there?"

"Veronica," I say gently and reach for her hand, but she pulls it away from me to roll out of bed.

"No! No. I refuse to believe this. I refuse to believe they are dead. They are alive. They're probably worried sick about us and have already filed a missing person's report. How do we know we weren't kidnapped or...or..." she stutters and licks her lips. "They probably have brainwashed us or something. We don't know these people, Violet." Veronica paces back and forth, chewing on her thumbnail like she always does when she's scared. "We need to get out of here."

"Veronica—"

"No, it's just like you to always give people the benefit of the doubt! The truth is, we don't know these men."

A wave of defense rolls through me. I get out of the bed next, readying myself for an argument. "I give them the benefit of the doubt because they saved us. They carried us from that boat and gave us medical treatment. They haven't harmed us at all. They have given us no reason at all for us to think they have brainwashed us and actually—" I scoff and hit the side of my head when I stare at her "—Do you know how crazy you sound? Brainwashing? Are you kidding me? And how could you think that when I am standing here telling you that I saw Mom and Dad die. Me." I slam my hand against my chest, signaling to myself. "I did. While you and Victoria were in the cabin like you were supposed to be, I wasn't. I experienced wave after wave hitting us in the face. I saw the cut on Mom's forehead as we held one another's hands. We fell off the side, and I held on to the rail, Veronica. Half of my body was engulfed in freezing cold water, and I watched the waves take her away while she screamed. Did you hear her scream?" A tear drips down my face as I take a step closer to her.

"Stop it! Stop. The both of you, just stop," Victoria pleads, crawling off her bed to Veronica's since it's closer to where we are standing.

But I don't stop. "Were you the one who watched the mast swing and hit dad in the back of the head? Did you watch his limp body fall overboard?"

"Violet!" Victoria scolds me.

"Did you?" I scream at Veronica, and she jumps from the sound of my voice. Her eyes are locked on the floor, too afraid to look at me. "No. You didn't. Don't stand there and say these people are brainwashing us when I lived the truth. These men have been kind. They could have left us out there to die. It wouldn't have taken that much longer. So maybe instead of being a brat, be fucking grateful that we are alive!" I yell at the top of my lungs. My voice cracks, and my throat is raw from the amount of force I have to use.

Veronica slides down the wall onto the floor and pulls her legs to her chest, burying her face between her knees as she cries. "I don't want them to be dead. I didn't get to say goodbye."

I kneel on the ground and wrap my arms around her. "I didn't either. It all happened so fast."

"What are we going to do?" she sniffles.

I sit back and shrug my shoulders. "I don't know, but at least we are together."

"Do you really trust these guys?" Victoria asks, sitting cross-legged on the bed.

"I do. There is one, his name is Kansas. He's been very

kind to me, so if you need anything, I'm sure he will help you two too."

"Everything okay in here?" a man with an eye-patch asks. A man I've never seen before.

I hold my hand out to Victoria, and she climbs off the bed and huddles against my side. "Who are you?" I ask, spreading my arms to protect my sisters.

His eye darts back and forth between us and he grins. "I'm One-Eye. I'm a friend of Kansas. He had to go on a run today, since he is acting VP, but he wanted me to make sure you ladies were alright."

A slender dark haired woman stands next to him and my defenses settle a bit. She has bags of clothes in each of her hands. "I got it from here, One-Eye." She pats him on his giant shoulder that looks like it could break her neck with a shove. "I think it's better if they talk to a woman."

"I can speak woman," One-Eye grumbles, displeased that he's doubted.

Victoria snickers quietly, and then hisses when I pinch her to shut up.

"One-Eye," the woman pushes his body, and he doesn't move. "Go. I got this."

"Arrow said he would give some of his juice boxes—"

"I don't care what Arrow said right now. Let me handle this, please. I have some experience, remember?"

"Fine, but don't come running to me when you can't speak woman." He points a finger in her face, and she pinches her lips shut to hide a smile as he bounds down the hall.

She enters the room and closes the door behind her, setting the bags on the floor. "Hi. I'm sorry I haven't come by sooner to introduce myself, but all of us here at the clubhouse wanted to give you your space until you felt better. I'm Scarlett. I'm engaged to Boomer, the man who is in charge."

"The President. That's what Kansas said."

"Yes, that's right," Scarlett says, tucking her espresso-colored hair behind her ear. She's pretty, with big blue eyes and a soft smile that would make it easy for someone to trust her. "You must be Violet." Her eyes land on me, and I push my sister's back a bit more.

"How do you know my name?"

"Kansas updates us on how you're doing. Plus, he says you have wild curly hair and the prettiest eyes he has ever seen, so it has to be you."

I blush from the unexpected compliment. "He said that?"

"I think you've got yourself a fan," Scarlett winks at me.

I shouldn't be so excited to hear that, but I am. I have some sort of feelings for Kansas, and while I don't know what they are just yet, I know they make my heart speed up. He's kind, smart, and obviously brave. All qualities that any woman would be attracted to.

Oh, and let's not forget how handsome he is.

He is so gorgeous. I've never seen a man look like him. He even has a nose ring, a small hoop that sits snug against his nostril. I've never been attracted to a man who looks like Kansas. My Dad would tell me guys like him are bad news, and I always believed him.

Until now.

"I think he might have a fan too."

I'm pulled away by my thoughts of Kansas when Scarlett gives me a cheeky smile while handing me a plastic bag. I scoff. "I don't even know him."

"He's one of the good ones."

"We aren't here for you to get a boyfriend, Violet," Veronica smarts off, snatching the plastic bag from Scarlett's hand.

"Hey, don't be rude to her. She's helping us. They aren't the enemy."

"God, a guy gives you the smallest amount of attention and you turn into one of those girls."

I narrow my eyes at my sister. "I'm not one of those girls. I've spent the last few days with Kansas, and he has been nothing but kind to me. You need to stop being such a bitch."

"Okay, all of you are pretty testy right now, for good reason. You're exhausted, hungry, and probably feeling a bit weak. I know you're sad too. Your emotions all over the place, so I'll let it slide."

Scarlett squats down and her elbows are on her knees as she looks us over. "Listen, we are the nice guys, but we don't handle bullshit very well. If I were you, I'd drop the attitude. We are helping you, using our resources, and I'm bringing you clothes that actually fit. Shower. Change. And then Boomer wants to talk to the three of you. Just follow the hall down until you get to the main room." She stands, leaving me swallowing to coat my dry throat. "What are your names again?"

"Veronica," my sister croaks.

"I'm Victoria."

"Well, I'll give you a heads up about Kansas. He's been through enough to not get flack from teenagers such as yourselves. I know you've been through a lot, but I have a family to protect too, and Kansas is a part of that. He doesn't go around getting googly-eyed over hair and eyes with every woman he sees. He isn't like that. I expect you all to be out in the main room in fifteen minutes. Lunch will be waiting, okay?"

"Thank you, Scarlett. We appreciate the gesture. I'll talk to my sisters about using their manners." I accuse Veronica with a hard stare.

"*Sorry,*" she mouths.

"Great. I'm glad you ladies are feeling better." Scarlett straightens to her full height and throws her hair over her shoulder as she leaves, leaving the door open behind her.

I stand up, annoyed and pissed off at Veronica. I lift the bag in the air and then bring it down, slapping her with it.

"What…stop!"

"I can't—" I hit her again "—believe you!" the plastic crinkles when I raise the bag over my shoulder and swing it on top of her head.

"Ow! Violet, that hurts."

"I don't care if it hurts. You are being unbelievable. After everything we have been through, after everything they have done for us, and you act like that?" I lift it one more time and Victoria slips in front of her older sister blocking my attack. "Get out of the way."

"I think we all just need to calm down and take a breather and do what Scarlett said to do. Maybe our mood won't be so bad once we shower and eat. You know how hangry Veronica gets."

"Fine. I'll meet you out there. Don't go without me. I need to make sure Veronica keeps her trap shut."

"I won't say a word, Violet. I'm sorry. I'm stressed out."

"Yeah, all of us are." I clutch the bag in my hand, and without a second look, I stomp out the door to head to my room, then slam it shut. I throw the bag in the bathroom, and the plastic hits the wall with a dull thud before falling to the ground.

These emotions are pent up inside me, and all I want to do is scream. I'm not going to be able to be the role model my sisters need, especially Veronica. Even on a good day, she's always on a warpath. I run to the bed and punch the mattress.

That feels good.

Really good.

I punch it again and the blanket indents with the size of my fist. I alternate hands, going back and forth punching the mattress until I'm sweating. The sweat mixes with the tears, and when I can't lift my arms anymore, I sag against the bed.

Tired.

Defeated.

Lost.

I snatch the pillow and throw my face into it. I scream into it until I run out of air, and my lungs are begging me to inhale.

"Better." My voice is muffled by the feathers. Tossing the pillow to the side, I inhale fresh air, my emotions a little more under control than they were before I walked into the room.

This life is going to be a big adjustment.

I drag my feet across the floor to the bathroom and flinch when I look in the mirror. Jesus, I look like I just crashed onto the shore. My curly hair is a mess and stained with blood. Blood doesn't turn blonde hair red, right? It doesn't actually stain...

No, that's stupid.

"Can't believe I let him see me like this," I mumble, peeling off his shirt and sweatpants. I hold in a grunt; my muscles ache and pinch as I lean into the shower and grip the handle, turning it to blazing hot.

I step inside and groan when the hot water hits my back.

It feels good, so much better than the icy cold caress of the sea. I wrap my fingers around the silver handlebar, using it as support to hold my body up. Leaning my head back, the water slowly soaks into the mass of my hair, and there's a slight pain where I have those stitches.

I'm probably not supposed to be washing my hair, but I don't care. I feel disgusting, and I just want to bathe. If anything, Pulse, or is it Fabio? I honestly can't remember which one is the correct name now...

Anyway, he can stitch me back up if need be.

I lean down and grab the peaches and cream shampoo, pouring a good size amount into my hand. I scrub my hair, careful to keep away from the stitches. The aroma of peaches mingles with the steam, and as I inhale, I relax. It reminds me of summertime with my parents. Mom always made peach cobbler every Saturday, and now...

That familiar sting is back behind my eyes, so I angle my head in the water and let the water wash away the sorrow.

There will be no more peach cobbler Saturdays.

I do a quick wash of my body next and thank the heavens when I see a razor. Looks new and unused, with the protector still on the blades. I lift my arms and drop them immediately when I see the situation.

Oh my god.

I hope Kansas hasn't seen them.

I look down and inspect other areas.

My legs look like Chewbacca, and don't get me started on what's going on between my legs. It's a danger zone down there. I snag the conditioner and nearly drench my entire body in it, then shave until I'm no longer a lost animal out in the wild.

When I'm done, I dry off and I'm relieved when I see panties still in the package and a tank top with a built-in bra. I get dressed, slipping on my black cheeky undies, then soft shorts along with a plain black shirt that says 'Ruthless Kings Atlantic City' on it.

I'm thankful there is not a brush because everyone knows curly hair cannot be brushed, not if we want it to look normal. So I leave it be. When I get to the hallway, my sisters are waiting. Both of them have their hair in a wet, messy bun, their eyes are red from crying, and they are wearing the same shirt I am.

"Ready?" Victoria asks.

"As I'll ever be."

I slip my arm through Veronica's and give her a tired smile. It's all I can muster right now. "I don't think it will be as bad as we think."

"I hope not. We have enough on our plates," Veronica says.

"We will get through it. We always do."

"Hey, look." Victoria points to the pictures on the wall. "They all look so happy. Oh, who is that?" her voice deepens, and I peek around her to see her looking at a man who is way too old for her.

I push her down the hall, and she giggles. "Keep dreaming. He is way too old for you. Anyone here is."

"But he is so handsome. I wonder who he is," she sighs, practically having hearts in her eyes.

Great. My sixteen-year-old sister is crushing on a biker. Maybe I need to get us out of here. "You can wonder until you're eighteen, but not a day until then."

"Pshh, whatever," she waves away my attempt at being authoritative.

When we get to the main room, a group of men are sitting on the couch. One is playing with pliers while another is whittling a piece of wood into a sharp point.

"Oh my god, that's him," Victoria gulps, then stands behind me.

Yeah, she's not ready for this.

None of us are.

My eyes drift to the pool table where a few men have stopped their game. There are more solids than there are stripes and whoever is winning is really kicking ass.

A young guy stands from the couch, tall, in shape, and for some reason, the first thing I notice is that he is missing a finger. I gulp when he walks toward us, and the men all stand at the same time.

They are all massive.

I look over everyone to find Kansas, and he isn't here.

I'm all on my own.

I pull the 'Mom' move again and stretch my arms out to protect my sisters. A patch on his cut says 'President' and then, to my horror, the name underneath says 'Boomer.'

Fuck.

"Ladies," he eyes me, grinning when he sees I'm protecting Victoria and Veronica. "Follow me, would you?"

Victoria whispers in my ear, "Oh my god, we are going to die."

"We are not going to die," I talk out of the side of my mouth so only she can hear me.

When we get into the room, there's a large table in the middle stretching from side to side to accommodate everyone.

"Take a seat," he says.

Like I'm going to disregard a man who only has nine

66

fingers. I scoot by him, keeping my sisters behind me and my arms spread. He looks amused as we inch through the tight space, since he doesn't move.

We take the closest seats, and then one after the other the members start to file in. I keep my eyes on Victoria as she watches all of them.

Until one with the name patch 'Satyr' walks in. She looks away, and he hasn't noticed her, but her cheeks are flaming red.

Great. I have another thing I need to add to my list of worries.

"I have a few things I want to talk to you about," Boomer starts to say and then digs into a black duffel bag and places square packages on the tabletop.

"We aren't going to be your drug mules!" Veronica slams her palm on the table. "We are getting out of here. Right now." She stands up and grips Victoria by the arm, but a man named Arrow steps in front of the door, folding his hands in front of him. "Get out of my way."

"Veronica—" I begin to say, but Boomer stops me.

"Actually, Veronica. We were hoping you could explain why your boat crashed onto my shore and dumped about fifty pounds of cocaine."

"What?" I feel like I've been slapped. "What are you talking about?"

"Sit back down, please," Boomer gestures to my sisters. "You're Veronica. And you must be Victoria, right?"

She nods, hiding behind Veronica.

"Well, I can not keep up with three names beginning with V, so you're going to be Ronni. Okay?"

"Fine," Veronica gives an eye roll, pretending not to be

afraid. I know her better than that. She's scared out of her mind right now

"Where is Kansas?" I ask, wishing he were here.

"On a run. Now, don't change the subject. Why were you sailing with all these drugs?"

"Those aren't ours," I say. "I don't know what the hell you're talking about. That was my—" it dawns on me that the boat was my father's. "Oh my god." I bow my head and cover my mouth with my hand.

"What?" Victoria asks in an innocent voice.

"We don't have anything to do with those drugs," Veronica declares, standing and leaning across the table to poke Boomer in the chest.

"Veronica!" I try to pull her down to her seat, but she shrugs out of my touch.

"Those drugs aren't ours." She pokes him again and he looks down to where she is touching him, and he snags her wrist.

He presses his fingers on pressure points which has Veronica whimpering and her knees threatening to give out. "I'll say this one time. No one fucking touches me, especially another woman. Now, you're underage, and it's the only reason why I'm not kicking you out on the fucking street for the disrespect that's been leaving your mouth. You are safe here, but I need to know where these fucking drugs were going and who is expecting them. Newsflash, princess, someone is without their drugs and they are going to want them."

"I swear, we don't know anything about the drugs. It had to be my dad. It's his boat."

Boomer lets go of my sister's wrist and his threat works because Veronica shuts up quickly.

68

"I heard your parents were on the boat, but didn't make it. I'm sorry for your loss. We have had a loss as well, so I know how much that hurts."

"Thank you," I say, staring at the large white packages in front of us. "I swear, I don't know anything about the drugs. I had no idea that's what we were doing sailing. We always sail to New York City from the Florida Keys this time of year. It's a big family trip."

"You can't honestly believe this biker is saying Dad was a drug dealer." Veronica shoots me with hot daggers in her eyes. "Dad was well off, but he didn't deal drugs."

"So you wouldn't mind giving us his name and us finding out for ourselves then?" Boomer asks, throwing something red and round into the air before catching it and doing it all over again.

All I know is it has a fuse on it and that means I need to stay away.

"Go right ahead," Veronica says, a smugness to her tone as she leans back and folds her arms across her chest. "Daddy was a lawyer."

"Daddy sniffed snow, girl," a man across from the table jabs at us. His patch says Void. Everyone looks at us like we know nothing about the world.

And right now, I guess we don't.

Staring at the drugs in front of me, I'm about to learn a lot more about my Dad than I want to.

I'm scared we are about to be thrown into a world we have no idea about.

A world we weren't prepared for. A
world that we are not ready for.

Kansas

CHAPTER FIVE

WARDEN AND BANE OPEN THE LARGE WAREHOUSE BOOMER bought a few weeks ago. The metal doors slide apart, revealing the empty inside. I peek into the rearview and see Decay flicking his lighter on and off. Wolf is next to him, drinking a bottle of vodka at eleven in the morning. No one has said anything to him about how much he drinks. We are letting him work through Abigale's death. He has been a train wreck. There's a sense of dread everywhere still since her passing is so recent and Wolf hasn't been able to pick himself up from the heartbreak.

He's losing himself in it.

He's only with me right now because Prez wanted him to get out of the clubhouse.

"Alright, come on," Warden raises his voice, so I can hear him from where he is standing.

I press on the gas, and the tires crunch along the gravel and ice before hitting the edge of the concrete floor of the warehouse. The truck dips, and the grumbling of the diesel is louder once we are in the enclosed space. The light from outside casts along inside, and as the doors shut, the light recedes, engulfing us in darkness.

The buzz of electricity sounds when one of the twins flips on the lights. I get flashbacks of being strung up in the barn, metal chains wrapped around my wrist, and a collar wrapped around my neck. The warehouse looks similar, only instead of being made of wood, it's made of metal.

"You okay?" Decay asks me.

I meet his eyes in the rearview and nod. "Yeah, I'm fine. Sorry." I get out of the truck, and the rest of the guys follow suit.

All except Wolf.

"You coming?" I question him as he takes another sip.

"No." He doesn't say why, but I see him staring at a picture of him and Abigale on his phone.

I leave him be.

Colt begins to walk over to him, but I grip the back of his cut and sling him back. "Don't. Leave the man alone. He needs us to respect his space."

"I just want to make sure he is okay," Colt says.

"Of course he isn't. We have work to do and somewhere else to be in three hours. We have a few business meetings today so let's take care of this bullshit. Leave Wolf alone, okay?"

"You got it, Kansas," Warden and Bane say at the same time.

Fucking hell, how am I supposed to tell them apart when they have the exact same tattoos now?

"So are we going to gut this guy or what?"

Ah, never mind. Bane is the act instead of think type, while Warden thinks before he acts. It's the only thing I have to go by.

Bane rubs his hands together manically. "Let's do this."

I toss the keys to him, and he catches them one-handed. "Go on, then."

"Seriously?" he nearly squeals with excitement.

It's like giving a kid cash for the ice cream truck. "Yeah, go."

"I'm so excited... and I just can't hide it," he sings as he skips to the tailgate of the truck. He slips the key inside the hole, twists it, then grabs the handle to pull it down. He reaches inside and yanks the goods from the back and tosses him on the floor.

"Well, well, well, if it isn't the woman beater and kidnapper," Bane greets, kicking our captive in the back.

"Please!" he tries to crawl away by using his elbows and knees, moving across the floor like a worm. "I won't ever do it again. I won't, please," he begs and cries, spittle dripping from his chin as he realizes just how much of a piece of shit he really is.

One-Eye isn't here with us only because Alicia asked him not to be. If it wasn't for her, no doubt One-Eye would be here right now getting retribution. This is the man who kidnapped Kimmy and hit Alicia. If there is one thing the Kings do not do, it's hit a woman.

Bane has stepped over our captive and takes a step forward every time the abuser takes an inch as he worms his way to the doors.

Warden and Colt are placing a massive blue tarp down for easy cleanup, and Decay is leaning against the truck, watching the scene unfold.

Well, I got a job to do, and the sooner I'm done, the sooner I can get back to Violet—I mean—the club.

I wanted to be there so bad today because Boomer was going to talk to her and her sisters about the drugs. I didn't want her to feel ganged up on, and I know that's how it can feel when you're surrounded by bikers who most likely have killed.

But since I am acting VP and Sergeant at Arms right now, I have a lot of responsibility on my shoulders and Boomer is trusting me to do what he can't. So as much as it pains me to be away from Violet, I have to be.

The first thing I'm doing when I get back though is asking her out.

I have no right to. The last thing she needs is some guy trying to have her fall in love with him with all the shit she has going on right now.

But I have to, something tells me if I don't try, I'll regret it forever, and I don't want to live a life full of regrets.

Which also reminds me that I need to call my own mom, who does not need to know the details of my job, or I'd get a long lecture full of damn tears. Then I'd feel a whole shit ton of guilt. It's just better for her to think I'm in a club who rides bikes to go look at the leaves change every autumn.

Ignorance is bliss sometimes.

"Bane, stop playing around and get him over here," I bark. My voice echoes off the metal walls. Boomer bought this warehouse and this land for one thing and one thing only.

Privacy.

The Ruthless Kings Atlantic City officially owns ten acres near the ocean and a warehouse that's surrounded by the woods.

No one can hear us.

No one can see us.

We are all alone, and there is no hope for this asshole.

Bane grips the man by his hair and drags him across the floor.

"No! No! Let me go. Let me go," he screams, struggling against the zip-ties binding his wrists. The skin turns white from the pressure, and his hands turn an ugly shade of purple.

When Bane gets to the tarp, he slides Alicia's abuser across the tarp, crinkling it along the way. In two steps, I strike my hand out like a snake latching on to its prey with its fangs. Wrapping my hand around his throat, I squeeze and lift him off his feet, making sure my grip chokes him.

I don't know what Alicia saw in this man. He's short, not well-groomed, a bit of a beer belly but nothing too awful, and he has shaggy, stringy hair that hasn't been washed in a few days. It's hard to look at this man and know he is Kimmy's father. The man has no idea how lucky he was, and he threw it all away when he hit Alicia.

Now, One-Eye and Alicia are just friends, and he is very protective of her, but I'm not blind. The man is head over heels for that woman, and I don't think she has the slightest idea.

"You can scream." I lift him higher as my voice deepens. "You can cry," I add as Bane lowers the hook from the ceiling. It clanks on its way down, since the thick chain is wrapped around a wheel Bane has to crank. "You can beg," I growl, bringing his face closer to mine. He's so close I can smell the stench of his morning breath. "You can even pray."

The hook lowers, and I raise him higher, then press

his back against the hook until my eardrums ring from the sound escaping his throat. The flesh tears and blood begins to drip onto the tarp. I keep pushing until the hook punctures through his shoulder and keeps him hanging there like a dead fucking fish.

"But nothing you do will help you. Your prayers won't be answered. Your screams won't be heard. Your tears? They won't be cared for." Blood rains from his wounds and flows down his chest.

I bend down and pick up a steel pipe. It's as long as a broomstick and has the same circumference. I throw it in the air and catch it.

Without saying another word, I slam the pipe against his body. His ribs crack on the first swing with a sick, satisfying crunch. He screams just like I knew he would.

"Don't paralyze him. I got plans," Decay advises me.

"No problem. I'll stay above the waist." I slam the rod against his back, right across his shoulders. I hit the hook too, making it sink deeper into his body.

He lurches, vomiting onto the tarp while flopping around just like a fish would.

"Bane? Warden?" I hold the pipe out to them, and Warden grins, kicks off the crate he is sitting on, and takes the weapon from me.

I watch Warden walk circles around our hanging meat sack. He analyzes him and then stares at his hands that are bound. He smirks, and with a loud grunt, instead of swinging the rod, he takes the end and shoves it through the palms of the man's hands.

Like fucking butter, Warden glides the pipe through his zip-tied hands. The screams fall on deaf ears at this point, and when Warden yanks the pipe back, there is a perfect circle cut out of the meat of his hands. I can see right through them.

Warden flings the flesh off the pipe and tosses it to Bane. He does the same thing only shoving it through the shoulder that doesn't have a hook in it.

"It's impressive you're staying conscious for this," I taunt, catching the long, steel pipe in my hand as Bane throws it.

Decay comes up next, and he lights a blow torch with his lighter. He sits on the tarp under our victim and makes a gesture for Bane to lift him higher. Decay pulls out a packet of cigarettes and slides one out, offering one to our victim. "Want one?" he asks.

The man's teeth chatter, and he doesn't answer.

"No? Okay," Decay shrugs, lighting the smoke with his blow torch. He takes a big puff and blows it out right as Bane cranks the lever again and slowly the limp body lifts.

He doesn't remain limp for long. The pain from the hook and the weight of his body against it pulls when he is raised into the air.

"I offered you a cigarette, man," Decay tries to raise his voice louder than the screams. "For this purpose. See? I'm nicer than these guys. Want to know why?" Decay asks.

"Just ki—kill me," the man stutters.

"In due time. I want to see you dance first." Decay presses his finger against the trigger of the blow torch. The fire comes out so hot, it's blue.

"What?" The man's eyes round as Decay slides under him.

He hovers the torch just below the man's feet. Not enough to burn, but enough to make it very hot and uncomfortable.

Our captive begins to wiggle and tries to lift his legs higher to get away from the hot flame.

"You dance so beautifully," Decay admires, then presses the torch closer to his feet until the smell of burnt flesh begins to fill the space.

Warden, Bane, and Colt chuckle.

"Colt?" I ask the man to take a step forward to join in.

"Don't mind if I do," he says, taking the pipe from my hand. Without missing a beat, he slams the rod between the man's legs.

"Oooh," all of us groan as if we feel the pain. Nothing hurts as bad as a kick in the balls. Not even fire under the feet.

He pukes again, and this time there's blood in it.

Having this tarp down really made the difference. Cleanup is going to be a breeze.

Colt throws the pipe back to me, and I twirl it like a baton, then place it right under the guy's chin to make him look at me. "This is what happens to pieces of shit like you. The world's a better place without liars, cheaters, and abusers. You won't be missed."

"My daughter—" the man chokes on his own blood.

"—Will forget you even existed," I finish for him and toss the steel rod onto the ground, then reach behind me and grab my gun from my waistband. "Imagine what you know being in... Kansas, and then imagine being here. It's a lot different, right?"

He nods, grunting in pain.

I press the barrel right against his heart and cock the gun. "Well, you aren't in fucking Kansas anymore." The gunshot rings out. His body falls limp when a chunk of his chest goes missing.

"That was fucking awesome," Bane says, peeking in from the other side of the hole, staring at me with… I don't know what that is. Respect? Admiration?

"Get him down, clean the hook, and roll him up. We're going to throw him in the ocean next with a few weights," I order, pulling a joint from my pocket and snagging Decay's torch.

"Hey," he gripes.

I inhale deep and hand him his toy back while I relax. Fuck, that feels good. They roll the body in the tarp like a burrito, and while I watch, the only thing I can think about is Violet. Would she approve of this?

Not many women would.

She might be better off without me because I don't plan on changing. Approval isn't needed in this way of life, it's just a bonus if it's offered.

I check on Wolf and he's passed out with an empty bottle on the floor. Maybe I'm better off without her anyway. I don't want to end up like Wolf.

Half dead and barely alive.

If love hurts that bad, I don't know if I fucking want it.

CHAPTER SIX

Violet

W E'VE BEEN MOVED TO OTHER ROOMS IN THE CLUBHOUSE NOW and are no longer in the medical wing. What's even better is that we have our own space. I don't have to share with my sisters, which is a good thing since the thought of being around Veronica right now makes me feel a bit murderous. I need space. I need time to think about who my parents were, and if I really knew anything about them at all.

The long family trips we always took, I'm starting to realize it wasn't about family time, but a job. We traveled up and down the east coast throughout the year. We were homeschooled by our Mom, so we had more time to do things together as a family. But if what Boomer said is true, then it was really so Dad could deliver his drugs.

We had a lot of money. A big house, boats, skis, vacation homes, and I never questioned it. I just thought Dad was the best lawyer around.

I know they loved us. We had the best parents. They never lacked in love, but how can I forgive them for being drug dealers?

All I can hope is maybe the Theodore Winston, my Dad, was set up somehow. Maybe, just maybe, the drugs were planted in our boat. It's a long shot.

I sit in the middle of the bed and exhale so deep, my entire upper body sags. I glance around the room, feeling defeated. I can tell this place was a motel before, but whoever renovated it did a great job at making it feel warm and cozy like a home. The walls are painted a warm beige, and there is an accent wall colored in bright burnt orange with a gold star hanging in the middle of it. The bed is King size, with a four-post canopy bed. There's a sheer metallic gold material hanging from the ceiling to drape down on all sides of the bed. It's gorgeous.

I grab a pillow and hold it close to my chest. For the first time in a long time, I've never felt so lost. What do we do? Where do we go? Do I have us go back home? Of course I do, right? I mean, it's what we know. It's where we are from. Staying here makes zero sense.

A knock on the door sounds, and I debate on answering it. It's late. I don't feel like talking to my sisters. I want to turn on the TV and get lost in House Hunters or something and not think. I want my brain to turn to mush for the night.

So I ignore whoever is at the door.

Bang, bang, bang.

I groan and throw the pillow off the bed, then tiptoe to the door to look through the peephole.

Fudge.

It's Kansas.

I stay silent and watch him mumble something to himself. I shift my gaze away and flatten my hands against the door, nibbling on my lip.

He clears his throat and knocks again.

I fluff my hair to get my curls nice and bouncy. Taking a deep breath, I wrap my hand around the gold knob and twist. I open the door all the way and make sure to greet him with a smile. "Hey."

His shoulders sag in relief when he sees me and offers me a grin in return. "Hi."

Hearing his voice after not hearing it all day has made my mood so much better. A cold wind blows, and my bare legs shiver when a few flakes of snow swoop in and swirl around my feet. "Come in, come in. You must be freezing."

"Yeah, thanks." He takes a step forward, and snow and ice fall onto the welcome mat as he cleans off the bottoms of his shoes.

He takes up so much space. I knew he was a big guy but seeing him up close like this makes me realize how small I am in comparison. I crane my neck back to get a good look at him, and he stares down at me with those gorgeous hazel eyes and cold red cheeks.

I close the door with a soft click as he shrugs off his jacket.

I can't help it. I watch as he does the most basic thing a person can do. Taking off a jacket isn't a big deal, but it is when he does it. Kansas slides one arm out of the jacket, showing a plain green Henley shirt. My god, it's hugging all of his muscles. I can tell he works out. I can see the ropes of muscle in his arm. The shirt stretches over his bicep, and when he shrugs off the other sleeve, then hangs the coat on the hook next to the door, I swallow a whimper.

The man should only be allowed to wear a Henley.

Eeek. Oh my god.

His nipples are hard, and I can see they are pierced.

Look away. Don't get caught.

I can't help it. I see the outline of two metal bars, and my lips begin to tingle for a taste...

I wrap my arms around my waist to stop myself from reaching out, then sit down on the couch that's in front of the coffee table. If I give myself space from Kansas, that will be good. I scoot all the way in the corner and crisscross applesauce my legs.

"How are you feeling?" he asks, proceeding to take a seat on the couch too.

Of course my plan would fail.

There's only one cushion of space between us, and he wraps one arm around the back of the sofa, then stretches the other across the arm of the couch. He's getting real comfortable, making himself right at home. He stretches, pressing his back against the edge of the sofa, and there is a nasty crack that travels up his spine that causes him to moan.

Yeah, my eyes are zeroed in on his nipples. The material of the shirt is so thin that the metal glints ever so slightly.

Can he please stop stretching? For goodness' sake, a woman can only handle so much.

"Hmm, what?"

He asked a question, right? I need to answer it.

He smirks. It's crooked and cocky, tilting his cheek just to the right to show a damn dimple.

A dimple.

He knows exactly what he is doing.

This man exists to torture all of womankind. I don't stand a chance.

"I asked how you are feeling? I'm sorry I wasn't there for the meeting. I had to go on a run for Prez." He reaches over and tugs on one of my curls. He pulls it all the way down and lets go, watching it bounce in place. "Oh, sorry. I like to watch the spring."

"It's alright. I know, my hair is crazy—"

"—It's gorgeous. Don't let anyone tell you any different."

I shift under his gaze as we lock eyes, staring longingly at one another longer than necessary—again. My heart begins to throb every second that passes with every second he doesn't look away. I read somewhere that chemistry can be created between two people if they stare into each other's eyes for ten seconds.

I believe it now, because I can hardly breathe the longer we stare. My palms sweat. My tongue goes dry, and I'm noticing aspects of his face that I wouldn't typically pay attention to, like the small dash of freckles scattered across his nose, and the tattoo on the left side of his face. It's tiny, hardly noticeable, but it's at the outer corner of his eye resting on his cheekbone—a heart. Never in a million years would I think that would be attractive or masculine, but he makes it work. His chin is square and there is a dip right under his bottom lip.

He is a handsome devil that makes me want to rebel against every warning my mom instilled in me about a man like him.

Kansas scoots over, and I gasp when his fingers graze over the side of my arm as he settles in front of me. "Are you ever going to tell me how you are?" he asks for the third time, still never breaking eye contact with me. It's intimidating. "How is your head? Does it hurt?"

The blue flecks in his green irises have me lost in the sea all over again.

"I'm okay," I finally remember how to speak. "My head is fine, but um…" I cough to clear my throat. "Boomer said that he thinks someone is going to come looking for their drugs since they weren't delivered, but I swear, Kansas, I didn't know. I still don't know if what he thinks of my dad is real. I almost can't. I would feel like everything was a lie."

I let all of my worries spill from me in one breath, and I inhale a long deep breath when I need air. I cover my eyes with my palm and laugh, but it's tinted with despair and embarrassment. "I'm sorry. I didn't realize how much I wanted to talk about it. It scares me."

Kansas tugs my hand down from my face and his wide, calloused index finger rubs across the top of my hand. "You don't have to apologize. I'm happy to listen, and don't ever feel like you have to hide yourself from me. I like looking at you, Springs," he says, still staring into the windows of my soul. "Talk to me about what else is on your mind."

He likes looking at me. Can I misinterpret that? Do friends say that to one another? I've never had a male friend before. "I like looking at you too." I don't even know if he can hear me with how quiet I'm speaking. There's a fever running through me making me hot, and If I'm sweating, I hope it isn't noticeable.

How embarrassing would that be? Oh, I'm just melting

into a pile of goo from how close he is, no big deal. I'm such a virgin. I bet he doesn't like that. He seems like the kind of guy that takes girls to bed every night.

And that thought has a pang stinging my chest. I don't want him to be with anyone else, but I can't claim him. He is far from being mine. For all I know, he'll be having sex tonight. "Mmm, see there it is. This is why I like looking at you. You speak with your eyes. They are always so expressive, and right now, whatever you are thinking, you didn't like it."

I can't tell him the truth. That's too personal. "Um—" I push my hair behind my ear and turn toward him so I'm directly facing him more than I was. My knees bump his. He has one leg tucked under his butt and the other is down, foot flat on the floor. "—I was just thinking about what will happen if our name is associated with drugs. Boomer said it might mean trouble. So does that mean I can't take my sisters home? I don't know what to do next." It's still the truth. I am scared of what happens next.

His fingers slide under my chin, and he lifts my head. "I don't think it's safe for you to go home. If you're wanting to go get your things, that much I can understand, but I don't think it's a good idea to live there again. If someone is looking for their product, the first place they are going to look is your home. Drug dealers, mob bosses, whoever the clientele is, they aren't the kind of people someone fucks over. They will come looking. It's best if you stay here. Besides—" he pushes his knee against mine again, so we are touching, "—I don't want you to go. I hope that's okay to say. I know you've been through a lot, but I want to get to know you better. And I know how that sounds, it sounds like I'm wanting you to stay for selfish reasons, but I'm not new to this way of life. I know you need to be safe. And you and your sisters are safe here. I promise."

"You want to get to know me?"

His fingers slide across my jaw, and his fingers turn into his entire palm as he cups my cheek. "I really do."

"You don't..." I lick my lips as my nerves get the best of me. "You don't have a girlfriend?" I whisper. Then I realize I am making assumptions. "Boyfriend?"

"Boyfriend?" he chuckles, his brows lifting in surprise.

"Oh, I don't mean to say you look gay, I just didn't want to assume—"

"—No girlfriend. No boyfriend. I was hoping you and I could go out sometime? Just me and you. I know your life has been turned upside down, but I'm hoping I can be the person to turn it right side up again. If not, I'm more than happy to be your friend."

"Do you want to be? My friend?"

He pinches his lips together as his eyes dart all over my face. He gives me a tight smile. "Honestly, I have plenty of friends, Springs. I want more than that with you."

"Why?" He can have anyone he wants, yet he wants to get to know me.

"That's what I want to figure out. I've never wanted more than what I've had. I've never needed more, but now I do."

"I'd like that," I admit, pressing my cheek harder against his palm.

"Tomorrow?"

I nod, not wanting him to go just yet, but I know this is about to come to an end with how he is withdrawing his hand from my face. I turn into the wide palm, smelling the musk of his skin, and I can taste the salt on his flesh.

"I don't want you to go." I don't mean to say it, but he feels so good. I don't expect such a gentle touch from him, especially with his tattooed hands against my plain skin.

He's trouble.

And my heart is all about it.

"I have to. If I don't, we will get into that bed and we will do things that I've thought about since the moment I saw you. If I don't leave—" his voice deepens, and I imagine it's what he sounds like after staying up too late at night, full of rasp but not the need to rest. "—I'll kiss you."

I snap my eyes up to his, shifting my weight under his sights.

"And I won't just kiss you. I'll deepen it. I'll slip my tongue inside so I can taste you. And then when that isn't enough, because I know it won't be, I'll take off your shirt to touch your skin." He inches closer to my face, his lips hovering right above mine. My eyes flutter when he drifts to the side and caresses his lips on my cheek. "But then that won't be enough."

My chest is rising in beats that would match a tempo of a raging bass. "No?"

"No. Fuck no. I'd take off your pants and dip my fingers into your panties to feel how wet you are, but then that wouldn't be enough." Hot puffs of breath leave his lips as he roams his lips down my neck. The space between my legs pulsates and wetness coating my panties. "Then I'd want to taste too. I'd somehow manage to rip my lips from yours and kiss your pussy until you're coming on my tongue."

I whimper and lean away from him, gripping the armrest of the couch for dear life.

"But then that wouldn't be enough," he growls, almost

angry. "I'd need to slide my cock inside you and feel you grip me."

Oh, god. "Would it be enough then?"

"No," he states, drifting his hand up my torso, following the curve.

"No?" I repeat, a bit surprised. What else would a man want?

"I have a feeling I'll always want more when it comes to you. It's why I'm going to go. I'm going to walk out that door, and I'll pick you up tomorrow night for our date like a real gentleman should."

"Are you a gentleman?"

"No, but I want to be for you."

"So if I said—" I whine pathetically as he peppers a kiss along my collarbone. "When I tell you I'm a virgin, you'll be okay with that?"

He grips me by my hips and throws me around like I weigh nothing, until I find myself pinned against the wall by the couch. I'm barely standing on my own two feet, his fingers digging into the bone, which is the only thing keeping me upright.

"You've never been with anyone? Look at me," he snaps, gripping the top of my neck to force me to look at him.

I shake my head, and I feel the sway of my curls bounce around me.

"Fuck," he rocks my hips against him, and his erection rubs against me, igniting a new fire that I've never felt before.

"Is that bad?"

"No. You have no idea how much..." a frustrated groan leaves him, vibrating his chest until I can feel it against mine. The stubble on his cheek scratches mine, and he kisses me right next to the edge of my mouth. "I'm going to go. I'm going to walk out that door, say goodnight, and go to my room where I'm going to jack myself off thinking about you."

"Kansas," I moan, half-tempted to say the hell with it and let him take me right here and now.

"Don't say my name like that. Fuck me, don't say it like that. You're turning me into a weak man." He steps away, breaking the erotic contact and readjusting himself, which only makes me yearn for him more when I see the outline of his cock.

I stay exactly where I am, frozen against the wall, too afraid to move or I might break this spell I'm under.

"Goodnight, Violet."

"Goodnight," I say through choppy, unstable breaths.

I watch him leave, his firm ass hugging against his boot-cut jeans. He grabs his coat and opens the door, and the untamed air swirls in again, bringing the scent of salt and snow.

"Violet?"

I turn around to see the door halfway shut and his back turned to me, so I can't see his face.

"Kansas?"

"Dream of me." He slams the door closed, and I'm left with unsatisfied heat between my legs.

Dream of me.

It would be impossible to not dream of Kansas.

The man, *not* the state.

KANSAS

Kansas

UNITED STATES

CHAPTER SEVEN

THE WINTER AIR DOES NOTHING TO COOL MY HEATED SKIN. I'M ON fucking fire for her. I'm going out of my fucking mind with how much I want her. Every time I breathe, the air fogs, but it isn't frozen. No, I doubt it. It's smoke from the inferno inside me.

I've fucked a lot of women. I've had the need for sex just like every other man that needed to scratch an itch, but the need for Violet is so much more than that. It's an all-consuming rage. It's the need to claim her, over and over again. It's as if I need to get a certain point across for her to understand how much she needs to know she's mine.

It's premature for me to say, but I know it. I don't care how long I have to wait; I'll prove we will be good together.

And then I'll get between her legs, a place no man has ever been, and make my fucking point.

I kick the door open to my room, place my boot on the wood, and push it shut. I throw my coat on the floor, toe off my boots, and then lock the door.

I can't have her yet, but that doesn't mean I can't imagine it while I pleasure myself. In jerky, hurried motions I yank off my shirt, toss it on the floor, then tug my pants. These are my tighter jeans. They hug my thighs a bit more than the others, so I have to pull on the denim a bit harder than what I normally do.

"Fuck," I grumble when they get stuck around my ankle. I hop to the bed, tugging on each pant leg until I'm able to fall onto the mattress. God, why did I wear these jeans? I wore them for her. When I got back from the run, I changed and knew these pants were tighter and would show off my body a bit more.

I forgot how much of a pain in the ass they were to get off.

Lifting my legs, I grab each pant leg and pull, finally getting the bunched-up material around my feet free. I throw the jeans behind me and catch my breath as I stare up at the ceiling. My cock is hard, pointing out of the waistband of my underwear.

I flip over onto my stomach and crawl forward so I can reach my nightstand and open the drawer. I'm going to say this: how I masturbate compared to how other men masturbate might be a little different. Don't get me wrong, I love a good ol' fashioned with only the hand, but I get more pleasure by getting a few toys out.

And thinking of Violet definitely has me wanting to

91

use all of them. I need more than to fuck my fist. I need a mind-blowing, earth-shattering sensation that will help ease the fire searing through my veins.

My cock is so fucking hard it hurts, and as I stretch against the bed to wrap my fingers around the handle of the nightstand, I moan from the friction rubbing against me. I grab the fleshlight and prostate massager and toss them on the bed, along with the vibrating cock ring and lube. A lot of men jerk-off to just orgasm.

I get it, I do that sometimes too, but I love to feel pleasure.

The prostate massager is one of my favorites. I'm straight. Always have been and always will be, and a lot of the time men think of the prostate as something gay men explore. No. I'm comfortable to know that I like my body explored, and the prostate is a magic fucking button waiting to be pushed. I'm not wanting to get fucked or anything like that. It isn't my thing, but playing with me?

That's my fucking thing.

Makes me feel good.

That's all I want.

I flip to my back, dipping my fingers into the waistband of my briefs and tugging them down to free my erection at last. The fat head slaps against my stomach and already I'm leaking precome all over my belly. I'm a big man. I've learned how to please myself, because there have been many instances where a woman doesn't want to fuck because of my size. The last thing I want to do is hurt anyone.

So when I want to fuck and don't feel like going to the bar and maybe getting turned down once they see my cock, I stay in.

And I'm glad, because I've learned a lot about myself.

I click the bottle of lube open and drizzle a few drops along myself, hissing since it's a little cold. The twelve-inch length jerks, and my sack pulls tight to my body as I wrap my fist around myself. I slide the lube around and the flesh shines against the light. I stroke myself a few times, my cock hardening more when I think of Violet trying to wrap her slender fingers around me. I bet her forefinger and thumb wouldn't even touch.

She'd be amazed. Her big eyes would widen further, the violet irises bright as a tulip in bloom as she explored her first cock. A tremor wracks through my body at the thought. I wonder if I'd be too much for her. In my fantasy, I'm not.

My Springs loves my cock. She's lapping at it with her tongue, trying her best to please me. She has both hands around the length, pumping simultaneously as she has half of me down her throat.

"Oh, that's it," I groan into the empty room. My legs spread open, and I reach for the prostate massager, dragging it across the plump vein filling my shaft to get it slick with lubricant. It's an interesting device. It looks a lot like a butt plug, but it has more of a handle to it that settles against the crease.

There's a little discomfort at first as I push it past the tight ring of muscle. Yeah, that's the part I don't like. Once it's all the way in, it settles right against the prostate, which has my cock leaking and pathetic sounds leaving from between my lips. My legs tremble while I roll to grab the remote that controls the vibration, and I shout when the movement causes it to slide in a little deeper.

"Fuccckkk," I draw out, and a sheen of sweat drapes over my skin instantly.

I crank the remote to three, which won't make me come

too fast, but will keep me right on the edge while I play around with the other toys.

A low buzz fills the air, and my arm slams against the bed. I fist the sheets, tugging on them as the massager does its job. My cock spurts more precome, red and angry from the amount of fucking need coursing through me right now.

The need to come.

The need to be with her.

The need to feel good.

Fuck, it's all too much. My body aches to the core.

I think of her hands drifting down my body, her mouth wrapping around my cock as the massager rubs against me. She doesn't judge. She loves it. She sucks me, licking me like a damn lollipop, and it brings me closer and closer to orgasm.

"Jesus fucking Christ. Oh god." My back arches off the bed. I can't take it anymore. It's all too much. The pleasure is bringing pain, but the good kind. The kind I want more of and less of at the same time.

I lick the sweat off the top of my lip as I tilt my chin to my chest, staring at my dripping slit. The thick muscle is a deep red, pulled as tight as it can grow, and every few seconds it jumps from the static charge the prostate messager gives me.

Men really need to get over themselves, because this feels so goddamn good.

I pinch my pierced nipples and give them a good twist, grunting when it adds to the wild sensation. "I'm going to come. So fucking good. Yes," I hiss, tugging on the bars through the tight beads. I've never come without an actual touch.

Violet is driving me insane.

"Violet," I say her name when the heat in my cock becomes too much. "Violet." My chest rises and falls in erratic, broken beats. "Violet!" I shout, watching as jets of come land on my belly. I continue playing with my nipples, roughly twisting the bars as my orgasm waves through me.

I don't stop there.

I'm not a one and done type of man.

As the massager pulsates on my over sensitive prostate, my cock stays hard, and I reach to the other side of the bed and grab the cock ring. I slide it through a thick white puddle to make it slick as I slide it down my girth until it's settled at the base.

Next, the fleshlight.

It doesn't feel as good as the real thing, but it gets the job done.

I scoop some come onto my cock and slip myself through the tight hold of the fleshlight. It's a soft silicone material and fakes the feel of what a pussy is like. Nothing can compare to a tight, hot, wet cunt, no matter the toys they invent.

"Ah, sonofabitch, that's fucking good, baby," I pretend to say to Violet, wishing it was her lowering herself on my dick instead of this toy.

Now, I jack myself like I promised I would.

The wet sounds fill the air as I fuck the fleshlight. I thrust my hips up, needing the extra friction, but then the fucking toy presses against my prostate harder. My neck strains as I bend back, stretching my body out as pleasure zips through me.

Fuck.

Nothing has ever felt this good. I think of those round

eyes staring back at me as she rides me. Her hands are on my chest, her hips rocking back and forth as she takes every single inch of my cock. She's whimpering my name. Her eyes roll to the back of her head, and she's coming, milking me for my come.

And that's all it takes.

I'm coming a second time, and the power behind this orgasm is greater than the last. A stream of white hits me under my chin, neck, and chest. It's just as much as it was the first time.

"Violet," her name is a hushed secret admitted into the room, a fallen whisper drifting through the air like a snowflake.

I pull the massager from me and sag against the bed, spent, exhausted, sweaty, and a damn mess. My muscles are at ease, and my mind is a blank slate, but the need for her is still pushing me to the edge. I want so bad just to fall off the cliff and jump into her waters.

The thought of being with her gives me a great orgasm, but I bet actually being with her will give me the best.

I sit up, swaying from how lightheaded I feel and grab the massager from the bed, then hold onto my softening cock in the fleshlight so I don't make a mess on the floor.

There used to be a time in my life where I ignored pleasure. I didn't care about how good it felt to touch myself, I only wanted the end goal. I found it annoying, like a job to make myself come. It had been a dare to walk into an Adult store when I was nineteen and Nigel was visiting. Fucking Nigel. I was so mad at him for making me go in there, but when I did, it was like the world opened up, and there were these possibilities I didn't know about.

I bought something that day. Nigel thought it was a joke, and that's what I let him believe. I didn't use that toy for about five years. It sat in my drawer until I got up the nerve, and a good handful of women who didn't want to have sex because of my size.

And then I educated myself.

Hell, sometimes I get more pleasure out of masturbating and using new toys than I do having sex with women I hardly know.

I doubt that will be the case with Violet.

I toss the toys in the tub and turn on the shower. A few hairs on my chest pinch as the come dries. My skin begins to itch, so I step into the hot spray and it roams over the front of my body. My mind begins to wander as I stand there as the steam rises, and the water causes my skin to turn pink.

Violet is the woman I've been waiting for, the one my heart has always yearned for, the one I can prove to myself that I'm nothing like my father for.

Despite how many times I've told myself I'm not, I don't think there will ever be a part of me that fully believes that. Leaving her alone would be the best thing. It would probably save her a lot of hurt in the future.

But I can't.

Washing off my body and my hair, I climb out of the tub and decide to let nature takes its course. I don't know what will happen, but I cannot live my life in fear and miss out on probably the best thing that can ever happen to me.

I hate my father even more for creating this self-doubt constantly inside me. Stepping out of the shower, I grab a towel and wrap it around my waist.

Thud, thud, thud.

Someone bangs on the door, shaking the entire room. "Kansas, we need to go! Boomer is calling Church!" Arrow shouts through the closed door.

"Oh, come on," I bitch and moan. It's late. What the fuck is he doing calling Church? I was about to go to bed. I feel so fucking sleepy and relaxed. Church is going to get me all riled up again, and I won't be able to go to bed. "Damn it." I stomp forward, clutching onto the towel so it doesn't fall.

"Kansas!"

"I fucking hear you, Arrow. I'm getting dressed. I just got out of the shower." Even though there is a door in the way, I can hear him slurping on his juice box.

"Okay, I'll wait."

"I don't need a babysitter, Arrow. You can go."

"It's okay. I don't mind," he says, his juice box sounding again.

I pinch the bridge of my nose and count to five to gather my patience before slipping on a pair of sweatpants. I snag a Ruthless Kings Atlantic City hoodie from the drawer too. It's blue with a black Kings emblem on the back and my name on the front left side of my chest. I slip on my boots and don't bother tying them before I swing the door open.

Arrow is standing right in front of my door, a tiny fucking red straw in his mouth while he holds an apple juice box that's smaller than his hand. He looks like he could crush it with just a hard stare. His eyes lift from the ground, and when he sees me, he grins around his straw.

He has the worst habit of biting the very tip of it. I don't know how he is able to get any juice through it. "Hey, Kansas," he greets.

"Hey, brother." I lean in and give him a quick hug and a few slaps on the back. Me, Arrow, and One-Eye all have a bond

98

unlike anyone else here. Being a part of the old chapter and going through what we went through, it's impossible not to be closer than the average people. We were strung up for weeks in that barn, and the only thing we had was each other to make sure we survived.

There was a time or two that One-Eye had us worried. They burnt his eye out and didn't bother treating it. It got infected, and he lost consciousness a few times as the infection got into his blood.

It was by far the scariest fucking experience of my entire life. I'm not afraid of a lot of things, but those nights in the barn will haunt me forever.

"What's Church about?" I ask him as we walk down the pathway. It's covered in salt so the ice melts and none of us bust our asses. We would too if our ice-skating skills—or lack thereof—are anything to go off of.

"I don't know. He just wanted me to round the troops. Plus, he wants to know how today went."

"Fuck. I forgot to update him. That's my fault."

"I know. You were too eager to see your new little lady friend," Arrow teases, peeking at me through the corner of his eye as he drinks his juice.

How is there any left in that little square box?

"Shut up," I mumble, stuffing my hands in the hoodie pocket.

"I knew it. You like her!"

"Shut up," I sing into the starry night.

"Hey, I think it's great. I've never seen you with someone for longer than a night."

"Just... let's keep it to ourselves okay? I don't want to fuck it up."

"Why?" he asks.

He steps in front of me to block the door so I can't open it. "Arrow," I complain.

His brows push together, and his hand lands on my shoulder, lifting his gaze at me to catch my line of sight. "Why do you think you will? Does this have anything to do with your dad?"

"Aw, who has daddy issues?" Homer shuffles his feet along the icy ground, taking his time so he doesn't slip and fall.

I roll my eyes and push Arrow to the side. "No one, let's go meet Boomer. He isn't going to wait forever."

"Want some weed to cheer you up? I'll give you an entire baggy. That's like an eighth. That should last you a night," Homer says, pushing between Arrow and me as I open the door.

"A night? That's gotta be what, three or four joints? How much do you smoke, Homer?"

"What the fuck is it to you, boy scout?" he snips at me. "It's for my fragile ego. I'm a delicate fucking flower."

"Poison Ivy is not delicate, Homer."

"Fuck you, Arrow. I'll give you a reason to itch your ass! I'll shove my foot so far up your—"

A loud pop and a small spark lands right at our feet shutting us up. The three of us lift our heads to see Prez standing there with a box of bang snaps in his hand. Without saying another word, he throws a handful at us, and they land right on our boots. We jump backward to try and get away from them, but he keeps throwing them until we are dancing.

Pop. Pop. Pop.

Arrow swings Homer up into his arms, and Homer starts slapping Arrow in the chest. "Put me down. This is a bunch of damn hootenanny."

"But your rice crispy bones!" Arrow shouts when the bang snaps pop against his juice box.

Boomer has impeccable aim.

"You piss me off." Homer fights Arrow every step of the way, struggling against him, and Arrow is bending, squatting, stretching his arms so Homer doesn't fall out of them.

"Will—" I jump out of the way as another round of bang snaps hit the floor "—you two," I'm tap dancing at this point, "—stop bitching!"

Boomer tosses his head back and laughs, gathering a crowd of the rest of the guys.

"Can I throw some, Prez?" Teeth asks, tucking his pliers into his pocket and rubbing his hands together.

"Be my guest, Teeth. It seems they aren't going to learn to stop bickering no matter how many I throw, so let's just have fun."

"Prez, I'm not a part of this," I explain to defend myself.

"I know. I'm just having fun." Boomer grins, tossing another handful of fireworks at my feet like he is blowing lucky dice.

"Okay, Prez. We will stop. I'm getting tired. Homer's bones weigh more than he looks," Arrow stands on his tiptoes and turns to the side to miss another round of snaps from Teeth.

I give Homer a dirty look to shut him up, and he grinds his jaws together to keep himself silent.

"Aw, I wanted a go at it," Void pouts.

"Me too," Nails chimes in.

"Well, I have a few things to say, and then everyone can have fun throwing bang snaps at each other. Conference room. Now. I won't say it again." Boomer eyes all of us before heading into the Church.

Boomer is younger than most of the members here, besides Warden and Bane. Some might think it's odd for a man to be Prez so young, and it is, but he's fucking proven himself more than other Presidents that have been in the position for years. Everyone listens to Boomer. He doesn't fuck around, and he isn't afraid to blow anyone up, so since I prefer my head attached to my body, I head into the conference room and take a seat next to Prez since I'm acting VP.

"Where's Wolf?" Pulse asks as he pulls out a chair across the table and sits down.

"Don't worry about him. He's fine," Boomer states, taking the seat at the head of the table.

Which means he probably isn't fine.

Once everyone is settled, Warden closes the door. He and Bane stay in the main room since they are prospects and can't join in on the meetings just yet.

"Kansas, how did today go?" he questions, plopping his boots on the table.

"Alicia and Kimmy can sleep at night. That guy is fish food."

"Thanks, brother," One-Eye gives me an appreciative nod.

"Anytime," I say happily. "The businesses on the other hand are going to be a bit more difficult. I saw three strip clubs today. Only one agreed to split ownership to give us thirty percent. The rest aren't interested in selling to us for obvious reasons."

"We'll keep working them. Give me the name of the guy who agreed, and I'll go visit him tomorrow."

"You got it, Prez. I'll text you after the meeting."

Boomer rubs his temples as he takes a deep breath. "Boys,

we got a fucking problem on our hands now. No thanks to your new friend, Kansas."

I straighten, leaning over the table, preparing to defend her.

"And we don't have problems yet, but it's only a matter of time. After putting out a few feelers underground, Theodore Winston's name is not only well known, but he was the fucking man to go to for the best drugs. He was known for his cocaine."

"—Fuck."

"—Damn it."

"—What's this mean for us?"

"—Are the girls going to leave? We don't want this kind of trouble."

One by one the guys speak up until the conversation is loud between everyone, and I can't understand what they are saying.

"Okay, okay, calm down," Prez shouts over us, but it doesn't work on anyone, they only get louder. He digs into his pocket and gathers more bang snaps, throwing them on the table as loud as he can.

"I said shut the fuck up!" he roars after the fireworks pop. His chest is heaving, and he slams his fists on the table, his blonde hair falling into his face. "The girls are safer here. No, we don't want trouble like this, but it was only a matter of time. Jesus, I swear if I have the luck Reaper has with his members, I'm going to bang my head up against the wall. These girls need us. They can't go home."

"Do we know who is missing their drugs, Prez?" Colt asks.

Homer passes a blunt around to Boomer and Prez tilts

his head back, takes an inhale, and blows the smoke in the air. "We sure fucking do, boys. We sure fucking do."

He doesn't say anything else and leaves us hanging on his words. Every member is staring at him, waiting for him to drop the bomb, but he takes another hit of the blunt. The embers are orange as the paper burns and the scent of weed fills the air.

"Prez," I say his name in a way to stop delaying, and he swings his feet to the floor and scoots forward.

He passes the roach to Homer and blows a lungful of smoke in the air. "Lorcan O'Crowely."

"Fuck," I curse when I hear the name.

"Who is that?" Void and a few others ask.

Me, Arrow, and One-Eye know who it is. It's hard not to when we live in our kind of world on the east coast.

"Kansas. Do the honors," Prez tells me, and One-Eye and Arrow are both wearing the same, dreadful expressions on their face.

I sigh and turn in my seat to look at the rest of the guys. "O'Crowely is the head of the Irish mob in New York City. He's in deep with cartels. His networking is huge. He has guys in prison working from prison. He has reach all around the world. He kills first and asks questions later. He isn't like Moretti, the Syndicate Boss in Vegas. He's much more vicious. The Irish do not fuck around. He is known for his drug empire. He will look for his drugs, and I bet he knows everything there is to know about Violet and her sisters. He's smart. It won't be long until he searches here."

"Why? How would he look here?" Decay questions. "Seems like a needle in a haystack. We are worrying when we don't have to."

"O'Crowely has men everywhere. This isn't the syndicate boss in Vegas who rules fucking Vegas, Decay. This is O'Crowely. He rules half of the country, he supplies half of the country with drugs and weapons, and he doesn't give a fuck who dies along the way. He will look here, because I bet anything he has eyes here. He has eyes everywhere. This is not fucking good. This is the last thing we wanted." I run my fingers through my hair and start wondering how the hell I'm going to keep Violet safe. I can't let anything happen to her.

"You might know him by something else," Boomer adds, dragging his hand over the smooth tabletop. "The Irish Crow?"

And there it is.

Everyone curses.

"Lucky us. Kansas, you'll explain to Violet what's going on and how much danger they are in."

"Of course," I answer quickly.

"Why can't we just give him his drugs and be done with it?" Teeth asks, then leans back in his chair and spreads his arms wide like he has found the answer to the universe.

"Because you're acting like you're dealing with a rational man. He isn't known for second chances. In his eyes, Violet's dad fucked him over so he will want not only his drugs, but payback."

"But her dad died in the storm," Homer's old voice shakes.

"He doesn't care," I finish. "In his eyes, her dad should have been able to handle it, and because he couldn't, he died failing. O'Crowely doesn't like failures."

"He's going to hate us then," Prez jokes since we are a bunch of misfits.

105

A few guys laugh, but it doesn't break the tension.

"How long do you think we have before we have trouble?" I ask, thinking about all the ways we need to be ready and how I can make this clubhouse safer. I need to prepare the girls and show them some self-defense moves to protect themselves. They need guns too.

"Honestly, I wouldn't be surprised if he were already on his way here."

When it comes to time, I refuse for anyone to fuck with any of mine. My father took enough from me.

I won't let O'Crowely do the same.

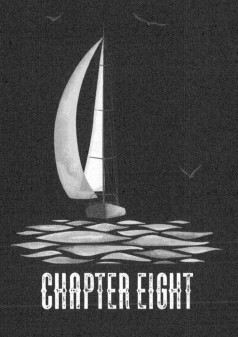

CHAPTER EIGHT

Violet

"So you're going to go out with him? You're going to leave us here with people we don't know?" Veronica scoffs, crossing her arms as she plops on the bed. She's pouting. Nearly eighteen years old and pouting.

"That's your fault. I'm not going to miss out on an opportunity to be happy because you feel like being a brat about this situation. You're the one choosing to be unhappy with the situation. You're the one being rude to badass bikers. You are. Don't blame me for choosing happiness."

I grab a pair of skinny jeans from the shelf and hold them in the air, shaking them at Veronica. "Do you see this? You see these clothes? Scarlett went shopping for us. She did this.

She cared enough while she doesn't even know us. You're not being appreciative. We have a roof over our heads. We have food. We have clothes. We could have died, Veronica. We could have ended up on a shore where no one found us and we froze to death, but we didn't. We ended up here, and I'm thankful for that, so grow the fuck up, Veronica."

It feels good to rant. She's being so impossible and while she's usually the one with more attitude, being disrespectful isn't like her. I won't have it. "And you aren't the only one who misses Mom and Dad, if this is what this is about. I miss them too, but guess what? There's a good chance they lied to us our entire lives. So maybe instead of being mad at the world, be mad at them. I am." I snag a burnt orange sweater from a hanger and head to the bathroom to get ready.

"I agree with Violet," Victoria's small voice whispers.

"No one asked you," Veronica snips.

I glare at her in the mirror. "Hey! Enough. Don't talk to your sister like that. You're being a bitch. You hate it here so bad; nothing is stopping you from heading home." I tug the sweater over my head and gather the strands of my hair to untuck it from the material. "I should warn you, if you do, there's a good chance a drug dealer will find you. So go ahead, leave at your own risk." I don't want her to leave. I'd be too worried, but I have this habit of saying things I don't mean when I'm pissed off.

Isn't that the worst thing about anger? It takes over, engulfing you in a thick cloud, suffocating you, boiling your blood, loosening your tongue until all that's left is to explode. Words are spit out like rancid venom and while the momentary relief feels good, the damage is done.

And sometimes, there is no mending what words have broken.

I have to do a dance to fit the dark blue skinny jeans. My ass is much bigger than it looks. I do a few squats and stretch the material, then tug on the waistband. Good god, these are tight. I'm not going to be able to breathe for the entire date.

It will be fine.

"You don't mean that," Veronica says with emotion choking her throat.

I turn my head over my shoulder and act casual as I take a peek at her. "No? Isn't that what you want? Isn't that what all of this is about, Veronica?" I flip my hair and grab the hairspray and spritz it onto my roots to give my coils some discipline. I don't need them getting out of hand tonight. I flip my head over again and realize there isn't much else I can do.

I stare at her through the mirror again and she wraps her arms around her knees and pulls them to her chest, setting her chin on top of them. "You know it isn't."

"Then you need to figure out why you are treating those around you like complete garbage. I won't stand for it. Put in some effort, Veronica. We might be here a while."

"You're right. I'm sorry."

I spin around, shocked that she just admitted defeat. I push off the bathroom counter and exhale while heading over to her. I wrap her in a hug and hold on tight. "I love you, and I'm sorry our lives have changed. We have to adapt or we won't make it, okay?"

"Okay," she nods, throwing her arms around my neck.

"Come here." I gesture to Victoria to join us, and she knee-walks across the bed, wrapping an arm around me and the other around Veronica.

"I love you both so much," I whisper. "We're all we've got. No matter what, we stick together, okay?"

"Okay," nods Victoria.

"Okay," repeats Veronica.

A knock on the door interrupts our moment.

"Oh my god, that's him." I break our hug and lean back, catching Veronica wiping a tear off her cheek. "Do I look okay?" I give them a spin.

"Gorgeous as always," Victoria comments, giving me a big grin as she sits down next to Veronica.

I skip to the door about to burst with excitement and nerves. I've been on dates before, but none like this. None where I felt like this could be the beginning of something really special.

He knocks again, and my hand is frozen on the doorknob. Oh my god, what if he is *the guy*? My guy. The guy I'm going to spend the rest of my life with?

"Are you going to let him in?" Veronica asks.

I stare at the knob, and I see myself in the reflection. I'm terrified. "What if he is the guy? What if I ruin it? I don't want to ruin it." I keep my voice low so he can't hear me, but my sisters can.

"You really like him, don't you?"

I nod to Victoria, remembering the times he held me through my bad dreams, something he hasn't done lately, and I miss it. I miss him holding me.

"Violet?" His heart-thundering voice has me panicking.

"What do I do?" I whisper hiss and take a step away from the door. "Oh my god, what do I do?"

Veronica flies off the bed and grips me by my arms. "You're going to get yourself together. Stop freaking out. Go out and have a good time. If he is the guy, then your night is going to be the best. Don't keep him waiting, Violet."

"You're right," I breathe and take a minute to calm myself. I'm freaking out for no reason.

"Sorry, Kansas! She's putting on her shoes. She'll be right out," she shouts so he can hear her through the door.

"Oh, okay. Thanks, Ronni," he replies.

He sounds so sexy. I don't know how I'll make it through the night.

"Ronni. That's going to take getting used to," she grumbles. "Okay, go put on your boots and grab that cute peacoat."

"Thank you." I squeeze her hand and then bolt to the closet. I slip on a pair of black riding boots that go to the knee, then yank the plum-colored peacoat from the hanger and put it on. I run out to them again and give them another spin. "So?"

"Perfect. Now go," she says, swinging the door wide open before I can second guess myself again.

I'm left staring at Kansas, who is standing right outside the doorway looking good enough to eat. He's wearing a gray beanie on his head that's pulled down low right above his brows. It has the color of his eyes popping. The shirt he is wearing is another Henley, spread tight across his chest to show his pecs.

To make the outfit even better, the color of the shirt is orange.

We match.

His pants hug his thighs too, just like the ones from yesterday.

"You look beautiful," his voice bathes me in the same warmth a fire whiskey leaves behind. "Great minds think alike." He grins, noticing we are wearing the same color. "Here, I uh… I got you these. I hope they are alright." He awkwardly holds out a bouquet of red roses. I know they are just flowers, but coming from him, they have me liking him even more.

"I love them. Thank you," I tell him, inhaling the sweet scent of the flowers.

"I'll take those and put them in water. You two have fun." Veronica snatches the bouquet of roses out of my hand, places her hand in the middle of my back, and shoves me out the door.

Then slams it behind me while the clicks and clacks of metal sound as she locks the door.

It's cold out here, but the sky is clear, and the stars are out by the zillions. The moon isn't out just yet, and the ocean is gently crashing onto the shore, the ice slowly melting since spring is around the corner.

I'm left standing directly eye level with his chest. The breeze carries his scent to my nose, rain and leather, which has me wanting to bury my face against his neck like a weirdo. I want to inhale him all day.

I want to be like clingwrap and glue myself to him so he can never get rid of me.

That doesn't sound too insane, right?

"You look very handsome," I finally say to break the silence, lifting my hand to fix the collar of his jacket. My fingers brush against the side of his neck, and he growls, pressing himself against my hand so the touch lasts. "Very." The word is as soft and breathless as a feather between us.

"You make it hard to be a gentleman." He rubs his nose down my wrist and brushes his lips against the skin.

"Who says I want you to be?" I can't believe I just said that, but it was the first thing to come to my mind. I know I'm supposed to be a good girl. I'm not supposed to have sex on the first date. Just a kiss at the end, maybe, but he makes me want to throw all caution to the wind.

Is that what my mom had been worried about when she said, "Violet, bad boys are bad news."

And damn, she was right.

I've dated preppy boys who wore polo shirts and khakis, and I never wanted them like I want Kansas. What is it about his appeal? Is it the danger aspect? The not-so-clean-shaven look?

He jerks his head up and then slams me against the door. One hand on my hip, the other caging my head in. "You have no idea just how much I want to break a promise I made to myself when it comes to you."

"What..." I press my hands against his chest and swallow when I feel the strength held within the walls of his chest. "What promise?"

"I swore I would do everything by the book when it comes to you, and that means, no matter how much I want to kiss you, no matter how much I want to peel these clothes off you, I'm not going to."

His lips are so close. They are right there. Right in front of me. All it will take is another gust of wind to push us together. "Why would you do that?" I follow his head with mine as he pulls away. I just want a quick peck, a little taste that will last me throughout the night.

"Because you deserve that. Honestly, I don't want to fuck this up with sex right off the bat. I want to do right by you, no matter how fucking hard it is and how much it tests my willpower."

"Awwwww."

I close my eyes when I hear my sisters on the other side. "They are watching us, aren't they?"

He chuckles, then leans in placing a kiss on my forehead. "Yep. They're looking out the window."

"Can we go now? Before they watch the entire date we are about to have at the door?"

He straightens, towering to his six-foot-four height, and holds out his arm. "I'd love to get the night started."

I blink up at him and loop my arm through his until my hand rests on his forearm. So damn muscular.

"Bye, ladies," he calls back to my sisters, who curse and drop the curtain to hide from us.

Yeah, like that helps. It's too late to be incognito.

My boot slips on a patch of ice and I squeal, flinging my arms into the air. There's that second when you know you're about to bust your ass and it's going to hurt. Where you think 'Fuck, I hope no one can see this' or 'I hope I don't break anything.'

And of course, I'm falling next to the one person I don't want to fall in front of.

"I got ya!" he yells, swooping his massive arms around me.

I have my eyes squeezed shut waiting for my body to hit the ground, but it never comes. My back is resting against his knee, and he still has a strong hold of me. I peek an eye open and see his face come into view. I feel like I'm in the moment of one of those fairytale movies. He saved me from hurting myself, and now I'm lost in the forest of his eyes.

His hand drifts down to my hip, then works its way up again, cupping the side of my neck. Our clouds of frozen breath mingle, and I wait for him to kiss me.

This would be the perfect time for a kiss, damn it.

But he doesn't. He lifts me up and sets me on my feet. "Are you okay?"

No, I am not okay.

How many more instances will there be for a perfect first kiss? That fall was golden material for him to use.

"Thank you for saving my life," I tease, holding onto his arm again as we walk through the breezeway of the clubhouse to get to the parking lot.

"Anytime, Springs," he says, opening the passenger side door for me.

"You're opening my door?" I lift a brow impressed. "I'm not going to be able to get up in the seat—Oh!" He catches me off guard and picks me up, setting me in the truck. He buckles me in too. The strap of the seatbelt digs between my breasts, and he stares at my chest, biting his bottom lip before lifting his eyes to mine.

"If you're surprised by me opening your door, you haven't been dating the right men," he states, yanking on the strap to tighten it so I'm secure. I gasp when his knuckles rub across my nipple, and I don't know if it was intentional, but I want him to do it again.

And again.

"You're probably right."

"Springs, I am right. As I said, I'm going to be a gentleman tonight. Be ready to constantly be impressed by me," he winks.

He closes the door, and I can't help but watch him out of the windshield as he walks around the front to get to the driver's side.

"I'm already impressed," I whisper into the empty cab.

Anymore and I'll be in love with him.

Kansas

UNITED STATES

CHAPTER NINE

I SHOULD HAVE FUCKING KISSED HER WHEN I HAD THE CHANCE. I had made up this entire plan for the evening: open doors, pull out chairs, pay for the meal, and kiss her goodnight. It was perfect, but then she had to step out of her room looking like a dream. I held myself back from kissing her, and that was fine. What's will for, if it isn't meant to be tested?

Then she had to go and fall, scaring me half to fucking death. I barely caught her in time, and she blinked those lavender eyes at me, and I almost said, 'fuck the plan!' She had no idea just how close I was to losing control. I deserve a reward for how I have contained myself.

She's kind of like a gift you see before Christmas. You want to unwrap it, but you can't, and it drives you nuts trying to figure out what's being hidden.

Actually, she's the warning label pasted on the side of the box.

And let's face it, no one reads those.

"Thank you for dinner," she says as I help her put her pea-coat on.

"Anytime," I find myself repeating for the second time tonight.

She buttons her coat, and I hold her against me for a second, letting my nose bury in her hair and the warmth of her body seeping into mine. The clattering of silverware against plates fades and the loud roar of conversations around us are muted. The faint glow of the candle in the middle of the table illuminates against the different shades of blonde in her hair.

I could slow dance with her in this room and turn the slow burn between us into a raging, untamable wildfire.

"Is it too early to say that I don't want this night to end?" I brush my lips across the shell of her ear, squeezing her biceps as emotions trample my heart.

She turns in my arms and shakes her head, her wild curls bouncing with every move of her body. "I don't want it to end either."

"Good. I have plans for us. I just wanted to see what you were going to say."

She playfully punches me in the side. I feign agony and clutch my side. "Ouch, that hurt," I whine, grabbing onto the back of the chair to hold myself up.

"Oh, please. Nothing could hurt you," she rolls her eyes.

I smirk, but the time for playfulness is over. I hold out my hand for her to take, and when her fingers slide between mine, I bring them to my lips and give her knuckles a kiss. "I'm not invincible. Everyone has a weakness."

"What's yours?" she asks, following behind me as I lead us out of the restaurant.

I have a feeling I'm looking at it.

I open the door for her so she can exit first onto the back deck. There are strings of lights everywhere, hanging in half circles along the beams. The bulbs themselves are plain, but it gives the deck a vintage, rustic appearance. The back deck overlooks the park where the skating rink is along with a few other vendors. It's the perfect spot to go after dinner to walk, talk, and get to know one another. A dinner and movie don't allow for much conversation to happen, and if I'm going to be sitting in the dark with her, it's going to be in bed.

"Do you need help down the stairs or do you think you can do it?" I tease, holding out my hand once more for her to take for support. I want her to. I want her to always reach for me, even when she doesn't need help, even when she's more than capable of doing it on her own, I want her to always need me.

"Wow, reminding me of one of the most embarrassing moments of my life?" Violet places her hand in mine anyway. Sparks dance along my skin, trailing up my arm.

She's on the last step and she slips again. Her arms flail, swinging like a windmill as she tries not to fall backward, but it's too late.

Lucky for her, I have quick reflexes.

I snatch her around the waist with my arm and swing her from the steps to the ground, keeping my hand on the dip of her hips. The soft wool of the peacoat rubs against my fingers, and her hands clutch onto the lapels of my jacket.

Here I am, finding myself in the same predicament as earlier. Her chest is heaving, her lips are a bright red from the cold, and her eyes... those fucking eyes are lilac dreams. When I fall asleep at night, I know that's all I'll see.

But the plan I have in my head doesn't fit with what is happening. Our first kiss isn't supposed to happen like this. I bend down and press a kiss just to the side of her mouth, and her lips come next to my ear. An audible shaky breath tickles a hot spot right on the side of my neck and goosebumps arise.

It's winter outside.

But the heat of a thousand summers is brewing between us.

Against my better judgement, I set her on her feet, and if I'm not mistaken, she seems disappointed.

I am too.

I have a method to my madness, I swear. I want to kiss her, but I want to feel when the right time will be. This isn't like kissing a cut slut. This is different. This kiss matters. It's important. The first kiss tells all, and I want her to think 'I want him to be my last kiss.'

I want to be the first.

The last.

And the everything in between.

So yeah, the perfect time matters because she matters to me.

I slip our hands together, and we start to head down the sidewalk that loops around the skating rink.

"Do you want a hot chocolate?" I point to the vendor just ahead to the right. It's a small cart hooked to a truck.

"Lava Chocolate?" she reads the name of the business stamped across the side of the truck and trailer.

"Yeah. It's cold out, and it will warm us up. It'll taste good too."

"Okay, well, I'm getting the biggest size there is."

I hurry ahead of her and stuff my hands in my coat pockets, turn around, and walk backwards so I can see her. "You like things big, Violet?" I grin.

She blushes and looks away from me. Her curly hair bounces with every step she takes.

"Kansas..." she turns coy, trying her best not to laugh, but I see the glint in her eyes, the way her teeth nibble on her bottom lip as she thinks of those... *big* things.

I'm doing research. This entire conversation is for selfish reasons.

"Listen, I just need to know how much money I'll be needing to dish out on every date. If you want a supersize drink every time we go out, that's expensive. So I just need to know if big things... are *your* thing, Springs."

If I'm not mistaken, there's a swing to her hips as she struts toward me. She's determined to see my joke through. "The more, the merrier, in my opinion," she says in an even, strong tone.

"Is that right?" We stop at Lava Chocolate and wait in line. There are a few people ahead of us, a couple snuggling against each other and a kid around ten wearing one of those fur hats with a raccoon tail.

Good for him.

"Yep," she says as-a-matter-of-factly.

"What if you can't finish it?" I clear my throat when an image of her lowering herself on my cock flashes in my mind. She's trying her best to take it all, but she can't. She doesn't stop trying though. She lowers herself until she is at the hilt, stretched out and full.

"I always finish my big drinks, Kansas."

She says that just as I take a step and the kid grabs his drink. He turns around, but I'm too busy staring at Violet, dumbfounded like a big fucking idiot. I run right into him, his hot chocolate falling to the ground. When it hits, the lid pops off, and steaming hot chocolate spills all over my boots.

"Hey, watch where you're going, pal!" the ten-year-old sasses me. "Look what you made me do. You owe me another drink, asshat."

Where the hell did this kid learn to speak like that?

Violet snickers, and I have no choice but to get my wallet out. "Here." I give him twenty bucks. "Scram. It was an accident."

"Forty and I won't cause a scene."

"Take what you have before I give you a swirly, kid."

The freckled-faced monster takes a step back and runs away, crying for his mommy and daddy.

"A swirly? Now, that's just mean. Are you a bully, Kansas?" Violet asks, taking a step forward at the same time I do. We are officially the second in line.

"No. I just don't like brats who try to extort me."

"Well, there goes my plan, gosh."

I dip my head and reach my arm behind my neck, scratching the middle of my back as I take a peek at her with a grin. She's always got me smiling for some reason.

"I'm kidding. I don't need your money, remember?" she hip bumps me.

I love the lightheartedness of the conversation, but when she brings up money, it reminds me of the issue at hand.

Her dad is—was—the biggest drug dealer on the east coast. How do I casually bring that up in the middle of a perfect date?

"What can I get you two love-birds?" the man behind the window asks. He's got flaming red hair and a beard that goes on for miles. Luckily, it's covered with a hairnet.

"I'll take your *biggest* hot chocolate. With extra marsh-mallows, please."

She's out to kill me. She knows exactly what she's talking about. I bet she isn't as innocent as she seems.

"A Big and Dirty for the lady!" he hollers behind him to another worker, a woman who is melting fresh chocolate.

"Big and Dirty coming up!" she echoes.

"Oh my god," Violet whispers so only I can hear.

I bend down and whisper in her ear, "What? You don't like it *Big* and *Dirty*, Springs?" I straighten before she can answer and place an elbow down on the counter. "I'll take the same, please."

"Another Big and Dirty!" he shouts over his shoulder.

Okay. I might have only said I wanted the same thing so I can see her reaction.

"Another Big and Dirty!" his employee repeats.

Violet is staring at the ground, but her cheeks are full and plump, telling me she's smiling underneath all that hair.

"Do you want whipped cream on top?" he asks.

"Oh yeah, whipped cream is the perfect topping on any-thing. Wouldn't you agree, sir?" I ask, tapping my fingers on the counter and doing my best not to laugh.

"Definitely," he replies in a professional manner, not un-derstanding the underlying meaning of what's being said.

She nudges me in the side, giggling silently, and I love that we kind of have our own inside joke now.

"Two Big and Dirties." He places them on the silver counter in front of us along with a red napkin that says 'Lava

Chocolate' in a black cursive outline in a thin square box. "Enjoy."

"Oh, we will. Thank you." I grab the drinks and hand Violet hers.

She wraps hers around the black cup with a red lid, and as we walk away, she bursts out laughing, then snorts. "Oh god," she tries to cover her mouth to muffle the sound, but it only makes her laugh harder.

Which means she is snorting every other second.

It's fucking adorable.

Another perfect time to kiss her, but I won't, simply because I want to hear her laugh.

"I will never be able to drink hot chocolate the same without thinking of this moment." She wraps her lips around the opening in the lid and takes the first sip. She groans in enjoyment, licking the bit of whipped cream off the top of her lip right where the cupid's bow is. "This is by far the best hot chocolate I have ever had."

"Is it the biggest, dirtiest thing you've ever had in your mouth?"

"So what if it is? I'm not ashamed of that."

I'm mid-swallow when she says that, and it has the hot liquid going down the wrong way. My eyes begin to water as I cough.

"Are you okay? Not used to having something so filthy in your mouth?" She sips her hot chocolate, watching me out of the corner of her eye.

"I will admit this is a first."

"Aw look at us, witnessing the loss of our virginities together. Cheers." She clinks our cups together, and my cock is starting to plump at what she said. Silence grows between us as we look at each other, and the gravity of her words start to sink in.

She is a virgin.

I am not, far from it, but if I would have known all those years ago that I would be in front of a woman like Violet, I would have saved myself for her.

"You know what I mean," she adds, drinking her hot chocolate to stop herself from saying anything else.

"I know." I move my drink into my other hand and hold out my free one for her to take. "Let's walk around the rink and watch people make fools of themselves."

She slaps her palm against mine and wraps her fingers through mine. "Sounds like the best plan ever."

The snow and ice crunch under our boots as we walk. We take our time, passing two old people sitting on a bench. The woman has her head on her husband's shoulders as they watch families ice skate together. He is wearing a black fedora and a brown tweed coat, while she is in ski gear that looks like it came from the eighties.

"So—" she begins to say but doesn't finish her thoughts.

"What?" I turn my body just in time before colliding with someone. "Excuse me, sorry."

"Is your real name Kansas?"

I nearly spit out my drink. "God, no," I laugh. "It isn't often I'm called by my given name. All the guys use our road names. Well, except for Colt. His name is Colton."

After a beat of waiting to hear more, she gestures with her hand for me to continue. "Are you going to tell me or leave me guessing?"

"Oh, sorry. My name is Amos Taylor."

"Amos," she whispers like she's trying to taste it on her tongue.

I've never liked my name, but I like it when she says it.

"I love it. It suits you. It's a name not heard of too often."

"Does that mean you think I'm not like all the hundreds of other guys out there with the name Kyle?"

We let out a small chuckle at the joke. "Most definitely not. You are uniquely your own. I've never met anyone like you before," she says.

"I'm not special," I mutter, pulling my brows together in thought.

"I'll have to disagree. I don't know many men who will hold someone they don't know throughout the night when that person is having nightmares and still not expect anything. You're sweet, Amos Taylor. Just about as sweet as this hot chocolate."

I snap my fingers and curse. "Damn, so much for accomplishing my end-of-month goals."

"I think you're doing pretty great," she whispers just as we stop at the top of the bridge that is across the skating rink.

We rest our elbows on the worn and weathered stone and glance over the frozen pond.

Another perfect moment for a kiss.

"Tell me about yourself. How did you get the name Kansas?" she asks.

And there goes the moment. Poof. Gone.

I let out a dreadful groan when she hits a topic I never speak of.

"Oh, we don't have to talk about it—"

"—No, it's okay. I want to tell you everything, it's just a hard subject for me."

Her gloved hand rubs over mine and squeezes, giving me the support I didn't realize I needed. I take a swig of hot chocolate to coat my throat. "I'm from Tulsa, Oklahoma—"

"—I am sorry." She lays a hand against her chest, pretending to feel sorry for me.

"Thank you. That's it. That's the entire story. Being from Oklahoma just does that to people."

"Okay, I'm listening, I'm sorry. I just wanted to see you smile, and it worked, so…" she lifts a shoulder nonchalantly.

I tug one of those curls I love so much and watch it spring into place. "You're good at it. Never stop."

She tilts her head to the left and presses her head into my hand, wanting more of my touch. Is it impossible to love someone after one date? Is it possible to know I want to spend the rest of my life with her? I've never felt like this before, and I want to run with it.

Going back to the subject I despise, I narrow my eyes out to the pond to see a familiar face. It's Ted, the guy who works at the skating rink. He still has a cast on his leg from when he broke it during the snowstorm. I wave to him and he eagerly waves back.

"My Pops worked a lot. He had business trips every weekend, and it was just me and my mom. Well, after so long of dealing with Pops never being home, my Mom fell into depression. It was bad. She slept a lot, cried a lot, and stopped doing things around the house. I didn't realize how much she did until I had to pick up the slack."

"Oh, gosh. That's so much for a kid to deal with," she says.

"Yeah, it was, but I managed. I paid the bills, did all the cooking and cleaning and laundry and housework. I did my best to keep the house in working order, and every time I checked on Mom, a deep hatred for my Pops bloomed. All I remembered was hating him, but he wasn't a bad father. He wasn't abusive to me. He was supportive financially. He was literally the kind of dad kids wanted, but I always felt something was off about him. For a long time, I thought it was me that was broken. The older I became, the worse the feeling in my gut got, and I was so tired of seeing my Mom waste away. She's a good woman. She deserved happiness. And she was slowly dying, and I knew it was because of him." My voice is getting louder. The more I talk about this, the more unhinged I become.

Violet scoots closer to me until our arms touch, and I blow out a stressed breath. Just a simple motion brings me a few levels down from jumping off the ledge.

"I was playing baseball with my best friend Nigel—"

She interrupts me. "Do you still talk to Nigel?"

"Oh yeah, I haven't seen him in a few years, because the old chapter wouldn't allow it. They were terrible."

"Well, maybe this is the chance for you to see him now. Fly him here."

Damn it, I want to kiss her again.

"Yeah, I'll have to ask Prez."

"Okay, I'm sorry. I interrupted again. I'm listening."

I take off the lid and shake the cup against my lips to get some of the marshmallows. "It's okay. I like it," I say, chewing through the chocolate doused fluffiness. "Anyway, Nigel had the idea to follow my dad before he left on Friday. He left every weekend and didn't come back until Sunday night, sometimes Monday. So we followed him. From Tulsa to Wichita, Kansas. Where he had another family."

She gasps, holding onto my hand tightly.

"I saw them run outside to greet them. A little girl, boy, and the woman was pregnant. The marriage couldn't have been legal. He was married to my mom since she was able to file for divorce. It fucking killed me to see him with them. They had everything. He kept their home in great shape, unlike ours. He had a good relationship with their mom, unlike mine. Everything clicked. I knew why I hated him."

"Amos, I am so sorry. He is such an asshole for doing that to you and your mom."

"He came home, and I had thrown all his shit out on the lawn. He had the nerve to keep pictures of his family right under our noses. I was furious."

"Oh, Amos," she sighs.

"So when he got home, we kicked him out. I pointed his gun at his head. I said, "You aren't in Kansas anymore." Or something to that effect, and Pops ran out of the house. Nigel called me Kansas ever since, and the name just stuck."

She throws her arms around me and gives me a hug. "I am so sorry. You didn't deserve that."

I hold her close, soaking in the comfort she's willingly giving, and place my nose against her neck to inhale her fruity scent. My heart rate decreases, and I begin to relax.

"And you call yourself Kansas because of that? Oh my god, that's horrible," she snorts.

I lean back and smile. "It is, isn't it? I've never really thought about it before."

"How?" her eyes dart all over my face, that gorgeous smile of hers stretching her lips. "Maybe you're just a glutton for punishment."

"You may be right," I say, kissing her forehead.

"Well, I don't understand why your dad would do that. Seems both of our fathers lied to us."

I whirl back, flabbergasted that she knows.

"Don't act surprised. My sisters are the ones in denial. I'm not. I connected the dots, but by the look on your face, I guess I'm right, aren't I?"

Our boots thud against the stone as I start walking again. She's beside me, hand on my arm as we continue our leisurely stroll. "Prez called us into a meeting last night. I've been debating on how to tell you. I wasn't trying to hide it from you, I just didn't know how to bring it up on the first real date I've had in years."

"Hey—" she stops walking and holds onto my arm which has me turning around to face her. "I'm not mad. I know it isn't exactly the easiest conversation to bring up, but I wouldn't be mad at you. Him, yes. You, no. Was anything else said? I mean, what's happening with the drugs?" she says a little too loudly for my liking, and a few people turn their heads and give us odd looks.

I snag ahold of her elbow and drag her to the edge of the woods. "You've got to be careful with what you say around here. We don't want this community not trusting us. We are still forming bonds with them. The old chapter took advantage of them, and the fact that we can even show our faces in public without getting killed…"

"I'm sorry. I didn't know. It won't happen again."

"It's okay. I didn't tell you, so that's my fault." I run a hand through my cropped hair and stare up to the sky. "But apparently, your dad was the biggest, most well-known coke dealer on the east coast."

"Oh my god." She sways on her feet. "I need to sit down."

I take her hand and bring her to a nearby bench that has a fire pit in front of it, so we are warm. "That's not the worst."

"Of course it isn't." Violet picks at the edge of the napkin.

"The man the drugs belong to. Prez put feelers out and there is a man named Lorcan O'Crowely looking for the exact same amount of cocaine that we found in your Dad's boat."

Her eyes are glassy when worry, panic, and fear hit her all at once. "Who is that? Can't we just give him the drugs and be done with it?" she looks hopeful.

"He is an Irish mobster. He runs New York City. They call him The Irish Crow. He was in business with our previous Prez. He isn't the kind of guy that is understanding. He will want some form of payment for his delivery being late."

"So me and my sisters are at risk?"

"I'm afraid so. Until we know what to do with O'Crowely, your best bet is to stay with us, and selfishly, I'm happy about that. Selflessly, I'm sorry you can't go home."

"Home is about what's there. There's nothing there for us anymore. It's time to build a life and a home elsewhere." She stands up and takes a step closer to the fire.

The flames dance over her face, showing the expressions as she comes to terms with what I said. She'll be safe here with me, and I hope this is the place she decides to stay.

I think the home we could build together would be extraordinary.

Dreaming about it makes me want it more.

And there's that voice in the back of my head that mocks what I want.

What if this life isn't enough and I need another just like my Pops did?

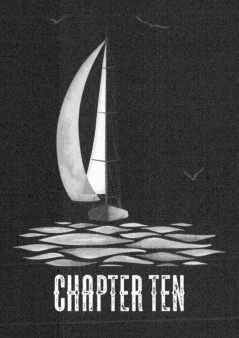

CHAPTER TEN

Violet

THE DRIVE BACK TO THE CLUBHOUSE IS A SILENT ONE. IT ISN'T uncomfortable or awkward, but safe and secure. I feel bad for not carrying on a conversation. I just have too much on my mind. The bomb that Amos dropped is a big one and it's still settling. It's not exactly easy to come to terms with the fact that an angry Irishmen that controls an entire city is after you and your family.

Amos puts the truck into park outside of the clubhouse, and the black building almost blends in with the night, which makes it difficult to see.

"You know I'm not going to let anything happen to you and your sisters, right? I'm going to protect you."

"How? I'm not going to let you put your life at risk for me. We aren't your responsibility. I'm who my sisters have now. It's up to me to protect them."

"And you are by choosing to stay here with us. If you leave, there is no telling what can happen if he finds you. You have to stay."

"But if we stay, your club could get hurt. I don't want that," I explain, turning in the passenger seat so I face him. "I don't want anything to happen to you."

"I'd rather take the chance than have you out there on your own. Don't be stubborn."

"Me?" I fake being insulted and open the door to get out. "I am far from stubborn."

"You better shut that door. I'm not done being a gentleman. Go on," he says, jutting his chin out toward the door. "Close it."

I huff out a breath and shut it again, blocking out the cold.

He gets out and walks around the front of the truck. Again, I'm watching him powerwalk through the built-up pile of snow, and he swipes a chunk of snow off the hood before getting to my door. Butterflies flap around in the chambers of my heart as he clicks the handle. Freezing air hits me, and he stretches out his hand to help me down.

This truck is gigantic.

"I'm going to need a stepladder to get in and out of this thing."

"Springs, there is no way I'm going to let a stepladder steal my thunder," he replies, holding my hand as he shuts the door.

The headlights flash when he presses the button on the

key fob to lock the truck. I'm bummed we are back here. I want us to crawl into the truck and drive so we can be alone. It's late, but I don't want to say goodnight.

I want to say good morning, but I don't have the courage to ask if he wants to spend the night. We don't have to have sex if he doesn't want to, I don't know if I'm ready for that, but maybe he'd just want to hang out? He has had too many opportunities to kiss me and hasn't, so I don't think he will. Which means I'm in the friendzone.

That's what it's called, right? When one person is interested and the other is not, the one that isn't interested politely just scoots us unwanteds to the side, yet continues to be nice.

Well, this is a terrible feeling that I never want to feel again. Rejection can go fuck itself.

I think I love him.

I won't be able to be his friend.

If he doesn't feel for me the way I feel for him, I'll need to leave.

We walk hand in hand down the breezeway and pass the door to the main room, where most of the members are hanging out. It's loud. Music is blaring. Loud laughs can be heard in the hallway. I bet everyone is having a good time in there.

Maybe that's where he wants to be?

"I can walk myself to my room," I'm barely able to push the words past my lips.

"What do you mean?" His boots come to a sudden stop, and the way his lips purse and brows drip tell me he isn't too happy with what I've said.

I'm not blind. I can read between the lines. "Listen, I know dating isn't your thing, and your friends are in the main room having a good time without you. I don't want to keep you back. I don't want you to think you have to walk me to my door when you aren't interested in me."

"What in—"

"—And don't feel bad about it. I get it. I want you to know I had a great time."

"What makes you think—"

I go on. "—I understand I have some baggage. I'm a walking time bomb right now and getting involved with me is crazy. I'm younger too and—"

"—Violet, I—"

I don't let him finish. "—I'm younger with no experience and that's a lot for a man your age to handle. Wait, that came out wrong. I'm not saying you're old, but you are older than me. In a good way. You aren't elderly or anything," I chuckle. God, I'm ruining this. I'm taking that shovel and digging my own grave. "I'm sure you are used to a certain kind of woman, and I'm not that."

"And what in the world makes you think—"

"—And I know all this is true because there have been ample—" he cuts me off by hauling me against him and crushing his lips onto mine.

Oh, wow.

His hands cup my face, and he angles his head to the side as our lips slide together. His lips are plump and soft, gently claiming my mouth in one of the best kisses to ever happen in human history. It has to be. His tongue dips between my lips, and I flick mine out too, not as confident as he is, but I want to taste him as well.

The hot chocolate lingers, and I drink it down, hoping something more than kissing will happen between us tonight. A fire brews in my belly, and I stand on my tiptoes, wrapping my arms around his neck, deepening the kiss. I push my chest against his, and he growls, pushing me against the side of the clubhouse. My back hits the brick wall and his fingers dig into my thighs. Amos lifts my legs, and I hook them over his hips.

He grinds his pelvis against mine, and I feel the hard bulge beneath his pants. It takes my breath away. I have to tilt my head back, which means the kiss is broken, but I need air. His lips trail down the side of my neck, nipping, licking, and kissing until he gets to the collar of my sweater. Those wide palms slide down to my ass and grip the thick globes. Knowing he is so close to my center, a gush of liquid heat escapes, soaking my panties.

My eyes hood when he kisses his way to my lips. He pushes our mouths together again. I whimper, skidding my fingertips up his sculpted physique. Even through his shirt, his stomach flexes, the muscles tightening under my touch. I trace every ridge and valley. A rumble vibrates his chest, the sound primal, animalistic, and threatening.

He sounds like he's about to tear my clothes off, and I want him to.

The kiss comes to another stop, and I lean forward, not ready for it to end yet. My lips are tingling and on the verge of going numb since it's cold out. Saliva pools in my mouth when I see his eyes bore into mine, lifting through voluminous lashes. It's a demented stare, one that tells me just how hungry he is for me.

He's starved, and a predator wanting his prey is a dangerous thing.

I'm cornered and don't stand a chance.

"What were you saying?" he asks, a plummet of icy breath puffing from his lips to mix with mine.

The back of my head hits the wall behind me, and I stare up to the sky. The column of my neck is exposed, bared to him, and he uses it to his advantage. Amos adores my feverish skin with more kisses.

"I was saying," I swallow, trying to catch my breath. "I was saying how you had a hundred—" I moan when he finds the spot right above my collarbone "—chances to kiss me, and you didn't."

"Just waiting for the right time. You kept blabbering, and I knew I had to shut you up."

"Is that all this is?" I keep my tone light as he nibbles on my earlobe.

"Fuck no," he growls. "I've been wanting to do this all night."

"Why didn't you?" I moan when the bulge of his erection presses against me again. I want to unzip his pants and free him. I want to see it, I want to touch it, I want to pleasure him.

I'm so nervous. What if I mess up?

"Because I wanted to get to know you. I wanted us to talk." He brings his head up from my neck to look at me. One hand stays around my waist while the other caresses the outline of my body before he grips onto my neck. It's a powerful, dominant move. If he wanted, he could hurt me with a flick of his wrist and break me right in two.

I didn't think I'd ever like being in the hands of someone so strong, but there's a thrill being in the clutches of a man that could kill me if he wanted to.

"I meant what I said. I didn't want to rush us. I wanted

more than I've had before when it comes to you, and now that I've had a taste, my worries are cemented now."

"What worries?"

"That kissing you—" he meshes his body against mine and those skilled fingers trace along my jaw "—that touching you wouldn't be enough."

"Oh."

He taps a quick kiss to my lips. "Yeah, oh." The tattoos along his neck dance as the tendons jump and the gold nose ring has a glint to it from the light casting from the breezeway.

Amos reminds me of the kind of man you don't want to see in the dark, but when you do, he yanks you into the dark with him.

And that's it.

You're lost in his abyss, and there is rarely a way out.

"Let me walk you to your door now," he says, groaning when he rubs his hands over my ass one last time. "Yeah, we have to now. I'm about to lose it. You're too fucking sexy." He squeezes the left cheek until I yelp from a pinch of pain, but I kind of like it. "Fuck, okay." I drop my legs, and he steps away from me. Cold replaces his warmth leaving me to shiver.

I rake my eyes down his body, but before I can get a good look at his bulge, he tilts my chin up with his fingers. "Come on, Springs. Let me finish this night as a gentleman. I can't make any promises tomorrow, though. I don't think I have it in me."

"I wouldn't want you to," I admit.

I've never felt like this before. There have been plenty of times in life I have been happy. There's the time Dad got me a new car, the time I got into a club even though I was under-age, then the other time when I got horseback riding lessons.

All made me happy, but that happiness was short-lived. The rush of joy wore off. All of those things were just material things I could have lived without.

But this feeling with Amos catapults me to another extreme. It surpasses happiness. It invades the corners of my heart and fills it with hope, dreams, and love.

It's ridiculous.

A ridiculous love that makes no sense. But to me, when I'm with him, it makes all the sense in the world.

We stop awkwardly at my door and we both let out a nervous laugh. What's there to be nervous about? It isn't like we just passionately made out against a wall, and I felt his cock between my legs. I step forward and slip my key in the knob to unlock the door, but for the third time tonight, I slip on ice, and he catches me.

He always catches me.

"I got you," he says, pushing my hair behind my ear as I stare up at him.

He bends down and kisses me. It's quick but heat still sizzles through my body. Before I can thrust my tongue between his lips, he pulls away and sets me on my feet. "Goodnight, Springs."

"Goodnight," I whisper, my voice hoarse from the need to burst from lust.

Our hands stay together for as long as they can before he is too far away, and like the clingwrap I consider myself to be when it comes to him, I curl my fingertips against his.

With one final step away from me, the contact breaks. "Night," he repeats, never taking his attention away from me.

"Night, Amos." I crack my door open, unable to look away from him when his nostrils flare when he hears his name.

Finding some amount of strength and composure, I thrust my shoulders back and step inside the room. I push the door closed, then sag against it, letting out a breath I didn't realize I was holding.

A part of me waits for him to come back, to knock on the door and take me, but seconds tick by, and he doesn't.

I love that he is a gentleman.

I just wish he wasn't being one right now, and I wish I had the balls to take matters into my own hands.

Kansas

CHAPTER ELEVEN

I KICK THE DOOR SHUT AND THROW MY JACKET ONTO THE COUCH. "Walking away was the right thing to do. You were a good man. Walking away..." I scratch the back of my head as I talk to myself "...Walking away was the only thing to do. She's a virgin. You don't want to push her. You like this woman," I keep jabbering as if my best friend is in the room. "You probably actually love her, but you don't know what love is yet, so you want to call it love, but you can't call it love. Walking away was the right thing, Kansas. Be proud of yourself."

I pace the floor beside the bed and replay the evening in my head, right down to the last sip she took of her Big and Dirty.

Perfect.

I know sex between us would have been amazing. "Don't fuck this up," I scold myself as I unbutton my pants and free my erection. "Oh, god," I breathe out. The bad thing about having a huge cock is when it gets hard in a pair of jeans and it's in an awkward position, it fucking hurts.

Yeah, I need to take care of this now or I won't be able to sleep.

I tug my shirt off and a whiff of her perfume hits me. My cock jerks and my lust is telling me to walk out that door and tell her to get on her knees and suck me.

"Nope," I tell myself. "I won't treat her like that. She deserves more." I bring my shirt to my nose and sniff to look for the spot that smells like her. When I find it, I inhale like a madman smelling a pair of fucking panties that have no business being in my hand and groan.

I wrap my hand around my cock and continue to smell her peach perfume. It's like she's right next to me. I imagine her on her knees, opening her mouth to take me in. She rubs her bottom lip across my slit to gather the precome. Her pink tongue flicks out, and she moans when she tastes me.

"Fuck, fuck, fuck." I thrust into my hand faster, my orgasm tickling my spine and pulling my sack against my body. I throw my head back and bury my face in the shirt, nearly suffocating myself with her scent. God, I bet she tastes like peaches too. I want to tongue fuck her virgin cunt until her come is overflowing in my mouth. She'd taste like peach tea, one of my favorite summertime drinks, and I'd help myself to another glass.

Then another.

I'd lick her sweet untouched lock, find the right

combination, undo the gates of her dam, and drink her water down until my thirst is quenched.

But I doubt it would be enough.

Something tells me it will never be.

"Violet. Violet, fuck baby, I'm coming," I moan into the room, tilt my head down, and watch the thick shaft swell before the white cream jets from me. My vision blurs from the intensity. "Ohhh, that's it." Five thick streams land in my other hand since I've cupped it over the tip, so I don't have to clean it off the wall and floor.

I stumble back and hit the couch. I sag, taking a minute to get my head on straight. I haven't come that hard in a long time. Not even since the other day with the toys. I shake my head, trying to gather enough energy to get up and wash my hands, but my cock is still hard, and lust is still pumping through my veins. I always have to come twice before my erection goes down.

I'm about to use my come as lube when there is a knock on the door.

Every muscle in my body tenses, and I stare at my hand that has come in the palm. My cock is jetting out from my pants and it shows no sign of going down.

Damn it.

Whoever it is, they will go away after a minute if I'm quiet.

"Kansas?"

I snap my head toward the door and inhale a sharp breath when I hear Violet's voice.

Oh, no

No, no, no. This can't be happening.

She knocks again, and this time it's frantic. "Amos, can we please talk?"

"Fuck," I whisper to myself. "Uh, just need a minute, okay?" I shout as I toss my shirt to the floor.

"Okay, thank you," she says.

I rush to the bathroom and turn the faucet on with my clean hand and wash the come down the drain. Next, I squirt way too much watermelon burst soap in my hand, but I'm nervous. I feel like I'm getting caught with my pants down—well, technically I am—and the fact that I just came is obvious. Wiping my hand on the towel, I hiss as I tuck myself in my jeans.

There is a trick when this happens to a man. All we have to do is lift our erection and safely squeeze it under the waistband so it can't be seen through the jeans. I open a drawer and snag a shirt.

Any shirt. It doesn't matter.

I tug my arms through the sleeves and open the door, seeing a brightly blushing Violet standing there. "Is everything okay?" I ask, glancing left and right to make sure no one is outside with her. "Come in." I pull her inside and double-check to make sure no one is watching her before closing the door.

"I want you to hear me out," she starts. "And don't interrupt me."

I cross my arms and prop myself against the wall to get comfortable. Seeing her again so soon is making it hard to pay attention to anything other than my cock tucked into my waistband. She's wearing her long, purple peacoat and it's buttoned. Her hair is just as crazy as it was when we left for our date, but something else shines in her eyes.

Determination.

"I know you were wanting tonight to go the way you wanted, but I wanted it to go a different way. I know it's fast.

I know I'm a virgin, and I don't have a clue as to what I'm doing, but I swear, I can learn. I want to please you. I want you, Amos. I've never wanted anyone like you before, and if you don't want me after one night, then… as awful as that would be, I can't imagine being with anyone else for my first time." She unbuttons her coat and lets the material slide down her shoulders. It falls to the floor in a useless heap and what stands before me has me pushing off the wall.

She's a goddess. The only power that has me willing to pray.

Her skin is the color of the clouds on a summer's day, and the nightie she's wearing is simple. It isn't overly sexy like a lot of lingerie. It isn't sheer lace and complicated straps. I don't like lingerie like that. Hers is perfect. It's elegant, a red silk slip that falls to her mid-thigh. There are lace accents down the plunging neckline, but that's it. The outfit brings out her sex appeal, it doesn't take away from it.

I never want her to wear anything else again. Only these. Forever.

She rubs her legs together and grabs her left arm with her right hand. She's insecure. I don't know why. The silk hugs her body as if it's tailor-made to it. Her thighs and ass are a bit thicker than what her normal clothes show, and my mouth waters while my cock leaks against my stomach.

In a split second, my body is against hers. I haven't touched her yet. I want to, but before I do, I need to make sure she knows what this means. She swallows and a droplet of sweat flows down the side of her neck. I can see her pulse thump along her throat. She's either nervous or scared, and if she's scared, this isn't the right thing to do. Not yet.

"You look fucking breathtaking, Springs." I move my

144

eyes downward, and I can see down the plunge of her slip, her cleavage perky and smooth. I want to run my tongue over the mounds and twist her nipples. Are they red? Pink? Big, small? I don't fucking care. I want to see them, taste them, give them the attention they deserve.

She blows out a relieved breath and smiles. "Yeah?" she asks, hopeful.

"Oh, fuck yeah, baby. You sure about this?" I run my fingers under the delicate strap of her nightie, sliding them up and down. I slip the left side off her shoulder and the bare skin tempts me to mark her. "Once we do this, it isn't one night. This isn't a fling. You get in my bed, you spread those flawless legs for me, you give yourself to me, you're fucking mine, Violet."

I squeeze a good chunk of her hair. My nails dig into her scalp as I yank her head back and bring our faces closer together. "I'm already on thin ice when it comes to you. When I came in here..." I walk toward her, and she takes a step back. She has no idea, but I'm guiding her to the bed.

"I jerked off to you, again. I came with your name leaving my lips. I want you. I've wanted you since I saw you blink those gorgeous eyes at me. So you need to be sure. I'm not a man who shares. I'm not a man who plays games. I'm laying it all out there on the table. I'm jealous and possessive. So when I say you're mine—" I throw her on the bed and watch her tits bounce before ripping my shirt off—"I also mean I'm yours too."

"Yes, god, yes. Please, Amos. Please," she begs me. "I want you." Violet roams her hands all over my chest, not knowing where to feel first.

I understand that. I feel like I finally have that Christmas

145

gift I've been waiting to unwrap, and now that I finally have it, I don't know what to do.

Experience doesn't matter. That's what I'm realizing right now. I have all the experience in the world, but with the right person like Violet, it all flies out the window. I'm too nervous. It's about more than reaching the end goal.

It's about what happens between now and then. Honestly, it's a lot of pressure. I care so fucking much. I don't want to mess this up.

"I'll be careful. You're safe with me. I'll take care of you," I inform her, needing her to know I'm not going to just thrust myself inside her and use her. No fucking way. I'm going to appreciate her for hours.

"I know, Amos. For my first time, I can't imagine anyone else."

I fall over her, caging her head in with my arms. I get lost in the beauty of her again, the delicate structure of her face, the high plains of her cheeks, the soft curve of her nose that has a dusting of freckles on it. "I'm your last too, Violet, just like you're mine. Maybe you don't know that yet, that's okay, but I do." I hold onto the sides of her neck and steal her lips into a searing, desperate kiss.

She whimpers down my throat, and I swallow it eagerly. My back tenses when her nails scratch down my spine, and on instinct I thrust my hips, wishing I were inside her. I slip my hands down her body, the silk slipping under my palm as I lift the hem by running my fingers up her thigh.

Her tits stretch the material with every breath she takes. The hard peaks of her nipples can be seen tenting the nightie, and it's erotic knowing they are hard, because she wants this so much. "I don't know if I want to take this off or keep it on

146

because you look so gorgeous in it," I say, sitting up on my knees and staring down at her. Her eyes are wide with anticipation and her curls are sprung all over my pillow.

She bends her knees, and the nightie slips down to her hips, making the decision easier than I thought. "Off it is," I growl, and in one fluid motion, pull the gown up and over her head. I throw it to the ground, not caring where it lands, when I see her naked for the first time.

I'm stunned silent. How the fuck am I supposed to handle something as gorgeous as her and not get carried away?

Her breasts are perfect, bigger than the palm of my hand, and her nipples are a cherry red that has me bending down. I suck one into my mouth needing a taste. She arches her back, whimpering when I flick my tongue over the bud.

I pluck and twist the other nipple, and while I'm playing with her, she rubs her hands over my pecs and finds my piercing. She pulls and twists, getting a groan from me. Out of all the women I've been with, no one has ever taken the time to play with my piercings. That's what they are there for. It feels so fucking good with the bite of pain.

Her nipple leaves my mouth with a wet pop, and I kiss my way down her stomach until I get to her pussy. "Fucking gorgeous," I rumble, pleased when I see trimmed hair and bare light-pink lips glistening, just waiting for me.

"You're overdressed," she interrupts me admiring her.

"I want you right now." I try to get her mind off me taking off my pants. There's big dick, then there is too big of dick, and that's where I land. I don't want to ruin this or scare her off or intimidate her.

"And before you can have me, I want you to take off your pants," she replies.

"Too fucking bad," I nearly snarl before latching my lips on her sweet piece of candy to satisfy my sweet tooth. She bucks and squirms, running her fingers through my hair. She tugs on the root, and I moan into her cunt, hoping her mind is off my pants.

I know it's inevitable, but I can buy time.

While I'm sucking on her clit, I slip a finger into her virgin hole. It's hot, tight, and slick with her vanilla frosting.

"Amos," she moans my real name. Something about it makes this moment a lot more intimate.

The girls I've been with scream Kansas.

And I hate Kansas.

Which in turn, kind of made me hate them.

"Amos, oh, don't stop."

Someone would have to shoot me dead right now in order for that to happen. I slip another finger in, and she takes it easily. I glance up to witness her kneading her breasts. I have the perfect view of her.

I insert a third finger, and she finally hisses from the discomfort, but I continue trying to figure out the code to her lock, flicking my tongue up and down, side to side. I write my name on this pussy, snarling as I open my mouth wider and suck in a part of her folds into my mouth. My arm lies across her stomach to hold her down, and I increase the pressure with my mouth, feasting like a king.

I'm finger fucking her long and hard now. Wet sounds fill the room along with her whines. She gets louder with every ticking second that passes. Her thighs begin to tremble and her stomach tenses. "Amos, I'm going to... you're going to make me come." She slaps me in the shoulder, which makes me grin around her clit.

Yeah, I'm proud of myself, so?

"Amos!"

I rip my face from her swollen pearl to watch as she orgasms for me. "Come on, baby. Fucking come for me." I scoot closer and pull her ass against my thighs, ramming my fingers into her and watching her hole swallow them without issue.

I can't wait to get inside.

"Amos," she whispers before detonating.

Her eyes go wide with shock, her mouth drops open on a silent scream, and when the first squirt of come hits my palm, she cries out.

Oh, fuck yes. I can't wait to feel this happen along my cock.

Her come splashes onto the bed, causing wet spots, but I don't care.

When she comes down from her high, I dip my head back down, slide my fingers out, and plunge my tongue in for a quick second. I sit up, then suck my fingers into my mouth and groan. "You taste so good, Springs. I could eat you all day."

"I'd let you," she slurs, stretching her arms over her head.

Her eyes fall to the tip of my cock poking out of the waistband. She licks her lips, and her arms reach for the button of my jeans.

I grab her wrist to stop her and take a deep breath. "Just know I'd never hurt you, okay?"

"I know that," she says with a smile, shaking her head like she can't believe I'd say such a thing. She unzips me next, the metal teeth grinding together as they get closer to freeing me.

My heart is pounding, wanting to leap out of my chest to see what her reaction is going to be. It's going to go one of two ways.

Violet tries tugging on my pants, but she can't get them off my hips, so I roll off the bed, turn around and shuck them off. She has a great view of my ass right now and she leans over the edge to steal a squeeze.

"So sexy," she purrs, her nails skating up and down my back. "Turn around, Amos. I want you. I really want to do this." She wraps her arms around my chest and kisses up my shoulder to my neck, sucking my earlobe into her mouth. She teases the flesh between her teeth, and I moan.

I finally turn around and spread my arms out.

She sits back and gasps, staring at my cock silently. I can't read her face. She's only shocked.

"Big and Dirty. I understand the joke now," she says out of nowhere.

I chuckle, which makes her laugh too, and jump on the bed. Crawling up her body, I place kisses in random places.

Next to her belly button, on her hip, against her ribs, in the middle of her chest. When I get to her face, I scoot up more, and her legs fall to the side naturally to let me in. I wait for her to say something else, to say anything, but she doesn't. Her palm rests against my cheek as she leans up and kisses me.

Wrapping my arms around her head, I deepen it, showing her how much I care about her and want her. The kiss quickly becomes frantic, and we are gasping, the out-of-control desire taking over our bodies. I reach down between us and wrap my hand around my cock to guide it to her entrance.

The tip hits against her, and she breaks the kiss to stare up at me through those lilac dreams. "I can't wait to feel you inside me, Amos. I can't wait," she repeats, pressing her forehead against mine.

Our palms come together, and our fingers slide home. We hold on tight as I push in, slow and steady as I stretch her with my girth. Our eyes lock, and I groan as her tight heat strangles me. I struggle to breathe because I'm on the verge of coming, she can't breathe because it hurts.

"Oh my god, you're so big. Amos, you feel so good."

I hit her barrier, and I want to go easy, but she takes me by surprise and thrusts herself down on me. I rip through her virginity, and she doesn't stop until she has taken every inch of me. My sack is nestled against her ass. She squeezes her eyes shut and does a few breathing techniques to push through the pain.

I grip her side and hiss to control myself. I was not expecting her to do that.

She relaxes and hooks her foot over my hip while hovering her lips against mine. "Make love to me, Amos. I want to feel every part of you take every part of me."

I slide all the way out, and we both moan as I slide back in. I have to watch where we are connected. A bit of blood is along my cock and a surge of possessiveness takes over. She's mine. All of her is mine.

Curling myself over her, I decide on long, deep thrusts, giving her every inch. "You take me so fucking good. You were made for me, Violet. You were made for my cock. Look at us. Watch us." I prop up on my elbow, and she sees the swell of my cock thrusting in and out. I cover her body again and use quick strokes, still long and deep, but a bit harder.

Our sounds mix together. The air becomes thick with body heat and sex, and our skin becomes slick with sweat while we slide against each other. We kiss, barely—the effort is cut short when we whimper and groan into each other's mouths because it feels so good.

I've never made love before, so while this is a first for her, it's a first for me too. The energy, the emotion, the feelings between us grow, the moment becoming sensational.

"I'm going to come," I warn her. "I can't hold back. You feel too fucking good. We feel too good," I admit, slamming our hands onto the bed and gripping onto her tight.

"Me too. Yes, Amos! Me too, yes. Oh, yes," she breaks, digging those nails into my hands as her pussy clenches around me, and she cries out, her entire body quaking under me.

"Fuck," I groan as I get closer. "Damn it! Ah, Violet," I grit through my teeth as I plant myself as far as I can, coming into her depths. With every spasm, I thrust, needing to get as far as I possibly can.

We're both a mess when we are done, and now when we kiss, it's languid and a bit messy. There's no finesse, but I don't care. I'm so wrung out and happy.

"I'll give you dirty tomorrow," I say, collapsing to my side, but still keeping us connected.

She bursts out laughing, which causes me to as well. I've never had this with someone. It's so… natural.

It hits me.

This is love.

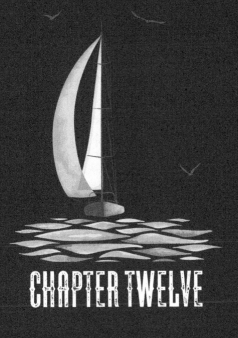

CHAPTER TWELVE

Violet

OH.
    My.
    God.
    I had sex last night, and it was mind-blowing. It was nothing like my friends back home warned me about. Everyone said the first time hurt. In a way, I guess it did. I didn't mind it though, and the pain was short-lived. Amos has got to have one of the biggest cocks in the world. When I saw it for the first time, I had doubts like any girl would, but I wasn't about to not feel him inside me after seeing how beautiful he was. He is as long as his forearm and as thick as his wrist.
    I can still feel just how big he is between my legs. I ache in

the best way. I'm tender, sore, and I remember him thrusting inside me for the first time. Nothing has ever felt better. He filled me to the brink where ecstasy and pain collide.

He is made to give pleasure.

And I was created to take it from him.

I stretch my arms above my head and smile, feeling the aches and pains all over my body. The pillow gives under me, and the blanket slides under my breasts. My nipples are rubbed raw and swollen from how much Amos sucked on them.

I'm not going to call him Kansas like everyone else, not when I know the real reason behind the name. He doesn't deserve that.

I stare at his back while he sleeps, admiring the muscles bulging, since his arms are stuffed under the pillow. There are a few scars along his back. They are thin and puckered. I trace them with my finger and wonder what could have done this to him. I lean down and press a kiss to the scars I have access to before rolling out of bed.

The mattress bounces as I get up, and when I turn around to give him one last look, that's when I see the spots of red on the sheets.

No.

I look between my legs and see dried come and blood along my thighs. This is so embarrassing. I freaking bled everywhere. I thought blood was a myth when it came to a woman losing her virginity. I haul ass to the bathroom and quietly shut the door, then bang my head against the wall. I hope he doesn't get upset when he sees his sheets are ruined.

I'll buy him new ones.

I take in the bathroom, appreciating how Amos has made it his. Three walls are painted gray while the wall where the sink sits is painted blue. There aren't any decorations. It's very 'bachelor.' There is a toothbrush holder that is black with a gold ring around it. Different, blue-colored towels are folded on a rack above the toilet.

There are fluffy black rugs on the hardwood floor, which is different from the floor in my bathroom. Mine has black and white checkers on it, but I like the worn hardwood look. It matches the style Amos seems to have.

The shower curtain is black, with gold hooks that hang on the rod that is attached to the wall. Other than that, the bathroom is pretty simple. I like it.

I lean down and turn on the shower. Once the water gets hot, I step in and make quick work of washing my body and hair. I pay careful attention to the space between my legs to clean up the mess we made.

That's when it hits me.

We didn't use a condom, and I'm not on birth control. I wait for the fear, the panic, the need to run out the door and go buy Plan-B, but it isn't there. I have a very nonchalant attitude about it right now, and I don't know if it is because I am still in a state of bliss, or if I really don't mind. I'll have to talk to him about it.

"I wonder if they even make condoms in his size," I mumble out loud as I think about our options. What if they don't? I could get on birth control, that doesn't bother me.

I twist the handle and shut the water off and slide the curtain back. Stepping out, my feet land on the fluffy rug, and I grab a fresh towel from the rack. I dry my hair first, then wrap the extra-large towel around my body.

It could be a dress.

I wince when I grab the knob and it clicks louder than I

want it to, then the hinges groan when I open the door. "Oh, come on," I whisper to it angrily. As if the door can understand me. I tiptoe to my purse that I threw on the couch last night and unzip it slowly.

Of course, the teeth grind extra loud when I don't want them to. I pause, tensing my shoulder as I take a peek at Amos to make sure I haven't woken him up. He flips to his back, and I wait for him to wake up, but he doesn't. Blowing out a relieved breath, I fish my phone out of the bag to check in with my sisters but find it dead.

"Balls," I curse. I don't have my charger.

When I came over last night, I didn't exactly pack. I tap my phone in my palm as I study the room for a charger. Nothing near the couch or TV, so I head to my side of the bed and open the drawer.

Nothing.

I creep around to Amos's side and grab the handle, slowly sliding it to reveal if there is a charger inside.

Oh my…

There are sex toys in here.

A lot of sex toys.

"What are you doing?" He snags my wrist to stop me from looking inside the drawer, but it's too late. I see everything. "You just go through people's stuff without asking?" he snips, slamming the drawer shut, and the loud sound causes me to jump.

"I'm sorry, I was looking for a charger," I explain, not understanding what the big deal is. "Are you mad?" I can tell he is panicked. His eyes are wide, and he is breathing hard.

He runs his hands over his messy bedhead, then rubs his palm down his face.

"Are you mad about me seeing the toys?"

"Listen, I'm allowed to want toys too. Just because I'm a man doesn't mean I don't like how toys feel." He sits up and leans against the headboard, unable to meet my eyes.

Oh, I see.

I sit down on the edge of the bed, and the edge of the towel stays tucked under my arm. "You are very defensive when I haven't even said anything, Amos."

"You don't need to. I know what you're thinking."

"Do you?" I ask, reaching to open the drawer again, but he slams it shut again. "Amos, what's the big deal? Why are you being like this?"

"Because you're going to think it's weird. I don't. I know you've noticed, but I have a really big dick, and not... not every woman I've been with wants to have sex with me when they see it, so I've learned to pleasure myself. I've branched out, and I'm not ashamed of that."

"Then why are you acting ashamed?" I ask gently, placing my hand on his arm. "I'm not judging you, and I know you aren't a saint. I know I wasn't your first—"

"—You're the first that matters, so it matters what you think."

I scoot closer to him and grab onto the hand holding the drawer shut and lift it off. "Then let me look. And yes, you have a giant dick, but I like it, so all those other girls can fuck off," I say with a slight attitude and a hint of jealousy.

"There are no other girls. Just you. I really believe you were made for my cock. You took me so fucking beautifully last night."

Blood burns my cheeks. "Amos," his name is breathless on my lips.

"Best night of my life." He brushes his thumb across my cheek.

"Even if I ruined your sheets? I'm sorry. I didn't think that would happen."

He looks to my side of the bed and pulls the sheet back to see two red spots. Amos growls, a deep rumble like the sound of a hundred bikes leaving his chest. "Ruined? You made them better. I'm never getting rid of these sheets."

I shake my head, cheeks on fire, and open the drawer again to change the subject. I pull out the first toy. "What's this for?" I ask.

"That's a cock ring. It wraps around the base of my cock and vibrates and holds my orgasm at bay. The longer I wait to come, the better it feels."

I look down to see his cock tenting the sheet, and I lick my lips when I'm feeling the rush of arousal again. "And this one?" I set the ring on the table and pull out something that looks like a cylinder pocket.

"It's a fleshlight."

"Why do you have a flashlight in your drawer?"

"No, a *flesh*light. I put my cock in there and jack myself off with it. I used that the other night just like I said I would," he growls.

"You put your cock in this tiny hole?"

"I fit in your tiny hole, didn't I?" he smirks.

I bite the side of my lip and place that toy next to the ring. "And this?" It reminds me of a butt-plug.

"Um..." His cheeks tint as he scratches the back of his head.

I've never seen Amos blush. He's nervous.

"That is a prostate massager. It uh... has a remote," his

voice croaks, and his suddenly bashful nature is making me grin. "It vibrates against my prostate."

"Oh, that sounds like it feels good."

He nods his head, watching me as I inspect the toy. I'm new to all of this, and maybe that's why I'm going into it unbiased. I don't have a problem with him having toys. I think it's great he took the time to learn what he likes and doesn't like. If people are judgmental, that's their problem, and he doesn't need them in his life.

"It does feel good," he admits.

"So, I have a question," I ask, just a bit curious.

"Ask me anything, Springs."

"Do you fuck yourself with anything?"

"No," he shakes his head. "I don't think I'm interested in that."

"Oh." I don't mean to sound disappointed, but I am.

"If you're asking if I have sex with men, the answer is no. I'm not attracted to men. I don't have issues with gay people, that's not what I'm saying," he clarifies.

"I didn't think that. I was just wondering... never mind."

"What? Tell me."

"Would you want to if it were me? Like if I fucked you with a toy or if I had a strap-on?" I've seen strap-ons used in porn before, so I know what they are.

"Wait, are you saying you're okay with this? You would actually consider doing that if I wanted it?"

I nod eagerly. "I think I'd like it."

"You're a dirty girl." He sits up and wraps a hand around my throat. "I don't like putting the massager in my ass, but it's worth it when I feel it press against my prostate. If you are wanting to try something like that, I'll have to think about it.

I'm not against it, but I'm not for it, so I don't know how I feel just yet. Give me time?" he asks.

"Yeah, no rush. I saw the toys, and my mind got ahead of me."

"I like that you're open about it. Not everyone is."

"I want to be your dirty girl," I admit, clenching the sheet in my hand and tugging it down to his thighs. His massive cock bobs and veins protrude in it to fill the beast. The tip is an angry red and there is a bit of our juices dried along his brown pubic hair.

"I'm going to go get cleaned up." He gives me a quick kiss and runs to the bathroom. I hear the sink turn on and a minute later he struts back out, cock swinging like a damn tree branch.

He is squeaky clean now.

Amos jumps on the bed and lies down, lacing his arms behind his head as he stares at me. "What are you thinking?" he asks.

"I'm thinking about how bad I want to see this massager drive you insane, and then I want to ride you as it's buzzing against your prostate." I grip his girthy shaft in my hand and squeeze. He flexes his hips, thrusting in the air. "Can I do that?"

He nods while his eyes roll to the back of his head when I bend down and lick the tip. "Fuck," he spits as I wrap my lips around the wide crown and suck him into my mouth. "I've never had anyone play with my toys with me," he groans as I flatten my tongue and trace his veins along his heavy flesh.

"Like you said," I stroke him. "We are made for each other. Why wouldn't I want to do this with you? I want to experience all the things with you, Amos. Things I don't know

160

about, things I'm curious about, things I never thought I'd try, but I'd try with you." I kiss the tip and lick the bead of pre-come off. It's salty.

I like it.

"Fuck yes, please," he groans.

I suck him down my throat again, and his fingers rub over my scalp until he cups the back of my head. He doesn't thrust his hip, thankfully. If he did, I'd die. There is no way I can fit him all.

I take as much as I can and stroke the other half of his length with one hand.

"For someone who has never done this before, you sure are fucking amazing at it." He lifts his head to watch me, then drops it against the pillow a second later when I grab the round orbs settled beneath his cock. They are big too, heavy with seed that's begging to be let out.

I pop off and wipe the corner of my mouth, then grab the massager. "What do I do with this?" I ask. "Do I just…" I'm embarrassed when I don't know what to do. "Do I…"

"I can do it," he says, reaching up to take it out of my hand, and I lift it higher in the air.

"No. I want to. I want you to tell me what to do. I want to learn. I want us to do this. I plan for you to do the same to me." I yelp when his arms wrap around my waist, and he flips me to my back. The toy falls out of my hand as I stare into his incredibly handsome face.

I trace his tattoos with my fingers along his neck, and his eyes hood.

"You want me to explore you like you want to explore me?" he asks.

I nod, sucking my bottom lip into my mouth. "Yes."

He tugs the edge out of the towel and whips it from my body. "You want me here?" His fingers slip between my legs and probe my hole. My forbidden star puckers as if I'm trying to suck him in.

"Yes, but…" I hook my legs around his waist and apply pressure to roll us again. He falls to his back, and I hover over his cock. As much as I want to slide down his impressive size, I fall onto my butt on the mattress, and I spread his legs.

He clears his throat, and another flush works its way from his neck to his face. The globes of his cheeks press against the mattress, firm and strong just like the trunks of his thighs.

"What do I do?" I want to make him comfortable.

He reaches for the nightstand again and pulls out a bottle of lubricant. "Just a little of this to help. Listen, I haven't ever done this with anyone before," his voice cracks, reminding me of a teenager hitting puberty.

"For a badass biker, you're a little shy." I drizzle a small amount of lube on the toy and click the cap shut.

"Well, it isn't every day I'm totally exposed," he chuckles nervously, and I notice his erection is flagging. "Maybe this isn't a good idea." He gets up to take the toy away from me, and I slap a hand on his chest pushing him back down.

I rake my nails down his chest. "Relax. It's just us. Me and you. If you don't want to, we can stop, but I'm wanting this." I wrap my hand around his cock and jerk. "I want to drive you crazy. I want to ride you while you're going out of your mind with your prostate being touched." His cock starts to thicken again to full mast, and I hum in approval. "I think you like the sound of that."

"I do," he moans, and the more I continue to jerk, the more he relaxes. His legs drop to the side more, and I slide the toy down his crease. "Just uh… don't fuck me with it. I'm nowhere near ready for that, remember? I said I'd think about it for you."

"I remember, Amos. I won't do anything you don't want me to." I find his hole and swallow. My hand begins to shake. "Do I just slip it in?"

"Until it can't anymore," he nods.

I push, but nothing happens, and I begin to panic. "I think I'm doing it wrong."

"You have to push harder at first. My god, I can't believe I just said that." He blows out a breath just as I push inside.

I do as he says and push in until the L-shaped handle is against his crease. "What do I do now?"

"The remote is in the drawer."

I dig around in the drawer for it, and when I see the round remote. I press a button with three plus signs. "And what does this do—"

"Oh, fuck!" he shouts, his back arching and his arms slapping onto the bed. He fists the sheets with his hands. "You're going to make me come if you don't turn that down!" he shouts, groaning loudly as the toy buzzes against his prostate. "Holy fuck. Jesus Christ, Violet. Fuck!"

Oh, I love this. I love seeing him squirm. Why don't women hear about men doing this more often?

His legs shake and his cock leaks all over his stomach, clear fluid sticking in his happy trail. "Does that feel good?" I purr at him, twisting my nipple between my fingers as I watch him rejoice in his pleasure.

"Fuck yes, it does."

I hit the button again to increase the vibration and his back bows again, and his abs clench. The tattoo of a frozen heart beats wildly, and I want to be the person to thaw it out. I dip my hand between my legs and slick my fingers through my folds. I'm soaked, and sore, but my hole aches to be filled with him.

"I'm going to come, Violet. I can't hold back."

I don't know what gets into me, but I push up onto my knees, situate myself over his cock, and slide down. Inch by inch I take him until I'm settled. I'm stretched and full of twelve inches of Amos, and for some reason, I want more. There's so much of him, but it's like I need to feel him in the marrow of my bones.

Every piece he gives me of himself isn't enough. I'm greedy and want more.

"You feel so fucking perfect," he whispers. He cups my breasts and pinches my sore nipples into tight buds.

I stare at the remote in my hand and lift a brow, wondering if he is catching on to my mischievous nature.

"Don't you dare. I can't take anymore. I'm barely holding it together." He has sweat beading across his face and on his upper lip. I bend forward and roughly kiss him, dipping my tongue into his mouth before tracing his lips and licking the sweat from his skin.

Click.

"Violet!" he cries, his fingers bruising my hips as he death grips my sides, thrusting into me as he comes. I feel his warmth trickle out of me and still hear the low buzz of the toy.

"You're a vixen," he gasps, wiping the sweat off his face with his hand. "My god, you have no idea how good that felt."

I lower the vibration setting and begin to rock against

him. "Maybe you should show me then," I say. "Show me how to fuck you, Amos," I beg as I fall back, then push forward. His cock almost hurts in this position. There's so much of him and not enough of me. My clit rubs against his pelvis, and I whimper, turning my head into my arm as I stretch them above my head.

"You are. You fucking belong up there, baby."

I speed up, quickening my hips. His heavy orbs slap against my ass, and the sounds that leave my mouth sound inhuman. They echo into the room. No doubt others can hear us. I don't care. I want the world to know how good Amos makes me feel.

I turn up the vibration again, feeling powerful with the remote in my hand.

He grinds his jaw together, and his hands on my hips help me rock faster. "Amos!" I slap my hands against his chest, the hard muscle flexing as I hold on tight. I fall down, unable to keep myself up from his cock splitting me. Our skin slides together, and I latch onto his earlobe, biting the soft skin as his hands roam over my ass as he rams into me.

"Tell me how much you like it," he snarls, fucking me so hard with every thrust that I cry out louder. "You like this big cock ruining you, don't you? You love it."

"Yes. I do. Don't stop. Please, don't stop."

"You're a filthy girl, aren't you?" he asks, running his finger down the crease of my ass, probing my forbidden hole. "You want me here too. You want me everywhere."

"Yes!" I flip my head back, and my hair fans over me. I hold my breasts as I ride him, harder, faster, harder, faster, wetter.

Oh my god, so wet.

"You're going to take every drop of come. You're hungry for it. You want whatever this big dick can give you."

"Amos," I whimper, my orgasm building to a dangerous proportion. It's bigger than the last one. My toes curl and tingles spread throughout my body. My belly flips and more liquid soaks us, which only causes his cock to slide in easier and faster than before.

I'm so close.

Click.

I don't mean to increase the vibration again, but I do. He growls as he jackknifes up, wrapping his arms around my waist. He changes the position, and I'm in a more seated position now. I drop my forearms to his shoulders, and we rock against one another, moaning together. He kisses the middle of my chest, and his forehead presses against my sternum. One hand fondles my breast while the other holds onto my thigh.

"I've never felt as good as I do with you," he says into my flesh.

I bob up and down, swirl my hips in a circle, and bend back until I'm flat against the bed. He is still in an upright position and he grazes his hand from my neck, over my tits, and down to my stomach. His hand dips between us and pinches my clit.

"Amos!" I'm so close. I'm still right on the edge, but I need more. "I can't. I need..."

"What do you need, Springs? I'll give it to you."

"I don't know," I whine as my orgasm continues to build.

He flips me onto my stomach, my legs straight and flat on the bed, and my face buried into the mattress. He shoves one finger into my ass, no ease, no caress, and fucks me hard at the same time.

"Yeah, there it is. You're close. That's all you needed. You needed yourself full of me."

I bite onto the mattress and scream when my vision sways, and I become lightheaded. My orgasm possesses me, tenses every muscle in my body as I explode, convulsing on his cock.

"Amos," I shout his name, and he falls over me, pounding me hard until he thrusts once, twice, and plants himself as far as he can.

"Violet," he groans adoringly into my neck, kissing the back of my nape as he comes.

I turn off the toy to stop the buzzing and throw it on the bed, my body spasming from the aftershocks.

Amos kisses down my spine, and it feels so amazing. I'm getting sleepy.

"I'm falling in love with you and it's scaring the hell of me."

I flip over and lean up on my elbows, still struggling to breathe, but I manage. His hair is damp, and he has red lines down his chest from my nails. His cock slips out of me and a trail of come spreads across my thigh from his slit.

"Yeah?" I ask hopefully.

"Yeah, Springs. You've got me all twisted up."

"I'm falling in love with you too."

"You scared?" he questions.

"Only for you to realize that you don't," I admit.

He cups my jaw and brings his lips to mine. "There's not a chance in hell of that."

I'm going to show him Kansas isn't who he is, it's just a state of mind.

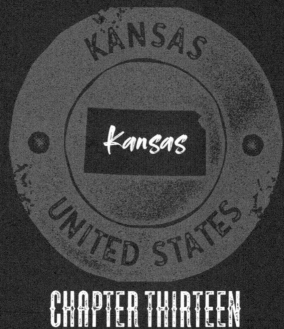

CHAPTER THIRTEEN

It's been three weeks of absolute fucking bliss.

The guy who wants his drugs hasn't been around yet, so we consider that a big fucking blessing. Right now, the only mess we are dealing with is Wolf.

There's a positive and a negative to him right now.

Positive, he has officially stopped the drunken bender. The negative? He has completely mentally checked out. He hasn't said a word in over two weeks.

Prez is still saying to give Wolf space, but I don't know if that's a good thing right now. I think he wants to be alone, but he doesn't need to be. I plan on talking to him today at some point. I don't like my friend being like this. I know he is grieving; god forbid anything happen to Violet. I don't know what I'd do. I don't even want to think about it.

But the darker mood Wolf gets in, the more worried about him I become.

Wolf and I go way back to when we were in the old chapter together. I'm not as close to him like I am One-Eye or Arrow, but I still care. He took care of the girls Venom kidnapped the best he could. I know he blames himself somehow for Abigale's death. We all have horrors from that chapter that we want to forget but will never be able to.

Whatever happened in that basement, whatever love story bloomed between Abigale and Wolf, it's changed him for life.

"Hey asshole. You didn't fucking take me to bingo. I missed seeing Elise." Homer kicks me in the leg while I'm changing the tire to an old Bobber. It's sick. If the guy that owned this took better care of the body, this motorcycle would be a beauty.

"I have other things going on in my life, Homer. I'm sorry."

"Oh, yeah. I know. You and Violet are so in love, Blah, blah. It was jackpot night, fucker. I could have won the five hundred bucks that you stole the last time."

"Hey, I won that fair and square. I had bingo. Twice! You're just jealous."

"I still think you cheated," he gripes.

"God, you're a senile old shit." I tighten the bolts to the tire. Arrow chuckles from the spot next to me as he changes out a fuel tank.

"What the fuck are you laughing at, Arrowhead?" Homer strolls over to Arrow and slaps him on the back of the head. "Didn't your mommy and daddy ever tell you to respect your elders?"

"I didn't realize elders meant dinosaurs, Homer. I am soooo sorry," Arrow says sarcastically.

"You young bucks don't know the meaning of respect." Homer pulls out a plastic bag and grabs a blunt.

"Homer, you can't smoke in here," I say for the hundredth time.

"It's for my damn headaches. Back off, Kansas." He ignores me and lights it up anyway, blowing the thick cloud of smoke in the air. "You're taking me next Friday," he points at me, the weed burning bright at the very end of the joint.

"Homer, the snow is starting to melt. Spring is around the corner. King's City Motorcycle Custom Repair and Body Shop is going to be getting busier. Over winter there wasn't much work, but now it's picking up. You might have to find someone else to take you."

"I'll take you, Homer," Arrow suggests.

"Ah, don't want you to. You smell funky."

"I do not smell funky. Kansas, tell him I don't smell funky."

I exhale and chuckle, tightening the last bolt on the tire. I throw the socket-wrench to the ground with a loud clatter. "You don't smell funky, Arrow. Homer, be nice."

"Kansas. I want you to take me. Please," Homer begs.

It isn't like Homer to beg.

"Fine, I'll take you. Only cause I don't have the heart to turn an old person down," I state.

"Good. I got to get it where I still can, right?" He puffs on his joint and Arrow holds out his hand. "The hell do you want, Arrowhead?"

"Give me a hit. Don't be greedy."

"Boy, don't be stupid. You know my rule. I do not puff, puff, pass. Get your own shit."

"Your bones are always going to be brittle old man, no matter how many joints you smoke."

Ah, shit. Here we go.

"You keep talking about my bones and one of these days, I'm going to knock you out with my fist."

I lean back and cross my arms over my chest to watch them bicker like they always do.

Arrow plucks the blunt from Homer's fingers and places it between his lips, inhaling. "And then your knuckles would snap, crackle, and pop. Just like those rice crispy treats." He blows the smoke out and Homer snatches his beloved weed back.

"I'm going to slit the tires of your bike."

"If you bend over, you'll throw out your back. Don't try so hard," Arrow tosses back at Homer. Anger fuels the lines etched on either side of his eyes.

Sometimes, I wonder if they mean to fight as bad as they do. Is it fun? Is it real? I can't tell anymore.

Homer grabs a tool from the box on the ground and throws it at Arrow. Arrow dodges it and it hits against the back wall. Luckily, this entire place is made of concrete so nothing can hurt it, but Arrow can get hurt if Homer throws something else.

Arrow wouldn't dare to hurt the old man. While a grumpy fuck, Arrow likes Homer, even if the feeling isn't mutual. "Okay, break time. Homer, go back to the clubhouse. Arrow, take five. Go get a juice box."

"Hey, you little baby. Go dwink frowm your wittle sippy cup," Homer talks like a baby, bringing his fists to his eyes pretending to cry.

Oh, that's just great.

"You know what? I will go get my juice box, and while I'm sipping on my favorite drink, you can go to the clubhouse and get your walker before you go to bingo. And when you get there, you'll lose."

Those are fighting words.

"You take that back!" Homer yells, jumping off the hood of a car and landing pretty decently for an old guy.

"No, I won't take it back. No one fucks with my juice boxes." Arrow pokes Homer in the chest.

"No one fucks with my bingo, bitch!" Homer jabs a finger in the middle of Arrow's chest in return.

"Jesus Christ," I mumble and head toward the front door, flipping the 'Open' sign to 'Closed.' I don't want to run off customers because these two knuckle heads can't see eye to eye for more than twenty seconds. My boots pound against the floor as I stomp my way toward them. I kick a few tools out of the way and push them away from one another.

They are yelling at the top of their lungs now. I can't even understand what they are saying. "Okay, that's enough!" I bellow, my voice bouncing off the metal and chrome of the bikes. "Homer. Home. Now. Arrow. Juice box." They don't move. Just linger and stare at one another.

"I said to go!" I kick another tool and it skitters across the floor. Arrow is the first to leave. His shoulders are tight and there is an oil stain across his white shirt. He gives Homer a dirty look before curling his lip and disappearing into the employee lounge where the kitchen is.

"What the fuck, Homer?" I wrap my arms around his shoulders and direct him outside where his motorcycle is. Water drips from the roof and pellets to the ground since the ice is melting from the warmer weather finally coming in.

"What? He started it."

"I don't care. I don't know why you two bumps heads so often but save it for the clubhouse. This is a place of business. And I'll be talking to Arrow too," I add, so he doesn't think I'm only giving him a lecture.

Homer flips me off and puts on his bucket helmet, starts his bike, and roars out of the parking lot. The only thing that gets worse other than Homer's age is his temper.

My phone buzzes in my pocket, and I pinch my eyes shut, not wanting to deal with whoever is on the other line. I head inside the shop again and dig my phone out of my pocket. Arrow is standing there, and I didn't know it was possible to angrily sip on a straw, but he is. He's sucking on it from the side of his mouth, one arm crossed over his chest.

"Hello?" I answer, fucking exhausted, and it's only three in the afternoon. I miss Violet. When I'm with her, it isn't crazy hectic. It's the opposite. It's laughter and comfort, safety. And the sex... Jesus, the fucking sex is out of this world. I've never had such a connection before.

I was so worried about being like my Pops, but now that I'm with Violet, knowing what love is like, I'm nothing like him. I'm a decent, good man who would never do that to my woman. Even with a gun to my head, I wouldn't do what my Pops did to me and Mom.

"Hey, sweetie."

Speaking of the devil.

"Hey, Mom. How are you?"

"Fine. I miss you. I haven't heard from you much. I wanted to make sure you were okay."

I curse silently, kicking myself in the ass. I have been a shithead. "I'm sorry. It's been a little hectic. I'll take you to

173

lunch on Saturday. How does that sound?" I ask, wanting to make it up to her. I should go to the jewelry store and pick her out a pair of sapphire earrings. It's her favorite gem, and she deserves it.

"Oh, I'd love that, sweetie. You want me to come there or you come here?"

"How about you come here so I can show you around? Stay a few days. Plus, there is…" I grin when I think about Violet.

"What is it, Amos? Is everything okay?"

"Yeah, everything is great. There's someone I want you to meet." The line falls silent between us, and I lift the phone away from my ear to make sure we are still connected. "Mom? You there?"

"Yes, I'm just wondering if I heard you right. You want me to meet someone? Is this a set up? You know I don't want to date."

Of course she would think I want to introduce her to someone, because I have never, not once, introduced a woman to my Mom. "No, Mom. I met someone."

She gasps and falls quiet again. "Really?"

I smile again. "Yeah. She's it, Mom."

"Oh my goodness. Tell me everything. Is she pretty? Is she smart? What's her name?"

"She's the most beautiful woman I've ever seen. She's brilliant and open-minded, kind, and open to learning new things. She's everything I've ever wanted. Her name is Violet."

"Oh, Violet. Such a lovely name. Am I going to finally get grandbabies?" she nearly screams into the phone. "I have to call everyone. I'm going to be a grandma!"

"Mom, no. I didn't say—"

"—I love you, sweetie. I'm so excited for you. I can't wait to meet her. I'll be there Saturday. I'm going to be a grandma!" she squeals again.

"Mom, wait—" but it's too late.

She's hung up on me.

I scratch my temple with the edge of my phone and try to figure out how I'm going to break the news that she isn't going to be a grandma yet. She's going to be so upset. She's been waiting years for me to settle down and give her grandchildren. I want kids, and I want them with Violet, but I doubt she's ready for something like that.

"I need another juice box. Homer has me all worked up."

I peer over my shoulder to see Arrow squeezing the small box in his hand until it's nothing but a folded-up piece of paper, then he tosses it on the ground. He huffs, mumbling under his breath as he marches into the employee lounge again. The door slams shut, and I'm left alone in the work bay.

Finally, some peace and quiet.

My phone chimes and it's a text from Mom.

It says, 'LOL.'

I reply and tell her, "LOL YOU TOO."

She thinks it stands for 'love you lots', and no matter how many times I tell her it means 'laugh out loud', it just won't sink in.

My phone buzzes again, and I groan, debating on throwing it against the wall. When I'm not busy, it doesn't ring. When I'm busy, it rings non-stop.

"Yeah?" I answer, pinching the bridge of my nose.

"Kansas, you need to get here now."

"Is everything okay, Prez?" I straighten. "Is it Violet?"

"No. No. Nothing like that. She went to go pick up her sisters from school. I have a few people here wanting to see you."

Right, a few weeks ago she enrolled them in Atlantic City High School. Veronica is hating it. Her attitude knows no bounds.

"See me? People? Who?" I question.

"Just get here and make them leave. They won't without talking to you. They even rented one of the apartments we built."

I go to reply but he hangs up on me before I can answer. "Why is everyone hanging up on me? I don't even know anyone else besides the club, Mom, and Nigel."

Nigel. What if he's come to visit me after traveling the world?

"Arrow!" I shout, tucking my phone in my pocket.

A door opens and closes, and I turn around to see him standing there sucking on two straws and holding two juice boxes.

Goodness. He really is mad.

"We need to go," I tell him, snagging my truck keys out of my pocket. Unlike some people, I do not ride my bike when it is fucking freezing out, and Arrow rode with me.

"Give me a second. I'm almost done with my boxes," he says around the straws.

I snag my leather jacket off the chair and slip it on. The sound of the boxes being emptied is accompanied by a loud slurping sound.

"Okay, ready." He tosses the boxes in the trash and grabs his coat too. "Let's blow this popsicle stand."

We step outside, and my boots step into slushy ice and water. "You realize we are about to go to the clubhouse where Homer is?"

"I'll ignore him. He pisses me off sometimes."

"Sometimes?" I tease as I open the truck door.

"Okay, all the time. What the hell is his problem with me?"

"What's your problem with him?" I throw my arm around the passenger seat and turn around to look out the back window. I can't look at the big fancy screen in the middle of the dash. It isn't the same or as effective. I reverse out of the spot and the slush squishes under the tires.

When the road is finally clear, I get us on the road and turn on the wipers. It's a shitty day. The clouds are heavy in the sky and rain has been sprinkling since the early morning.

"I just like to give him a hard time. I thought we were having fun, but I'm starting to really think he doesn't like me."

"I think he likes you. He only banters with you like that. He's just an ornery old shithead." I hope I'm right. The last thing I want to do is give false hope to Arrow.

Arrow is one of the good guys. Sure, he likes his juice boxes, but he's a complete badass and has a heart of gold. When I stood up to Venom, Arrow was at my side. He was strung up with me, and when I was whipped, he was shot with his own bow and arrows.

He hasn't been able to pick up his bow since.

"I hope so," he says. "I don't like it when people don't like me. I shouldn't care, but I do."

"Ah, that's what makes you so great, Arrow. Don't let Homer get to you." I slap his shoulder, trying to be as reassuring as I can.

"So why are we closing up shop two hours early?" he asks, rubbing his hands on his jeans. That's when I notice he has grease all over them and embedded under his nails.

"I don't know. Prez called. He said he needed me home because someone is there asking for me."

"Oh, old girlfriend?" he asks. "That'll be some drama."

I snort, flip on the blinker, and take the next left. "No. I don't have any old girlfriends. Violet doesn't have to worry about that."

"Even the old cut-sluts from the previous chapter?"

I shiver when I remember them. "Especially them. They knew the deal." I want to scrub my body clean when I think about them.

"Wonder who it is," he mumbles.

"We are about to find out," I tell him as I flip the blinker on again to take another left into the clubhouse parking lot.

The parking lot is finally safe to drive through, and I can see the waves crashing against the shore again instead of ice. I can't wait until summer. All I can think of lately is seeing Violet in a bikini that's a few sizes too small as we sit in the sand and catch some sun. I bet her skin is sensitive. I'd have to volunteer to rub her down with sunscreen, so she wouldn't burn.

Oh, the horror.

Ha. Not.

I can't wait to get my hands on that body and feel the sun's warmth against her gorgeous flesh.

I park the truck and get out, looping the key ring around my finger and swinging it. Arrow is right behind me, and the wind tunnels through the breezeway, brisk and fucking freezing.

I knock on Prez's office door, which has "PRESIDENT" stamped across the front in a metal plate.

"Come in," he shouts.

I swing it open and find him scribbling something down. "Prez, you wanted to see me?" I won't lie and say I'm not nervous. Last time my Prez wanted to see me, I was strung up in a barn and left for dead.

"Yeah, the people—"

"—You must be looking for us." Someone interrupts Prez, which has me turning around, slightly pissed off that they had the nerve. If they had any idea what Boomer was capable of, they wouldn't have dared.

"Kansas, do you know these people?" Boomer asks, folding his hands across his stomach.

I stare at the three of them and shake my head. "Never seen them before in my entire life. I think you have the wrong place. Sorry." I go to leave, but one of them blocks me. He is as tall as me, maybe a few years younger. "Listen, I don't know what you think—"

"—Are you not Amos Taylor?"

There he goes, interrupting again.

I don't like to hear my name from someone I don't know. I take a step back and cross my arms over my chest. Arrow slides between them and stands next to me, mocking my stance.

"Yeah, I'm Amos. What do you want?"

"I'm Carson," the man who blocked me introduces himself. "This is my sister Stevie and my youngest brother Brighton."

"Okay, that's really great. Nice to meet you. If you'll excuse me," I say, trying to leave again, but Carson's hand

179

presses against the middle of my chest. I look down, lifting a brow.

"We are the Taylors," he says slowly, waiting for the recognition to dawn on me.

It doesn't take long. The blood drains from my face as I stare at the three kids. The last time I saw them, I was sixteen. "Fuck off," I grumble, shoving him in the chest.

He stumbles back against the wall, and his sister grabs his arm to stop him from falling. "We are your siblings. We came here—"

It's my turn to interrupt him this time. I let my fist fly and slam it across his jaw. "You think I give a fuck why you are here? You think I give a damn about what you want? I don't. And let me make my point crystal fucking clear," I move my eyes over all of them, hoping they see the rage and how disinterested I am. "We are not family. We are not siblings. I don't even know you. As far as I'm concerned, you ruined many years of my life. Go back where you came from."

"Okay, I'll let you have that," he acknowledges, licking the blood off his lip.

"You better stop fucking talking before 'you' let me have another," I sneer. I hate him more now than I did when I saw him all those years ago. He kind of looks like me. Same brown hair, same eyes, same height… I guess he gets it from Pops like I do.

"Amos, we came from Kansas to see you. Please, listen," he begs. "We have been wanting to meet you for a long time, ever since Dad told us about you, but he got sick, and we didn't get the chance."

"Oh, did he finally die? So sad. I don't give a fuck." I try to leave again, but he grabs onto my arm. "Let go of me," I warn, popping my neck when the tension becomes too high.

180

"Dad needs a bone marrow transplant, and we aren't matches," he informs me.

I laugh sardonically until my sides hurt. I spin around slowly, glaring at Carson, then drop my eyes to Stevie and Brighton. "So the real reason you're here is to ask me if I'll get tested to see if I'm a match. You didn't actually come here to see me."

"We wanted to before, but we were nervous, then Dad got sick, and it strengthened the reason for us to find you. I know it doesn't look good, but he really needs it, Amos. Please—"

I grab him by the shirt and throw him against the wall, lifting him off his feet. Boomer stands up from his chair and Arrow takes a step forward to stop me before I hurt him.

"Don't hurt him, please," Stevie begs. I can hear the tears in her voice.

My heart clenches. I always wanted siblings. I always wanted a sister. I thought I would have been a good big brother. I would have protected her. They don't need me. They have each other.

I ignore her and cock my head to the side. "You think I really give a fuck what he needs after what he did to me and my mom? You think I care that he is dying? Let him fucking rot."

I let go of his shirt, and he drops to his feet. "Get out of here," I tell them. "What you want isn't here." I stomp down the breezeway to get out of there, wishing Violet were back or I'd go straight to her.

"I know he wasn't the best father to you, but he was to us. He was amazing, and he is our Dad. We don't want him to die."

I twirl around so fast, and I'm in Carson's face before he

can say anything else. A few of the club brothers come out of the main room and surround us. Stevie and Brighton get closer to Carson, and like the good big brother he is, he stands in front of them to protect them.

Laughing again, I hit the side of my head with my hand and say, "How stupid are you? Do you really think he was a good father to you? Are you that clueless? After he spent the weekend with you and his fake wife, he came to me and my Mom. His real wife. All those times he probably said some shit about working long hours? He was in Oklahoma during the week. How about the times he was gone during baseball season? His schedule changed. Yeah, that's because he came to all of my games. You think he was a bad father to me? He was the fucking best, but I hated him through it. You want to know why? Because I fucking knew something was wrong with him. My Mom was sick because of him, so I followed him one night, drove to Kansas, and saw him with you. You," I point to the youngest one. "You were still in Mommy's belly. None of you knew just how horrible he was. He wasn't a good father. He was fake. He played us. All of us. So take your want. Take your mission to save your father's life and go elsewhere. I'm not interested."

"I know!" he yells at me, shoving me in the chest.

Yep. We are related. Only Taylor men have that kind of temper.

"You don't think we know that? You don't think we were just as angry? But guess what? I had more good memories with him, than bad. I chose to not be angry about it. It was out of my control. He fucked up. It was a fucked-up thing he did to us, but he went to all of your games. He supported you. That's more than a lot of kids get. Can't you say that?"

"No, no I can't say that, because while he was with you, loving your mom and taking care of your house, I had to take care of my mom. I had to take care of the house that was falling apart. So fuck you, fuck what you need, and fuck him."

"We aren't going anywhere. We are family."

"Oh, fuck you, Carson. This is my family." I spread my arms out to show all of my brothers. "These are my brothers. I don't know you."

"We want to get to know you. He told us about you when he first got sick, and we were just as mad at him, but please—" Stevie pleads.

Fuck. I don't do well when it comes to women having tears in their eyes. My heart softens when I see the same hazel color I have.

"Please, you could save him. You're our last hope, and I know our intentions seem twisted, but we have always wanted to get to know you ever since we found out you existed. It hasn't been an easy ride of acceptance for us either."

I gently place my hand on her shoulder and clear my throat. "I'm sorry, Stevie. You've wasted your time. My life is where I want it to be, and that's no thanks to him."

"We will be renting that apartment. We aren't going anywhere. We don't want to be in Kansas. We want to be where you are. We even brought Dad here to the hospital."

"He is here?" I roar, shouting at Carson. "Are you kidding me?"

"I told you. We are here for the long haul." He tugs his sister out of my hold and wraps an arm around her. "We are family."

"Well, I hate to break it to ya, kid. But I'm not the man you've conjured up in your mind. I'm sorry about your dad, but he is no longer my old man. And you don't know what you've just walked into. This isn't a country club. You aren't in fucking Kansas anymore." I turn to leave again, fucking done with this conversation.

"I'll prospect then. You guys always want prospects, right?"

"Oh, shit," Satyr grumbles.

"Kid, this isn't one of those clubs your join to put on your resume," Prez states, taking a step between me and Carson.

"I want to be where my brother is, and if it's here, then it is here. I'll prospect."

"That ain't up to me," Prez states, confusing all the members.

"You're the President."

"I care about my members. Kansas is my acting VP and Sergeant at Arms. He is important and has been through enough in his life. It's up to him," Prez states.

All eyes are on me, so I say the only thing that comes to mind. "No. Go home. Sorry about your dad." And with that I walk away, turning my back to them.

Surprisingly, it hurts way more than I thought it would.

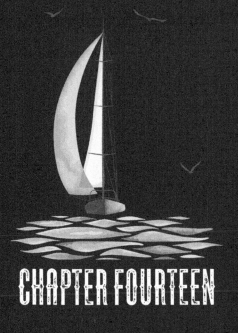

CHAPTER FOURTEEN

Violet

"UNREAL. YOUR SECOND WEEK OF SCHOOL AND YOU GOT suspended already?" I throw my purse in the car and slam the driver's side door closed. "Are you fucking kidding me? Seriously?"

I wait for Veronica to say something, to say anything, but she sits there with her arms crossed in the passenger seat. I turn to look at Victoria, who is twisting her hands in her lap, also silent. "Someone better talk to me or I swear…"

"What? You'll ground us? Please, you aren't Mom."

I slam my fist against the wheel and let out a frustrated sound. "You know what? I'm not Mom, but guess what? We are all we have, and I'm the oldest out of us which puts me in charge, and I don't care how much you don't like it. I won't let you walk all over me with your bad attitude, Veronica. How am I supposed to make our lives better when you aren't helping me? You're acting like a child. Tell me what happened today."

"It was my fault," Victoria cries from the backseat. Big fat tears are rolling down her face. "There has been this girl in my class who has been really mean to me. Veronica saw her push me into the locker. She grabbed the girl by her hair and tossed her on the ground and punched her and said, 'Stay away from my sister or this will be the last time your face looks this good.' It's my fault, Violet. I'm sorry, Veronica. I didn't want you to get suspended,'" she sobs, clutching onto her notebooks for safety.

I let out a breath of relief and drop my forehead to the wheel, then chuckle. "God, Veronica. Why didn't you say that? Did you kick her ass?"

Veronica whips her head toward me, rounding her eyes. "You aren't mad?"

I put the car in drive and start on our way home. "No. Not when it comes to your sister. Did you kick her ass?"

She smirks. "Yeah, I really did. She's going to have a black eye for school pictures."

"Good. Serves the bitch right for fucking with Victoria. You have my permission to kick anyone's ass who messes with her. Is that the only girl bothering you? What did she say?" I stare at Victoria through the rearview mirror when we get to the red light.

"There are others," she whispers.

"What? Who? Tell me their names," Veronica says. "When I get back to school, I'll kick their ass."

"It's okay," she says sadly.

"No, it isn't okay, Victoria. What happened? I didn't know you were getting bullied. What are they saying?"

"Just calling me names. It isn't a big deal."

"What names?" I ask her. She stays silent, so I press on. "What names, Victoria?"

"They call me brace-face and ugly. It's fine."

"I'm killing them," Veronica snarls and slouches in the seat, staring out the window.

"You are beautiful, Victoria. Those braces? You're going to have perfect teeth when they come off, and they are going to be jealous. That's all it is. They are jealous. Keep that in mind, okay? I know it's hard, but they will be the ones laughing in the end."

I hated high school too. Kids are brutal and often times, it's the bullies with the issues. "I know it's hard to stay positive, but you have to."

"I know," she whispers, flipping through her book.

"Maybe we can ask some of the guys to bring you to school on their bikes. That should scare some of them, right?"

She perks up at that idea. "You think they would? Oh gosh, that would be so cool, Violet."

"I'll talk to Kansas and set something up. I have no doubt he will do it for you."

"Oh my god, that would be so awesome. I hope it happens. What about tomorrow? The sooner the better."

"You bet. I'll talk to him when we get—" I almost say home, but I stop myself. I'm not sure if they see it that way yet. "—When we get to the clubhouse."

I turn on the radio and my sisters are in a happy mood again. Victoria is smiling and singing along, off-key and horrible while Veronica laughs as she sings too. I stare at her, then lift my gaze to the rearview mirror again. I've been waiting to hear them laugh like that again.

I focus on the road again, and the light ahead is green. I'm midway through the intersection when a vehicle out of nowhere slams against the driver's side. Metal crunches against metal, and my sister's screams ring my ears. Glass prickles across my skin, and my head jerks to the side. My body flies out of the seat, and I hit my head on the roof of the car. The seatbelt keeps me intact, but the car flips to the side. My eyes are blurry as I stare at the sparks flying against the pavement, and the passenger side window shatters.

But it doesn't stop there.

The car flips through the air and Victoria's books slam against the windshield. It's all happening in slow motion. I almost don't realize what is going on or happening. The car rolls and every other flip it's my side hitting the pavement, then it's Veronica's.

Scarlett is going to be so upset when she sees her car is totaled. It has to be, right?

The squealing of tires surrounds us as other vehicles try not to hit us.

When the car flips again, my body is limp. The vehicle falls to the side I'm on again, only to skid and hit against something. I can't tell what it is. The engine makes a clicking sound while smoke fills the cab. I cough and every part of my body hurts.

I taste blood as it trickles down my lip. I blink my eyes, trying to clear my vision, but I can't. "Veronica? Victoria?" I barely manage to say, but they don't answer. I yank on the seatbelt with all my might, but it doesn't matter. I'm too weak and injured to get out. My face is pressed against the bent metal, and I swallow as pain spreads up my left leg. I grimace and try to lift my head again.

"Veronica?" I try again. "Victoria?" I need to look at them, I need to see if they are okay, but I don't have the strength to turn my head.

"Oh my god, are you okay? Can anyone hear me?" someone shouts from outside the car. "They are really hurt. Someone call 911."

I want to beg for help, I want to speak, but I can't find my voice. I'm too tired. I'm scared. I'm so fucking scared. It's just me and my sisters. They can't die. I can't die. Life is starting over for us now. This can't be how things end.

"Hey, we are going to get you guys out of there, okay?" a man yells through the windshield. "Just hang on, okay? I need you to hang on."

"My sisters..." my voice breaks.

"It's all going to be okay," he reassures me.

I'm in and out of consciousness, fighting the urge to succumb to darkness. I'm so tired. I'm so sleepy. Sirens wail in the distance, and relief floods through me. Everything is going to be okay.

"Veronica, Victoria, help is coming. You hear that?" My voice is hoarse, and the stranger in front of me gets as close as he can to the windshield. The hood is bent and crumpled, reminding me of a piece of paper crumpled up. He gets as close as he can to the windshield, the smoke from the engine clouding his face.

He snaps his fingers. "Hey, no. Keep your eyes open. Tell me about yourself," he says. "Help is almost here."

"Tired," I slur. "Head hurts."

"I know, but your sisters need you to stay awake. We need information. Do you know your name?" he asks.

Tears brim my eyes when I try to move, but my leg stops me, the agony almost unbearable.

"I know you're tired, but talk to me. My name is Gregory. What's yours?" he says, poking his head through the windshield.

"Violet," I rasp.

"Violet. Such a pretty name. And your sisters?"

"Veronica and Victoria," I whimper, the pinch of pain causing me to look down to see a piece of glass in my thigh.

Oh, that really sucks.

"Goodness, I bet everyone gets your names mixed up since the names all start with V," he says. I can hear the smile in his voice, trying to remain in good spirits.

"My sisters... are they okay?"

"I can't see from here, Violet. The sirens are getting closer, though. Everything is going to be fine."

"Kansas," I mumble, fighting dizziness. "Take me to Kansas." My head lulls to the side of the scratched-up metal and glass digs into my skin.

"Hey, no, no. What's in Kansas? Your parents there?" My eyes droop, and he tries to keep me awake by shouting, "Violet, stay awake. I really need you to."

"Sir, I'm going to need you to step back."

"Thank God, you're here. There are three girls in there. They are really banged up. You have to help them," Gregory says through a panicked breath.

I hear loud crunching and a drill, maybe a saw of some sort, but I can't see anything. I've given in. I want to go to sleep. It all hurts.

"Stabilize the C-spine."

I turn my neck to see two firefighters. Or maybe paramedics, I can't tell. My vision is too blurry. They are getting Veronica out. She's lying still on the board. Her hand has fallen off the gurney and there's blood trickling down her finger.

"Hey." A paramedic crawls into the car and begins wrapping something around my neck. "We are going to get you out of here."

"My sister. Get my sister," I argue, doing my best to push him away from me.

"You have a piece of glass in your femoral artery. You're bleeding out. You are first priority," he says, leaning in to wrap the collar around my neck.

"I'm refusing..." I cough again. "Until my sister is out of this car."

He sighs, but he has to listen to me since I denied treatment. Pulse taught me that. He climbs into the back, and a few minutes go by before a yellow board comes through the window. When Victoria's secure, they lift her out, and I breathe easier knowing they are getting help.

"Don't fight me, okay? It's your turn now." He stabilizes my C-spine with a neck brace and cuts me out of the seatbelt when it won't come unbuckled. A burst of heat hits us in the face and a flurry of loud commotion outside the car has my heart rate spiking.

"You need to get out of there! The engine is on fire. It's going to blow!" someone screams over the blaze to inform us.

"I'm not leaving without her!" he shouts.

"I'm scared," I admit through the haze. "I'm so scared."

"I know, hey, I know you are." He takes my hand and squeezes, hooking me against him. "You're doing great,

Violet. Okay? You're going to be alright. There's no time to stabilize you further. We need to go."

I nod as he swings me into an awkward hold. I cry out when the glass moves deeper into my leg.

"I know," he says, crawling out the back window. When fresh air hits my face, he sets me on a gurney, and I stare up at the man who saved my life. His nametag says Wilson. "Thank you."

"Anytime, Violet," he smiles as they load me into the ambulance.

I'm starting to feel drowsy again.

"Her blood pressure is tanking. We need to go now."

"Take me to Kansas," I repeat through a twisted tongue.

Wilson shines a light in my eyes. "What's in Kansas, Violet? Talk to me."

"Everything," I whisper before giving into the darkness.

Everything is in Kansas.

Kansas

UNITED STATES

CHAPTER FIFTEEN

"How are you holding up?" Arrow asks, walking into my room with One-Eye, Satyr, and Void.

I'm sitting on the couch, feet up on the coffee table, watching a show I've never heard of on my sixty-inch flat-screen TV. Honestly, I'm not even paying attention to the show. My mind is reeling from meeting Carson, Stevie, and Brighton. I'm so mad at them. Deep down, I know it isn't their fault, but the audacity they have coming here to ask for my bone marrow for that man… it's unbelievable.

The guys take a seat next to me and Void places a six-pack of beer on the table. "Brought some goods too," he says, bringing out a plastic baggy that has a few tightly rolled blunts in it.

"I'm fine." I lean forward and snag a beer from the plastic. The can hisses when I crack it open, and I take a big gulp. "I thought you went with Violet, One-Eye?"

"I stayed behind because she threatened to cut my throat if she didn't get some space."

"Yeah, sounds like her," I chuckle when I think about her not getting her way. "I don't like that she's alone. She'll be okay, right?"

"She'll be fine, we haven't heard anything from the Irish guy, I think it's fine," he replies. "So how are you really doing?"

I huff and turn the channel on the TV. "I said I was fine."

"Oh yeah, you look real fine. No big deal, right? Just your brothers and sister coming to see you and asking for bone marrow for your old man that had a separate family. Yeah, you're just peachy," Void says sarcastically, reaching for a beer himself.

"Talk to us. What are you thinking?" One-Eye asks. Today he is wearing his fake eye, but I can tell it's bothering him. He hasn't been wearing it lately, and come to think of it, Alicia hasn't been around. I wonder if everything is okay.

"Where's Alicia?" I decide to use that information to change the subject.

"We didn't work out," he rubs his chest where his heart is. He sounds sad.

"What? What happened?" Satyr plops down next to him. "You two were adorable."

"I don't know. I wish I knew, but I don't know. She ended things with me. I guess maybe it's the fact that I'm missing an eye?" He chuckles, but there is no happiness in it.

"When did this happen?" Arrow grabs each person a beer, handing one to One-Eye.

"The other day. I didn't want to bring it up. There are other things going on that are more important than me and my relationship."

"I'm sorry," I say, hating that he is hurting. I know he really liked Alicia.

"It's alright. So," he sips his beer and leans back against the couch. "What are you going to do?"

Damn. That plan didn't last long.

I chug half my beer down and lift a shoulder. "Keep living my life how it is? I have a good thing going. I have lunch with my mom on Saturday, and I'm going to introduce her to Violet. I like how things are. I don't know them. I don't want to know them, and I sure as hell don't want anything to do with my Pops."

"You don't mean that," Satyr frowns.

"How the fuck would you know what I mean and don't mean?" I snap, squeezing the can until it dents. "You have no idea how it felt seeing them when I was sixteen. You don't know what it was like."

"No, I don't. But I know it isn't their fault. I know if I had a family, no matter the situation, I'd want to get to know them."

"Satyr, you guys are all I need. I don't need them."

"I think that's a lie you're telling yourself because you're so mad at your old man. You're taking it out on them." Satyr gulps down his beer, crushes the can, and tosses it like a basketball in the small trashcan near the door. The can hits the target and swishes it against the plastic-bag. "All trash, baby!" he cheers.

Talk about putting me in my place. "I'm not ready to talk to them," I admit, fiddling with the tab of the beer can. "They had this entire life with him, and I only had him part-time. I'm too fucking mad."

"They only had him part-time, too," he points out. If he was over with your family five days a week, if anything, you had him for longer than they did. At least for some of your life."

I hate to admit it, but he's right. Damn it.

"I'm just saying, don't let him die because you're mad. I have a feeling you'd regret it," he continues.

"You give good advice, Satyr," I tell him.

"I'm more than good looks. I'm smart too."

"I mean, you're brighter than a pink crayon, but I don't know if you're the sharpest tool in the shed," Void jabs and it causes the tension to break as we holler with laughter.

"Fuck you," Satyr flips Void off and chuckles, not giving a fuck about the joke.

The door is suddenly kicked in with a heavy slam while we are swallowing our beer. All of us pull out our weapons, and I cock my gun, pointing it at the intruder. I breathe a sigh of relief when it's Pulse. "What the fuck? You nearly got drenched in bullets."

"We need to go to the hospital now, Kansas. Everyone needs to get ready. Put down the beer." Pulse is sweating and stealing the beer from our hands and tossing them in the trash.

"What are you talking about? I'm not going to see my Pops. You can forget it."

"What? No. Don't you know?" he asks, sweat building on his top lip.

"Know what?"

"It's Violet. I just got a call from a friend of mine at the hospital. He remembered the members we had here, and she

196

kept asking people to take her to Kansas. It's bad, man. They got into a really bad car accident."

"What?" I choke and force myself to stand on shaking legs. "No, she was on her way here. She was only going to pick up her sisters."

"I don't know the whole story. All I know is that Violet, Victoria, and Veronica are all in the hospital and according to my friend, it isn't looking good."

"No." I run my fingers through my hair and stumble, slamming my leg against the coffee table. "No, she's fine. She has to be okay."

"Prez is waiting in the truck for you. We will follow behind. You aren't going to be alone."

A hundred thoughts run through my mind as I think about Violet. I'm panicked, I'm scared, and I'm in a daze. I need to be more put together than this. She needs me.

I walk out of the room, not looking where I'm going, but my boots take me there. Pulse is next to me and the other guys are behind us. Everything is numb. I can't think. She has to be okay. I haven't told her I loved her yet. I said I was falling in love with her, but I haven't said the words because I was waiting for the right time.

That's my problem. I've realized there is no such thing as the right time. It's only now. The present.

And I might have lost my chance.

"Amos—" Carson calls my name right as I get to the truck.

"Not now," Pulse says, holding his hand out to tell him to stop where he is.

"Amos, I need to talk to you."

I slam the passenger side door shut and stomp my way

forward, trying to hide the emotion brimming my eyes as I think about Violet. I wrap my hand around his throat and squeeze. "I need to go. I have more important things to do than talk to you about Pops. I'm going to the hospital. I'll be back." I release his neck and spin around, leaving him gasping for air.

Opening the door again, I climb in, and Carson runs up to the side of the truck. "Are you okay? What's going on?" he asks.

"My girlfriend was in a bad car accident. I'm not going to see Pops, so you can stop holding your breath. Prez, let's go."

When everyone is piled into the car, Prez reverses out of the parking lot, and Carson is left standing in front of the clubhouse alone. His hands are laced together on the top of his head as he watches us leave.

"I'm so sorry, Kansas," Scarlett mutters from beside me. She's sitting in the middle so she can be next to Boomer. "This has been an emotional day." Her hand slides into mine and squeezes. I hold onto her, not wanting to lose the connection just yet. It's like having my sister or Mom hold me. The simple touch is keeping me from completely losing it, and I hope Prez doesn't mind.

"Pulse, have you heard anything else while we've been driving?"

"No, I'm checking my phone but there is a video of the accident trending on Facebook," he says.

"What!" I roar in pure rage. "Let me fucking see."

"I don't think you want to," Satyr says, eyes on Pulse's phone screen, and he winces right as I hear the sound of metal hit metal.

I turn as much as the seat allows me and snatch the

phone out of Pulse's hands. I refresh the video and wait. It's taken from a car, and right now it's just of someone recording them and their significant other sharing a kiss. When they break apart, that's when I see Scarlett's car drive through the light and a black SUV slam against the driver's side.

"No!" I scream at the screen until my voice breaks, gasping in horror as my worst nightmares come true. "No, please."

A tear falls, blurring the video. Violet's car slides across the pavement. Sparks fly.

And then it begins to flip.

My stomach turns when I see a quick glimpse of Violet in the driver's seat. I hold a hand over my mouth when they smash against a pole, the one thing that stops the momentum of the car from flipping more. Smoke comes from the engine, and everyone is getting out of their cars, but not the man in the SUV.

"Who the hell is that?" I growl, waiting to see what the driver in the sedan chooses to do. Another tear drops onto the screen, and I wipe it away. There is so much noise, so much chaos in the video, and so many people go to help them. "They are leaving," I clutch the cell as the SUV reverses out of the scene. The fucked up front end speeds off down the opposite road, abandoning the destruction they caused. "They fucking left!"

I throw the phone against the dash, and it cracks in half. All I see is the car flipping. I shouldn't have watched it. Satyr was right.

"I can't help but wonder if it was O'Crowely," Prez mumbles, pressing the button to his hazards as we get to town. He speeds up, the engine revving with the loud horsepower as it bullets us down the street.

"You think he is here?"

"It's the only thing I can think of. Black SUV, leaves the scene, and underground has been quiet when it comes to him. Too quiet. I bet it was him, and he was doing exactly what I thought he would: collecting his debt."

"I'm going to fucking kill him." I wipe my cheek with the back of my hand and stare out the window to see the murky ocean waves rippling, mocking me with their strength.

"You don't kill a man like Lorcan O'Crowely. I'm sorry, Kansas, but this time, the fight might be to negotiate. Not kill."

"Fuck that. If I see him, I'm going to tear him in two for doing what he did to Violet. If that had been Scarlett, you would have his head." I hit the dash with my fist.

"I would have anyone's head, but his? I don't know. We need to be smart when it comes to him, because he is smarter."

I sit quietly as we get onto the highway. I stare at the sky-scrapers, and I'm kicking myself for not taking her downtown and exploring like she's been wanting to do. I was too scared to take her out in the open, for this reason, but she deserved more than the walls of the clubhouse.

Then, out of nowhere, it hits me that the phone I busted wasn't mine. Fuck. "I'll get you a new phone, Pulse. I'm sorry."

"Don't worry about it. I want to check on them just as badly as you do," he says.

I doubt that. He isn't in love with one of them, and if he were, I'd be worried.

"They are my patients too, remember?"

"Right," I say, forgetting that they were patients barely a month ago. "Are we almost there? How far is the hospital?" My leg shakes impatiently as we pass another exit sign that's covered in ice.

"Five minutes, maybe," Prez states, pressing the pedal to the floor.

"Just hurry," I beg. I hold a hand over my heart and rub the ache. Fuck, this hurts so bad. Losing my Pops that day while I held a gun to his head didn't hurt this bad. Maybe it's because I knew he didn't love us like he pretended to. Or maybe it's because I didn't love him as a son should have.

But I know love now. I know how it feels and how it is meant to feel. And damn it, it fucking hurts. I wouldn't change it for a thing.

I would hurt more if I never knew her love at all.

In a sea of beautiful, strong women, not only did I find my best friend, but I found the love of my life. A love like that, when it comes to pain, it really does knock the breath out of you. But when it's good... like really fucking good, it makes breathing easy.

The truck tires squeal as Boomer takes a right into a crowded parking lot. Cars are everywhere and right when we think there is an empty spot, a fucking smart car is there.

"Fuck!" I kick the dash with my foot. "Why do those cars exist? They are a waste of fucking space. Run over it," I tell Prez, spreading my arm out toward the stupid box car and staring at him like that's the only solution. It is.

"I'm going to drop you off in front. Pulse, go with him. We will find a parking spot and then we will find you inside. Just say we are family."

"We are," I grumble, irritated with myself that I haven't officially made her a part of the family yet. I want her last name to be mine. I want her to be my ol' lady, but I've been dragging my ass, once again waiting for the right time.

And I might have been waiting to see if I'd end up like my

dad. It's been one of my worst fears. I thought our blood was bad and eventually, I'd get the urge to ruin something good, but I haven't. I won't.

There's no way in hell I'd ever do that to Violet. If there was a choice, either cheat or have Prez blow me up with one of his grenades, I'd choose death every time.

The truck doesn't even come to a stop outside the Emergency Room before I'm opening the door and jumping out. I don't even bother shutting the door, I run toward the entrance, slipping on ice that hasn't turned to slush yet. The automatic doors take forever to open, and when the space is big enough for me to fit through, I slide in.

Again, I slip against the floor and notice the floor is wet with dirty water from the outside. Yeah, that's real safe. There isn't even a yellow sign on the floor warning people that it's wet. That's a lawsuit waiting to happen.

I take a big step to the left and wipe my boots across the carpet to dry them off before flying down the white tile floor. I skid to a stop in front of the front desk and slam my hands on the counter in front of a lady that seems less than thrilled to see me. She has dyed black hair and wrinkles around her lips. For some reason, she reminds me of someone who smokes ten packs a day.

"I'll be with you in a moment," she croaks.

Yeah, she's differently a smoker.

She's typing away on her computer, and I clench my jaw together. No, I will not wait a fucking moment. "Listen, lady. I'm a member of the Ruthless Kings MC of Atlantic City, and a group of us is about to walk through that door. I want an update by the time they walk in, do you understand me?" It isn't often I use my club as ammo, but this is an emergency.

She gulps and gives me her undivided attention. "What can I help you with?" Her long red nails clink against each other as she looks at me.

"My fiancée, her name is Violet Winston. She was in a car accident with her two sisters. They are here. How is she? How are they? Can you tell me anything?"

"Give me a minute to look up her information, okay?"

"Sure, sure. Please, just anything. I'm going out of my mind. She's everything to me. I can't... nothing can happen to her. Please," my voice breaks next when those damn emotions strangle my throat.

Her nails peck at the keyboard, and she finally starts to nod. "Okay, all three of them are in surgery. It's going to be a while. You might want to get comfortable."

"Surgery? Why? Why does she need surgery? Why do they? Are you sure?"

"I'm sure, sweetie. I'll have the doctor come give an update, okay? I promise," she tells me.

Yeah, that doesn't make me feel any better. I cup my hands over my face, tilt my head back and groan. How do people do this without going insane?

I find a worn seat and sit down.

No, I can't sit.

I stand.

Then I sit again.

And then I stand.

Fuck. How much time has passed? I glance at my watch, and I want to kill someone when I see only three minutes have gone by. Come on, what am I supposed to do?

This time when I sit, I stay there. I place my elbows on my knees and drop my head, trying to remember to breathe. My legs continue to shake, and the noises around me start to grind on my nerves. Someone coughs and it's wet and loud. A kid cries in the corner, splitting my eardrums. A woman is arguing with what sounds like her insurance company. A man four seats down from me is asleep and snoring like an oncoming train.

I cover my ears to block the noise out, and a hand lands on my shoulder. Lifting my head, I see Prez standing there. Scarlett takes a seat next to me and takes my hand again, her eyes showing sympathy and sadness.

"Any update?" he asks, taking to seat to the right of me.

I shake my head. "They are in surgery. All three of them."

God, I love Violet, but I've come to love her sisters like my own, even if Veronica is a little testy.

Void, Satyr, One-Eye, Colt, everyone walks through the door and takes the row of seats in front of me. Warden and Bane aren't their usual playful selves. They are sullen. Decay sits next to them along with Teeth, and then I see Pulse strutting up to the front desk.

"Of course, doctor," the same nurse that helps me tells him, then calls someone on the phone.

He takes three large strides before kneeling in front of me. "She's checking to see if I can have privileges here. If so, the first thing I am going to do is check on them, and I'll be back with an update."

"Yeah, okay. That would be..." My cheeks puff out when I exhale "...that would be great, Pulse. Thank you."

"Don't mention it." He stands up and the nurse waves her hand at him. "I'll be back." He runs to the desk, and I keep my fingers crossed that they give him those privileges because I don't think I can wait. I'm about to burst through those doors that are for personnel only.

If I did that, security would snag me and kick me out. I can't risk that.

"I know it's hard, but you need to calm down. You're shaking all over," Scarlett tries to soothe me. "She will be okay."

"I have privileges. I'll be back when I get some answers," Pulse says, giving me a reassuring smile.

There is nothing reassuring about this, but his efforts mean the world. "Thanks, Pulse." I watch him disappear between the doors and hang my head again. My neck aches with stress, and I rub it, trying to relieve the pressure.

Scarlett rubs the middle of my back in soothing circles and it helps my nerves. I take a deep breath and let it out. "There you go," she says softly. "Violet is strong. She'll be okay."

"I hope you're right," I whisper, then glimpse at her through my wet lashes. "I can't lose her, Scarlett. She's the start of the future I never knew I had. I need her. I love her so fucking much."

"Well, when she is out of surgery, you'll have to make her your ol' lady, won't you?"

"First fucking thing. When I see her open those eyes, you better fucking believe those are going to be the first words out of my mouth. I just need her to live. I need her to wake up, and I'm never going to waste another moment waiting for the right fucking moment."

I press the palms of my hands against my eyes and rub them, trying to get rid of the constant burn.

"I'm going to get some coffees you want some?" Warden asks as he stands, Bane right along with him. They do everything hand in hand.

"Yeah, that would be great," I say. "Thank you."

"Coffee for everyone?" Warden takes a tally. "Alright. We will be back. Keep us updated." The twins head out.

Boomer checks his phone, then tucks it back in his pocket. "I have Wolf seeing if O'Crowely is in town."

"Wolf? Is he able to focus right now?"

"He can't be in a hospital, so he volunteered to go on the hunt for the Irish fucker," Boomer sneers.

I get up from the chair. I can't sit anymore. I begin to pace, and before I know it, a half-hour has passed and Warden and Bane are back with coffee. The cup warms my hand just as the doors swing open, and Pulse arrives. He is in scrubs.

I've never seen him in scrubs. He looks like a real doctor now.

"Pulse." I dash to him, barely feeling the hot liquid spill from the cup onto my hand. "What is it? How is she? Is she okay?" All the members surround me, and Pulse stretches his neck from side to side.

He shuffles his weight on his feet. "The car accident was a bad one. Victoria will be in the hospital for a while. She cracked a few vertebrae in her spine, but she isn't paralyzed."

"Oh my god," Scarlett gasps.

"Veronica shattered the bones in her right arm and has a concussion."

"Violet—"

"—What about Violet?" I interrupt him.

"Well, the car hit her side, so her injuries were more severe. She nearly bled out. She had a piece of glass impaled in her femoral artery, internal injuries, a bruised spine, and her brain swelled. To relieve the pressure, they had to drill holes in her skull to get the excess bleeding and a clot. Everyone's surgery is going smoothly. Everyone has superficial wounds from the glass, some bruising, but hey, nothing time can't heal."

"They had to drill a hole in her head?" The coffee slips from my hand as I mumble the words. "Holes?"

"It's not as scary as it sounds. It's done more than you think. It's okay, she's fine, Kansas. They gave her blood transfusions to replace the blood she lost."

"When can I see her?" I sway on my feet, the lightheadedness causing me to lose balance. "I want to see her."

"They are wrapping up soon. When I know, you'll know, I swear."

I've been through and seen unimaginable things, but this is my worst nightmare.

Kansas wasn't this bad.

Jersey is so much worse.

Kansas

UNITED STATES

CHAPTER SIXTEEN

I T FEELS LIKE AN ETERNITY BEFORE PULSE COMES TO GET US TO SEE Violet and her sisters. Every step I take, it's like I'm trudging through mud or quicksand. Each step is more difficult than the last. The white tiled floor is slowly swallowing me whole. The fluorescent lights are too bright, stinging my swollen eyes.

"Remember, she will look worse than she really is. She's still asleep," Pulse informs me. "And only one at a time, I'm sorry guys. It's hospital regulation."

"It's okay. We will go see Veronica and Victoria. Go see Violet, Kansas." Prez slaps me on the back as he walks by with the guys, his arm around Scarlett to keep her close.

"I'll leave you alone. Just call me if you need me."

"Thanks, Pulse." I let out a shaky breath and grip the silver handle. Blood is rushing through my ears, and my heart is hammering against my chest with anxiety. Nausea brews as I press down on the door latch. The click of the lock and groan of the door opening is going to haunt me for years to come. The scent of the hospital floods my senses.

I hate the way it smells.

It's blood, plastic, and death, with a hint of cleaner to try and cover it up.

"Oh, Springs."

I break when I see her lying still on the bed, head wrapped, leg elevated, and black and blue bruises all over her beautiful face. There are small cuts from the glass, and I'm noticing a side of her head is shaved.

Her beautiful, wild curls are gone.

I close the door and hurry to her side, scooting a chair as close as I can. My hand trembles as it hovers over her hand. I'm afraid to touch her. What if I hurt her more? Even her slender fingers are cut, and the top of her knuckles are scraped.

Gently, I fold my fingers around her palm and hold up her arm, bringing her hand to my mouth as I press a kiss to it. I wish it made her better. I wish my kiss healed her like children believe it does when their parents kiss their boo-boos. Life isn't that easy. A kiss doesn't change the world.

Only time does.

"Violet," her name is twisted in agony around my tongue, dark and gritty with emotion.

I cry.

I let my strength go. I release my pride, my power, my dominance, all the things that make me the invincible man I've molded myself into—I let go.

Because I am not invincible. Violet is just as much a weakness as she is my strength.

Love fucking hurts, but the pain is worth it as long as her heart keeps beating.

"I love you," I rasp. "I love you. I love you. I love you," I chant as I feather kisses along the top of her hand. I hope she can hear me. "I wish I would have said that sooner," I say, wiping my wet cheeks on the sleeve of my shirt. "You are scaring the hell out of me. I never thought I'd ever be in this position, but loving you has changed me, and I really like the man I am with you, so you have to come back to me, okay? You can't leave me."

I sniffle, then rest my head against the mattress next to her. I never want to leave her side. I find peace in the heart monitor as it beeps, reassuring me she's alive. "You shouldn't have left alone. I can't believe you did that. You can't ever do that again. You call me or you have one of the guys with you. It's too dangerous for you to be out on your own. I'll never forgive myself that this happened to you. I should have been there. I should have saved you." I lift my hand and rub the one spot on her jaw that's not harmed by a bruise or a cut. "I am so sorry, Springs."

She doesn't reply. She's just as still as she was when I walked inside the room.

"You're so beautiful," I continue to talk to her. "You aren't alone, okay? I'm here every step of the way. You won't ever be alone again."

Her heart rate changes, and I glance up at the monitor, then to her face to see if she's waking up, but it's becoming slower, so slow the monitors start wailing, blinking red.

I fly out of my chair just as a team of doctors rush in,

210

along with Pulse. I grip the thick of my hair and give them room, scared out of my damn mind. "I didn't touch her. I didn't do anything. What's wrong with her? What happened!" I scream at them in the flurry of chaos. "Talk to me, goddamn it! Tell me!" The heart rate monitor flatlines, the constant low beep a sound that rips my heart right of my chest. "No, no, no. Please," I sob and Pulse grips me by the jaws and gives me a shake. "Why is this happening?"

"She has a pneumothorax. It can happen after surgery. Basically, she has an air bubble and it's traveling. We need to release the air."

"Fucking release it then!" I roar.

"They are going to needle aspirate. They will put a needle into her chest cavity, watch." He steps out of the way and points to the doctor that has the needle in his hand. "You see that?"

The doctor shoves a needle into her, causing me to flinch because I want to swoop in a save her myself. I know they are helping, but it almost looks like they are hurting her.

"Now he will pull back on the syringe," Pulse says.

The doctor does what he says, and the syringe is empty as he pulls back, hopefully, full of air. The monitor begins to beep again, and I bend over, pressing my hands against my knees, and let out a breath I didn't realize I was holding.

"There we go," the doctor states, staring at the needle before lying it on the tray next to him. "She's stable."

Pulse pats the middle of my back, and I shake my head. I should be more put together than this. While she isn't dead, I know what Wolf feels like now. I can't imagine how I'd be if she died. I'd be just like him. I'm already out of my mind.

"She's going to be okay," Pulse says. "I know it's scary,

and as I said, it's not as scary as it looks. I'm not saying her condition isn't serious, it is, but so far, nothing has happened that we don't have control of, okay? The first twenty-four hours are the worst. After that, it's hopeful she'll make it through without any other complications."

"Pulse, it's like I can't breathe," I gasp. "Why can't I be in more control?" I struggle to breathe again and press my hand against my heart. "My chest hurts." I inhale again, but it's like my throat is closing up or my lungs won't accept the air.

He pushes me into the chair as I stare at him with wide eyes.

"What's... happening..."

"You're having a panic attack," he says, pushing me into the seat. "You have to slow your breathing. Come on, follow my breaths."

"I can't. I can't!" I squeeze my eyes shut as my head swims in uncertainty and lack of oxygen.

He lifts his hand and slaps me across the face. The burn stings my cheek, and my jaw aches, and I don't have time to react before he backhands me again.

I shake my head, and my vision stabilizes. I can breathe. My lungs open, and I suck air in as if I'm starved for it. Pulse checks, well, my pulse, and he nods. "There we go. Calm down, brother. You'll be okay."

"Thank you," I mumble, exhausted.

"Sorry, sometimes a bit of pain brings people back to reality. I didn't want to hurt you."

"No, I appreciate it. I can't believe I reacted that way. I'm better than that."

"Kansas, no one is better than that. You have someone you love in a hospital bed fighting for her life. You witnessed her flatline. You saw a needle go into her chest. That isn't easy. Panic is normal. There isn't a manual to deal with an emotional disaster like this. I wish there were, but all you can do is adapt as you go. You're allowed to lose it. You're allowed to freak the fuck out. I would. I would be scared out of my mind."

"I am. I can't string together a cohesive thought. It's like my mind is going a hundred-miles-an-hour. I can't focus. It only makes me feel worse for Wolf. No wonder he is off-the-wall."

"Yeah, people deal differently. You aren't weak for being worried and scared, Kansas. It's okay."

I nod, leaning my head back against the wall. I stare at Violet, eyes still shut as if she didn't just flatline and have a needle in her chest.

"How are her sisters?" I should have asked earlier, but my focus has only been on Violet.

"They are doing really well. Victoria will need to be in a back brace for a while, and Veronica has pins and plates in her arm to repair the break, but they will wake up soon, sooner than Violet."

"Why is that?"

"Technically she had brain surgery. Patients always take longer to wake up from that. Be patient, she'll wake up. I'm going to go get something to drink. Do you want me to bring you anything?"

"Yeah, water would be great, thank you."

"Any snacks?"

I shake my head. "I couldn't eat right now, thanks though."

He leaves the room, and I can't help but notice how confident he is in a hospital setting. He is in his zone. I'm so damn thankful he is here. I trust him, and if I can trust him, then I have to believe she is going to be okay.

"I'm going to kill that asshole that did this to you and your sisters. I'm going to find him. I'll get retribution. I don't care what needs to be done or who I need to kill to do it. He will never hurt you again." I take her hand in mine again and place my head on the mattress next to her arm. "Not right now. Right now, I'm going to stay by your side. I can't be anywhere else when I know you're here."

I kiss her thumb. The faint scent of peaches somehow managed to survive on her skin. I inhale, close my eyes, and remember the first time I held her in my arms.

She was in a hospital bed.

"We really have to stop meeting like this," I say with a sad laugh.

I place her hand under my cheek, and my eyes drift, heavy from the emotional day and stress. As I said, I refuse to leave her. I'll sleep here for weeks if I have to.

I'm not sure how long I fall asleep for. Hours, minutes, I don't know, because I can't see the clock when I snap my eyes open. The room is dark, quiet, but I feel something.

My instincts are never off.

I reach into the back of my waistband and grab my gold-plated gun, aiming it at the corner of the room. "You better reveal yourself before I blow your fucking head off," I warn.

A beat passes with no answer, and I cock the weapon, the click louder than the beep of the machine. "I don't mind leaving a hole where your heart used to be."

A maniacal chuckle drifts from the shadows, sounding as vile as a villain in a movie.

"Yer a smart man, Amos Taylor." The light Irish lilt has my finger on the trigger.

The Irish fucking Crow. He's here.

I flip on the lamp on the side of the bed and am greeted with a tall, imposing man in a pristine suit, hands casually in his pockets, and a wicked grin on his face.

"How do you know me? You know what, I don't care. I'm going to fucking kill you," I grit through tight teeth.

"No, ye aren't." He takes a step out of the dark. "I didn't do this. Regardless of what my reputation says, I do not kill innocent women."

But he does kill women. At least that's what he implies.

"If you didn't, who did?" I ask.

"I'd like to know that too, considering these are my godchildren."

No.

Fucking.

Way.

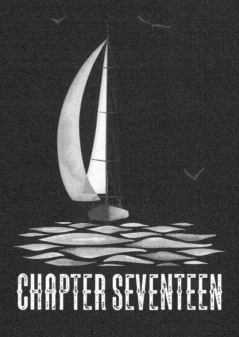

CHAPTER SEVENTEEN

Violet

BLINK MY EYES OPEN. THEY ARE HEAVY, GRITTY WITH SLEEP, AND I want to immediately fall back asleep, but the commotion in the room won't allow me. My head is pounding, and I need them to lower their voices, because *ow*.

"You expect me to believe that?"

That's Boomer. What is he doing here?

"Ta be frank, boyo, I don't give a fuck what ya believe."

Who the hell is that? He sounds Irish. I think. Am I dreaming? Is this a figment of my imagination?

"You can't be her godfather. Her dad couldn't have been that stupid."

That's Amos. He sounds furious.

"Ya better watch yer fucking tone when ya speak to me. You have no idea who I am and what I am capable of."

"I do. You are The Irish Crow. It's what they call you. I'm not stupid. You used to work with my old Prez."

"Ah, Venom. Horrible man. He owed me a lot of money when he died. I guess that's yer doing?" Irish man asks.

"That would be mine. Blew them to fucking bits just like I can you in a matter of seconds. You can shoot me, but you'd be stuck with a grenade at your feet. Boom." Boomer makes an explosion sound with his mouth. "A sweet red mist will coat the room with your Irish fucking filth."

"I like you," Irish says with an ironic laugh.

"Makes one of us," Amos sneers.

I manage to wiggle, and pain rolls up my leg. "Ouch," I grumble. It hurts to speak. My throat is dry and raw, and my leg feels like it's on fire.

"Violet." Amos hovers over my face.

I blink slowly and steadily, letting my mind come to the present on its own terms. His handsome face comes into view. He looks like crap. It looks like he hasn't shaved in a few days, and his eyes are ringed with red.

"Violet. You're awake. I love you." He presses a soft kiss on my lips, and I weakly lift my hand to press it against his face. "You scared the hell out of me."

If I had enough energy, I'd cry to hear him say that. I give him a tiny, tired smile instead. I'm so happy, but I know he can't see it. "I love you too. My sisters?" I ask, staring into the home of his hazel irises.

"They are okay. They woke up a few hours ago."

"Is an Irish man here? I'm so confused."

A few guys laugh in the background, but I can't tell who it is since I've closed my eyes for a minute.

"Remember the man we worried about finding you for the drugs?"

I nod, licking my dry, chapped lips.

"He's here. His name is Lorcan O'Crowely."

"He did this," I mumble, turning my head weakly to look at the man. Every fiber of my being hurts, and I point to him. "You almost killed me."

"He says he didn't do it," Amos growls, displeased. "And I don't know if I believe him. He claims to be your godfather."

"My Dad never mentioned it," I counter with evidence to prove he isn't.

"I have proof. If anything happened to them, you were supposed to come to me, but considering you're grown now, you are in charge of your sisters. Yer father and I were good friends, Violet. He spoke of his daughters constantly."

"Why didn't I know about you, then?"

He takes a step forward, and Amos holds out his hand to stop him from coming closer. "That's close enough."

Lorcan sits down in the chair and crosses an ankle over his knee. "It was important to yer father ye were not involved in this world. Our world. My world. It's a dangerous one, because I am a dangerous man. Ya weren't easy to find. I had to hire a private investigator. When yer father didn't deliver, I knew something had happened. He was always on top, punctual, and he communicated."

"They died in the storm," I whisper.

"I'm so sorry to hear that, Violet," Lorcan states. "But I assure you, I would not harm my family, well, unless they harmed me first. That's not the point."

And it isn't reassuring.

"So." He slaps his hands on the chair. "We need to find who did this to ya." His Irish accent comes out stronger in some sentences than others. "I'll kill them."

"I will," Amos inserts, taking my hand in his. "I want retribution. It's probably one of your men causing fucking problems."

"My men know better. How do we not know it isn't one of yours?"

Boomer tosses a grenade in his hand, and my heart rate kicks up a notch.

Please, don't drop that.

"Never. My men are loyal to the core." Boomer stands in front of Lorcan, glaring daggers with him, eye-to-eye.

"My men are smart and scared. They would never turn their back on me while they know what I can do to them," he states.

"Can someone get a doctor? I need pain meds and water."

"I can make you feel better, Violet," Pulse says, coming into view from the back corner.

"Pulse," I grin. "You're here."

"I can't let my favorite patients be seen by some other doctor. I'm territorial like that," he teases.

"I'm glad," I say. "Can you get everyone to lower their voices? My head hurts."

"Makes sense. You had holes drilled in it." He inserts a needle into the IV and a few seconds go by before the pain meds hit me.

Oh yeah, that's the stuff.

"No way," I gasp, staring at him open-mouthed.

"Yes way. Feel better?"

"Soooo much." I grin, not bothering to ask why I had holes drilled in my head. I'm not wanting to get into the details of my injuries right now. I remember the accident. It doesn't take a rocket scientist to figure out that I got fucked up.

"Okay, enough smiling at the doctor." Amos shoves Pulse out of the way and it makes me giggle.

Pulse throws his head back and laughs. "What can I say? Chicks dig a man who can save their lives." He shrugs as if it isn't a big deal.

"We are getting off-topic," Boomer grunts, pinching the bridge of his nose. "Not that I'm not happy you're okay, Violet. I am. It's so nice to see all three of you awake, but there is a man in here who has killed people for looking at him wrong."

"Guilty as charged," Lorcan preens, sitting straighter in his chair. "Though, I've heard of yer reputation, Ruthless Kings. Are ye so in a position to judge?"

Boomer's eyes flicker in rage, but I don't care. I have more important things to ask.

"Are you really my godfather?" I slur, staring at his intimidating face. He has a beard, square face, but I can't tell what color his eyes are. He's a big guy. He has wide shoulders, and the suit stretches across his chest so tight it might tear with the next deep breath he takes.

"I am. I swear on me life."

"Well, that's something. I know you care for your life," Boomer exhales in frustration. "So, what are we going to do? The girls stay with us. She's Kansas's ol' lady, but I know you. You are going to want something. Men like you always do."

"And if you were in my position, you'd want something

too." O'Crowely tugs on his suit sleeves, checking the time on his Rolex. "Do you have my shipment?" he asks.

"We do. We don't use drugs in the club."

"Funny way of saying you don't mind selling them." Lorcan twists Boomer's words. "I need a new contact here. My friend and dealer are dead. I can give you contact to his supplier, and you will get a cut. I like my shit on time, and when you make a delivery, you bring my goddaughters to see me."

"I feel like this is all happening because of me, and I don't like that," I mumble and yawn. "And I don't even know you," I point to Lorcan.

"Well, you do now. You're involved in the MC life now, there is no reason you can't be involved in mine. I've missed your entire lives because that was what your parents wanted."

"You've known my Dad that long?" I ask just as Amos places a cup under my mouth with a straw. I take a long gulp and groan, then suck on the straw like my life depends on it.

"Whoa, okay, slow down. Sips, Violet. Sips." Pulse takes the cup from Amos, and the straw slips from between my lips. "Dude, she shouldn't be drinking that fast."

"She's thirsty. She's been asleep for hours," Amos defends me.

"And she might throw it up."

"Christ on a bike, you Americans are gobshites. Let her drink the damn water." Lorcan steals the cup from Pulse and sets it in front of me, then folds his hands in his lap. "Do we have a deal or not?"

"What kind of drugs are we talking about?" Boomer leans against the end of the bed and tucks his thumbs in his belt loops as he stares down Lorcan.

"The kind that pays."

"I don't know. We've been thinking about getting into the marijuana industry, maybe open up shop for some medical-grade stuff."

O'Crowely lifts his chin and his brow rises again. A happy smile takes over when he stands. "A business is a good, discreet way of loading and unloading, my friend."

"We are not friends, O'Crowely," Boomer says.

"Ye better change yer attitude," Lorcan deepens his voice and takes a step forward, invading Boomer's space. "We are practically family now. Ye can't get rid of me. I'm the Irish Crow, ya know. And remember what a flock of crows is called." A silent threat hangs in the air.

"Don't act like you are doing this out of selflessness. Yes, your goddaughters are here, but you want something in return for your drugs not being delivered on time. That's selfish. If you really cared, wouldn't you just leave and not get us into business together?" Boomer asks.

It's like a soap opera. I dart my eyes to the Irishman, sipping my water while Amos is petting the top of my head. It feels good.

I love him.

He's so handsome.

I chuckle around the straw for no reason.

"Oh, someone is feeling good," Amos whispers into my ear.

"Make me feel even better," I slur, tapping the tip of his nose. "You know you wanna."

"When you're healed, there's nothing that will keep me out of your tight cunt." He keeps his voice low so no one can hear us.

My heart rate monitor kicks up when I think about us in this bed. "I don't feel anything now. I'm all drugged up. Let's do it." I grab his shirt and tug him close, and he grunts, almost falling out of the seat.

"Springs, you're injured. No way, plus, you're high."

A few guys chuckle behind him, and I lift a shoulder. "Feels good too."

"What am I going to do with you?" he says happily, pressing a kiss to my lips.

"Love me," my eyes begin to drift shut again.

"You'll never have to worry about a day where I don't do that."

Sweet talker.

"I am a businessman, Boomer. Money rules my world, and only now will I care for someone other than myself," Lorcan states. "I see opportunity everywhere, and this is an opportunity I will refuse to not take. Now, if ye will excuse me, I have two other goddaughters to see." Lorcan is next to my bed and bends down to kiss me on the forehead. Amos rumbles in displeasure, but I kind of like that I have someone else who is an extension of Mom and Dad. I might not know him, but my family did, and that brings me comfort.

Even if he sells drugs, kills people, and whatever else.

"I hope ye don't mind who I am and what I do," he says to me, brushing my hair back. "I really only stayed away because it was yer father's wish."

I live with men who have killed. "Bitches gotta pay rent, right?" I say sounding drunk and shrugging my shoulders uncaring.

Everyone stares at me slack-jawed until Boomer starts to laugh. It's a domino effect. O'Crowely and Amos cackle while the guys wipe under their eyes from laughing so hard.

What did I say? I don't know.

"Silly girl. I *own*. Renting is for poor people," he scoffs as he begins to leave, spine straight as he walks with impeccable posture for a man. "I'll be in touch, Boomer."

"I don't doubt it," Boomer grumbles, a bit disgruntled.

As soon as he leaves the room, a surge or wave of heavy power exits with him.

Arrow pipes up. "What's wrong with renting? I like renting. If it breaks, landlord fixes it, and it ain't my problem."

"Same," Teeth agrees.

"I want a juice box," Arrow announces. "I'm going to the cafeteria."

"Alright everyone, let's head out and give Violet some rest. We have broken enough rules today."

"Amos, don't go," I reach for his hand and press it against the cheek that doesn't hurt.

Or maybe it does.

I can't feel a damn thing.

"Never, Springs."

"Good." I close my eyes and try to get comfortable again. I forget who is with me and mutter, "I want Kansas."

"I'm here, Springs."

"Everything is in Kansas."

Kansas

UNITED STATES

CHAPTER EIGHTEEN

I REPLAY HER WORDS IN MY HEAD ABOUT A MILLION TIMES AS I watch her sleep. It's just been over a few hours since she admitted everything was in Kansas.

My heart swelled with joy, and then I began to overthink the actual meaning of it. What if everything is in Kansas? What if Kansas means my family? What if I need to talk to my Pops for the first time in over fifteen years? What if I need to embrace the three siblings I've always wanted nothing to do with, because I've been so fucking angry at them for taking my Pops away from me?

'Everything is in Kansas' is starting to have more meaning than she meant to imply. Fuck. I'm going to have to see him. I don't want to, but in order for me to fully move on with my life, to fully move on with Violet, I need to come to terms with what my past is.

My dad fucking sucks as a human being, but I have three siblings I could get to know. Family.

Hell, Violet just found out she has an Irish mobster as her godfather, and for the most part, she took it in stride. It could have been because she is high, but I guess we will know for sure tomorrow.

"Hey, how is she?" Pulse asks, peeking his head through the crack of the door.

"Can you stay with her for a bit? I need to…" I stand up, not wanting to let go of her hand, but knowing I have to, "…I need to go see my Pops."

Pulse whistles low as he steps into the room. "You're going to get tested for him?"

"I don't know about that yet, but he is in this hospital. If Violet can accept O'Crowely, then maybe, somehow—" I blow out some air and shake my head while scratching the side of my neck "—Maybe somehow I can get to know my brothers and sister. I don't know what I'm doing."

"Hey, doing something is better than doing nothing. I'm proud of you. Of course, I'll stay with her. Don't worry about it."

"I don't trust that Irish fuck. If you leave her, he could come in here and take her. I can't have that. I'm trusting you," I tell him.

"Brother, you don't have a thing to worry about. I'm going to read while I'll wait for you to come back."

"Thank you." I give her a quick peck on the lips. She stirs slightly, whimpers in pain, and her brows dip. I look up at the monitor, but she's okay.

"I'll give her some pain meds. It's about that time anyway. Go on, she'll be fine. Go while you have the nerve."

"I said I wouldn't leave her."

"You aren't leaving her alone, and you will be back. I doubt she will wake up. I'm going to really knock her out. She'll be thankful."

I whisper in her ear, "I'll be right back, Spring. I love you. I'm going to go see my Pops. He is here too." I kiss her on the cheek and straighten to my full height. "Do you know where I'd find someone who needs a bone marrow transplant?"

"Cancer ward, probably. I don't know where it is here, sorry. Someone will show you the way. Good luck."

I give him a stressed smile, but don't even show my teeth. When I walk out the door and close it behind me, I look left and right down the hall.

Fuck, which way did I even come from when we first got into her room? A doctor in a white coat scribbling something on a chart is power walking by, not looking at where he is going.

I pretend to be in his way, and he bumps into me. His chart clatters to the floor, and his pen rolls under a machine that's against the wall.

"I am so sorry! Are you okay?" he asks.

I bend down and pick up his chart, but I can't reach the pen. "Yes, thank you. It's okay. Don't worry about it."

"It isn't the first time I've run into someone. I really need to watch out where I'm going. Someone could get hurt."

"Good thing we are in a hospital, right?" I try to make a joke of it, but he doesn't laugh.

Tough crowd. Okay.

"So, I was wondering. Where would I find oncology?"

227

"You're going to want to go to the third floor. Front desk will help you from there."

"Thanks so much. Take care," I tell him and step to the right to make my way down the hall. I peek into Veronica and Victoria's room. They are sleeping and O'Crowely glares at me from the small, uncomfortable loveseat in Veronica's room.

I don't say a word to him, but he hasn't hurt them yet, so that's something. Shutting the door, I aimlessly walk toward the silver elevators. It's apparent that I have no idea where I'm going, but as long as I get to the third floor, I don't care how clueless I look.

There are a few nurses around me, gossiping at the nurse's station about a patient who likes to grab their ass when they walk away.

If they are complaining about patients, I can't imagine what they would say about bikers. I press the button and it dings, sliding the metal slabs open instantly. I step inside and the scent of bleach wafts heavily in my face, making my head spin.

Only one reason for bleach and that's to erase all signs of blood.

I hit 3 on the panel and the nurse winks at me as the door shuts.

Yeah, old me would have been all about that.

New me?

I'm a forever taken and faithful man.

"Thank you for choosing Atlantic City Hospital, the number one choice for patients who truly want to be cared for. From general surgery to family medicine, our highly-trained medical staff here at ACH will do everything in their power to make sure you and your loved ones feel as though you are at home—" the automatic voice fades when I step out onto the third floor.

Thank god I don't have to hear those lies anymore. There is nothing worse than hearing that on constant repeat. This place does not feel like home. Not even close.

The third floor is like entering another world. The walls are painted blue and it looks fresh, while the tile looks like it has signatures from every child that has entered this place.

Fuck. I hope they all survived.

This is depressing.

"Hi, can I help you?" a cheery, young blonde pipes up from behind the desk. She smiles, and her kindness warms up the horrible edge lingering in the air.

I step over as many names on the ground as I can. I don't know, I feel like it's bad luck if I step on them. If I step on a crack, I'll break my mother's back, that type of thing.

She has an amused expression stretching her lips as I finally make it to the counter.

"I hope you can help me. My Pops is here. His name is Taylor. Ronald Taylor."

The smile on her face dims and she nods. "He's going to be in room 356. You must be Amos."

"Uh, yeah," I nod, a bit uneasy.

"He talks a lot about his kids. We were wondering if you were going to show." She leans in and whispers, placing her hand against her mouth so no one can see her. "We had a bet going."

"And were you on the betting side that I would show or wouldn't?"

"Would. It's too hard to ignore a parent while they are in this condition."

"Well—" I pull out my wallet and slap twenty bucks on the counter. "I'm more surprised than you are for showing up here. Room 356?" I point my finger down the hall and take a step in that direction.

She points her French manicured finger into the other direction, the hall to the left. "That way," she directs.

"Thanks." I nod, giving her a quick salute.

"Hey, um, maybe when you're done and it isn't a bad time, you'd want to go out to get a drink?" she asks as I pass her.

"Sorry. Happily married man. I'm flattered, though."

"Oh, lucky lady," she says. "Unfair to women all around."

She's nice, but she's forward, I'll give her that. She's pretty, but nowhere near as pretty as my Violet. "Not unfair to me," I say, and after I say it, I realize it's insulting, so I don't look back and put one foot in front of the other.

I pass rooms as I go. Each one is more depressing than the last.

Names on the tile get fewer and further between and I still try to miss them, skipping over them. You know, just in case.

350.

352.

354.

I stop in the middle of the hallway before room 356. I can hear laughter, but the kind from a game show on a TV. My nerves are on fire in my stomach. My heart is beating a million miles an hour, and my palms are starting to sweat.

I can't do this.

Why the fuck am I here? Violet needs me. I spin on my heel to get the fuck out of here when I run smack into someone.

"Shit. I'm sorry—" I stop short when I see Carson standing there. Of course I'd run into him.

He is clearly stunned and takes a step back. "What are you doing here, Amos?"

"Violet got into a car accident with her sisters and it was pretty serious. I got to thinking of you guys and thought of Dad, but this was a mistake. I can't do this. I'm sorry, Carson. I just... I can't." It's nearly impossible to miss the names scribbled on the tile.

"You're all he has talked about," Carson says.

I'm almost at the end of the hall when he says that, and of course, I have to stop.

"He talks about all of your baseball games, and how he wishes he could have seen you grow up more, but he was proud of the man you became by standing up to him the way you did. He's always wondered about you and your mom."

Before I know it, I'm in Carson's space. "He doesn't have a right to ask about my mom after what he did to her."

"He knows that. I know that. I'm saying, he knows you are here. He has tried to keep up with you and ever since we moved here, you're all he has talked about. He doesn't deserve your kindness, but maybe..." he exhales "...maybe give it to him anyway? Be better than he was."

I snort and tilt my head back, trying not to smile. "For a younger brother, you're smarter than me. I don't know how I feel about that."

"I don't believe that for a minute. You had the strength to leave him. When I found out, I didn't. I know I seem like I'm rooting for him, and I'm by his side. I am, but I'm fucking mad at him, Amos. That hasn't changed, only my actions have. See him and while you're visiting him, maybe I can see Violet? See how she is? She'll be okay, right?" His understanding and kindness make it that much harder to hate him.

231

"Yeah, I think so. I don't know you too well, Carson. I'm not comfortable with you seeing her, especially in this condition. I'm sorry."

"I get it. I'll just wait in the waiting room."

"But maybe another time? I just... this is all very new to me."

"I understand. Give her my best, yeah?" he asks before walking away.

I haven't even told her they are here. What the hell is wrong with me?

"Let's get this over with," I tell myself. All this is too awkward for me to handle. It's like living in another dimension.

Room 356.

Here goes nothing.

I knock on the door as a wet cough fills the room. "Come in!" he shouts.

His words are barely understandable through the phlegm lodged in his throat. I make the biggest leap of my life and place my foot over the threshold. The room is nice and private. He doesn't share it with anyone. The bed is in the middle on the opposite wall so he can look out to see the view of the ocean. The TV hangs in the corner playing the game show the 'Price is Right', and the hiss of oxygen can be heard over the cheers of the audience.

He hasn't noticed me yet.

My god, he looks like hell. The years have not been kind to him. He looks ten years older than he really is. Dark spots and bruises cover his hands from the needle pricks, and he has dark circles under his eyes. He doesn't have hair, bald as the day he was born, and he is thin.

When I imagined he had cancer, I still imagined the man that I held at gunpoint. I figured he was unbreakable.

Karma is a bitch.

Fuck, I'm going to hell.

My angry side is a real dick.

I'm finally deep enough into the room when he sees me out of his peripheral vision. The same hazel eyes that I have, that Carson has, that Stevie and Brighton have, stare at me like they have never seen me before.

"You lost?" he asks, not even recognizing me.

I knew this was a fucking mistake. I try to leave, I try to move my feet, but they are glued to the ground. I'm stuck in this stare-off, unable to speak a word. I've waited for this moment for years. I've run this conversation over a hundred times in my head. I've planned for this day.

There's so much to say, and yet, I can't speak a word of it.

"Amos?" he whispers when it finally hits him who I am. "Amos, is that you?" his eyes water, and a tear flows out of the corner of his eye. "My boy—"

"—No. You don't get to call me that. You don't get to call me your son." My voice cracks, but I'm still able to speak in a deep, pissed-off tone through my teeth grinding together. "Don't call me that. I'm not here for you. I'm here for me, and I'm here for the siblings that I don't know, but I'm not here for you."

"I deserve that." He grabs a tissue from the nightstand and dabs it under his nose, then presses a button on the side of the bed that shuts off the TV. "I deserve that and more. I guess that's why I have cancer, right? Karma's a bitch."

Shit. We even think alike. There's something similar in this blood of ours then.

I sit in the chair that's settled next to the bed and see a vase of yellow, pink, and purple wildflowers with a card that says, "I love you— Stevie" sticking from the top of it.

"I'm still glad you came to see me. I have a lot to say," he gasps between words, pressing the oxygen mask over his mouth.

That part of me that's a dick thinks this is all just a show. He doesn't really need that mask to breathe. It's all a ruse. He is a professional conman, right? How am I supposed to believe this?

The evidence is staring at me in the face. He looks like shit. I rub my temples to get my thoughts together and try to ease the rage throbbing through every cell in my body.

"I know you have a lot of questions—"

"—No, not really. Not a lot. Just one." I hold up one finger. I lean against the back of the chair and get comfortable, widen the stance of my legs as I slouch. "Why?"

"Why," he repeats, nodding and clicking his tongue. "I've thought that every day ever since you held that gun to my head when you were sixteen."

"But not a moment before, right?"

He places the oxygen mask over his mouth again and the plastic fogs with every breath he takes. "Honestly? No," he admits. "I had gotten away with it for so long, I didn't think I'd get caught."

"You regret nothing? You just regret getting caught? Un-fucking-believable."

"That's not what I said." A nasty coughing spree takes over again. "I can't regret Carson, Stevie, or Brighton. I love them just like I love you."

"And Mom? What about her? You were fucking horrible to her."

"I regret that. Is... I don't have a right to ask, but is she better?"

"Much. Living a full and happy life." I leave out that I'm seeing her this Saturday. I don't want him to know.

"That's good. That's real good. She deserves that."

"She deserves everything, and I give it to her. Me. I became the man you couldn't be. I became the dependable one. I worked my ass off. I didn't finish high school because I had to get two jobs. I had to get my G.E.D. I provided. Me!" I hit my chest and sit forward.

"I took care of her when you didn't. I got her the help she needed. Now, she's a pottery instructor, doing what she loves. It pays surprisingly well, but I still take care of her so she can travel as much as she wants, so she can see the world how she wants because you took enough years from her. So don't you dare sit there and tell me what she deserves, because you don't know the first thing about what deserving means."

"I know."

"God, stop! Stop it!" I stand and smack the chair with my arm. "Stop being so... so..."

"Accepting?"

The air whooshes from my lungs as I place my hands on my hips. "Yeah, you're making the fighting pretty fucking hard to do."

"I don't want to fight, Amos. I'm too tired, and I've had many years to think about everything I've done, and I've tried to come up with an excuse, with a reason, and I don't have any. I wanted the best of both worlds. It was wrong, but I don't regret my kids, Amos. I don't. I can't."

I pluck one of the petals off of the flowers. It's soft and almost has a velvety surface to it. "I know. It's the one thing I can say about you. You loved us, but you were a shit husband.

And no matter your effort of being a good father, what you did made you a bad one."

"I know." His hand quakes when he reaches for the cup of water next to the flowers. "So you met Carson, Stevie, and Brighton? Carson is a lot like you. Tough. He doesn't take no shit."

"So I've noticed." I plop down the seat. "Stevie is nice."

"She's smart. The thinker of the bunch. And Brighton, well, he just turned sixteen so he's pretty moody, but shy."

"You sound proud of them." It hurts to say more than I want to admit. "You went back to Kansas when I kicked you out, didn't you?"

"I didn't know where else to go."

"And when did they find out? The truth, when did they know?"

"I've had lung cancer for years now. I've been in remission twice, but this time it isn't looking too promising. I told them when I was first diagnosed."

"Got to rid yourself of your sins before the sins take you, huh?" I scoff, not shocked in the least that that's what he would do.

"No, they deserved to know about you. I couldn't die knowing I didn't say a word about you. You're family."

"Why wait so long to tell the truth? Why not tell them sooner?"

"I didn't want to lose them too, but I figured I was losing them if I was dying anyway."

"—It's time for your daily medicine, Mr. Taylor. Oh! Look, you have a visitor. I'm his nurse, Ann." She's a plump woman, happy, and there is bright pink lipstick on her lips. She's a ray of sunshine. A dose I most desperately needed.

"Amos," I greet, putting our conversation on pause. It's time to end it anyway.

"I'll be out of your hair in a jiff." Her round fingers grip the small container the pills are in and gives them to Pops. "Toss and swallow," she tries to sound stern, and he follows her order. "Open." He opens his mouth to prove himself. "Good. Okay, I'll dash now," she giggles. "It's nice to meet you, Amos."

I catch her before she pushes the silver cart out of the room. "Hey, Ann. Where do I get tested to see if I'm a bone marrow match?"

"Oh my dear. Aren't you sweet? I'll grab a doctor, and he can send you to the right place." She closes the door, leaving me in a silent, awkward room with my Pops.

"You're really going to see if you're a match?"

"I'm not doing it for you," I say.

That's the bitch of it though.

I am doing it for him, and I hate myself a little for it.

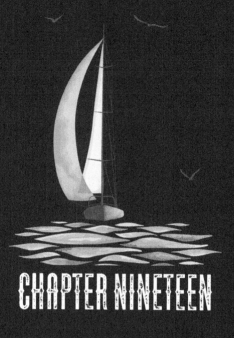

CHAPTER NINETEEN

Violet

"I'M FINE!" I SLAP AMOS'S HAND AWAY WHEN HE TRIES TO HELP me to the bathroom. "You are not going to keep helping me pee. I'm not helpless, damn it."

"I don't want you to hurt yourself, Springs. What if you fall or slip off the toilet and hit your head? Or your stitches in your leg—"

"My stitches dissolve. They are already dissolving. The glass stabbed me more than it slashed me, remember?" I hobble to the restroom, and he is right behind me. "Kansas!"

He inhales a sharp breath and stands in front of me, blocking my way to the toilet. "What did you just call

I roll my eyes and fold my arms over my chest. "I called you Kansas. Everyone does."

"You aren't everyone. You call me Amos. I like it when you call me Amos. It's like a pet name that's mine and mine alone."

"It's your name," I deadpan.

"A name that never gets used. The audacity," he scoffs, then twists the knob to open the door and bows, spreading his arm out. "Your toilet, my queen."

I narrow my eyes at him. "You are driving me nuts!" I limp into the bathroom and slam the door, locking it for good measure.

"Yeah? Well, when you slip off the toilet and piss yourself everywhere, don't come crying to me for help because I'm just going to say 'I told you so'!" he shouts from beyond the door.

I'm way too damn stubborn to say that. He should know better.

I love Amos.

So much.

So freaking much it hurts, but I've been home three weeks, and if it isn't him looking after me every second of every day, it's someone else. I need my space. I need to feel independent.

But this is the worst we have ever fought.

And it's hilarious.

I press my forehead against the door and laugh, and his deep chuckle from the other side has me unlocking and swinging the door open. He's standing there, shoulder against the frame, lifting those beautiful hazels at me through thick brown lashes. He has a crooked, mischievous smirk. He looks so sexy leaning like that.

Damn.

"I'm sorry I'm so grouchy."

He pulls the strings to my sweatpants and tugs me closer to him. My hands land on his chest and my eyes immediately fall to the sculpted lines I can see against the shirt.

"I'd be grouchy too if I were you. I bet you're all cramped up in here."

"I am. I'm going insane." I wrap my arms around his neck and stand on my good leg as I tilt to my tiptoe. "Can we get some fresh air and sit on the beach?" I rub my hands down his chest, and he grumbles, snatching my wrist between his index finger and thumb. I whimper, not from bruises or pain, but lust.

I've been wanting him for weeks, but he won't have sex with me because Pulse hasn't cleared me for sex.

"Will you behave?" he asks, kissing the tips of my fingers.

"Probably not."

"Then no," he grins.

"Kan—"

He silences his road name with a kiss. He presses me against the wall and hooks my good leg over his hip. "What did I tell you about calling me that?"

"I only do it to annoy you now," I giggle, my breath hitching when his thumb rubs over the flesh of my hip when my shirt rides up.

"You could never annoy me."

"I want you," I pant.

He proceeds to trace a few of the cuts from the glass around my neck. His brows furrow as his fingers dive down around the curve of my breasts until he is gliding them between them. "I want you too. I want you so bad."

"Then—"

"—I refuse to hurt you."

"You won't," I try to argue, but he backs away from me. "Amos?"

"Not until Pulse gives the go-ahead, Springs. It's your leg. I'm not going to risk busting those stitches and having you bleed to death because I want to give in and be twelve inches deep inside you." He strokes his erection through his gray sweatpants, and I can see every ridge, every vein, the crown of the thick head as it presses against the material. My mouth waters for a taste.

"Twelve inches would feel so good right about now," I say breathlessly.

He groans and slams the back of his fist against the wall behind him. "Damn it, no. No! You're getting into my head." He taps against his temple. "With your... fucking body and those lips. Christ. I need out of this room too."

"Amos—"

He grabs me by the shoulders, sliding his hands up and around my neck until his fingers are buried in my hair. "I love you and that is exactly why I am saying no. I want you more than my next breath, but I want you to live more. I want you to heal, and I want us to be able to move on with our lives, and it's already hard to do knowing the man that hit you and your sisters hasn't been caught yet. There's a lot on our plates, but you healing—" he tilts my head back and kisses my chin, "—you healing is the top priority, okay? He said another week. One more week and your clothes are off, that back is flat, those legs are spread, and I'm going to be so deep inside you, you'll feel me for an entire week after." He sucks my bottom lip into my mouth, tugs it down before letting it go softly. "How does that sound?"

"Why don't you feel for yourself?" I tempt him by insinuating how wet I am between my legs.

Which I most definitely am.

"You're trouble." He shakes a finger at me.

"Kansas! Church!" Arrow bellows from outside.

Always interrupted.

"I'll be right out," Amos shouts.

He sits down on the edge of the bed and holds out his arm, signaling me to come to him. I waddle over, dragging my injured leg behind me dramatically, and he laughs.

His smile is so damn gorgeous. I love seeing him happy.

I plop down on his lap, and his arm makes itself home around the dip of my waist like it always does.

"Make sure you—"

I exhale as I repeat his every word, "Make sure I lock the door and keep the gun next to me at all times. I know."

"Carson will be—"

"—Right outside. I know. I know." I flop down to the bed and crawl up it. I won't ever admit it to him, but it feels good to lie down. I might just take a nap because I'm already exhausted.

Not that I'd tell him that either.

Damn, I didn't even go to the bathroom. Ugh, there is nothing worse than getting comfortable and realizing you need to pee.

"I'm sorry it's like this, Springs." He gently tugs on one of my curls, then lets go like he always does to watch it bounce.

The section that had to get shaved is still pretty bare, and I surprisingly don't mind it. It makes me look edgy, when I'm far from it. Amos likes it too, so I might keep it, even after the cuts heal.

"It's okay. I guess if I had to be stuck within four walls, I'd want to be stuck within four walls with you."

He tucks the blanket under my chin and places the gun on the nightstand. "You have such a way with words."

"And you have such a way with weapons." I yawn, and my eyes begin to droop. "Hey, check on my sisters?" Veronica is doing much better than Victoria. Victoria is in a back brace, and she hates it. To a sixteen-year-old, being injured is a nightmare, but I'm thankful she's alive. That's all that matters.

"Always do, Springs. Get some rest."

"Mmmkay," I mumble as he shuts the door. After a minute he locks it for me, and I smile to myself. I always forget to lock the door even when he reminds me.

My leg throbs a bit, but it isn't anything I can't handle. Parts of me are still sore and achy from the accident. Every now and then I'll have a nightmare about it. Usually it ends with one of my sisters dying or both. Amos will hold me as I cry and then I'll fall right back asleep, safe and secure in his arms.

I shut my eyes and think about all the good things that have happened to try and make sure I have good dreams instead of bad ones. My sisters are safe, Amos got tested for a bone marrow transplant, and he is a match for his father. The type of cancer his father has doesn't always take bone marrow. The mortality rate is very high. This is kind of the last hurrah before nothing else works. There isn't a high positivity rate for this type of transplant to work with patients who have small cell lung cancer.

While his dad has been fighting for his life, he has gotten to know his siblings. It's been awkward a few times, but I can tell Amos is happy he decided to give them a chance. Plus, I really like Stevie. I think she and I could be close if the circumstances allow.

Oh, and I met his mom and she is so lovely. She came to see us, and she is the kindest soul. On top of all this, I have a dangerous Irish godfather who hasn't left Atlantic City and won't until we are all healed and the man who tried to kill me and my sisters is caught. He's scary, but he cares.

Yeah, bad things happened, but good things are happening too.

I'm lucky.

A wistful smile teases my lips as I get drowsier. My body feels light as sleep takes me. I'm in the in-between, where I'm half asleep but I'm aware of my surrounding, but as if they are a part of a dream.

The lock of the door clicks and the cool air sweeps in, rustling me a bit. Amos's footsteps are careful and quiet, so he doesn't wake me. So sweet.

Has the meeting ended already?

The bed dips, and he crawls up my body, straddling me. I keep my eyes closed, waiting to see what he will do next, and his fingers skid across my chest, touching me lightly. His lips are against my cheek and he inhales my hair like he always does.

"So sexy."

I snap my eyes open when I hear the unfamiliar voice. I open my mouth to scream, but a pillow is shoved over my face. I arch my body and try to fight him off, kicking and slapping his chest. I try to find his face blindly, but he keeps his head away from my reach.

The gun.

It's getting harder to breathe. My lungs burn, and my throat is raw from screaming. Tears are soaking the pillow smashed against my eyes, and I can feel the skin pulling along the stitches in my leg.

I will not die like this. Not after what I've survived.

My hand slaps against the nightstand for the gun, but it isn't there.

"You think he loves you?" The stranger applies more pressure against my face. "He will never love you. He belongs to me, you fucking whore."

My hand hits the lamp, and I curl my fingers around the post, lift it, and with all the strength I have left, I swing. It connects with his head, and he falls to the side. I throw the pillow off my face and take a big gulp of air. I roll off the bed and run to the door, but the intruder grabs my ankle.

I hit the ground hard, my jaw snapping against the floor. My teeth clink together, and he grips me by the hips to drag me back onto the bed.

While I'm able to, I scream as loud as I can until my lungs are wrung out. I lift my good leg and smash my heel against his face and scurry off the bed. I unlock the door and run outside, barefoot. The ice is freezing against my skin, causing goosebumps to rise.

"Amos! Amos!" in desperation and fear, I cry out his name.

"Not a chance." A hand covers my mouth, and he drags me off the porch, my knee smashing against the wood. "He loves me, you know. Me. Not you. It will always be me. You're nothing but a bed warmer."

He grips onto my hair, my sore scalp, and I try to scream again from the pain. I'm still sore from surgery.

"You were supposed to fucking die in the crash, bitch. And now I have to do it myself."

My feet hit the sand, and I still fight him the best I can, but I can't get my feet under me. Ice cold water hits my ankles, and it feels like knives digging into my flesh. He dunks my head in the water, keeping a firm grip on my shirt.

I can't see him through the water's surface. It's a blur. I'm blinded.

And I'm going to die.

It gets to the point that I have to open my mouth. My head is brimming with pressure, and I have to breathe in, but I know it won't be air. It will be water.

It's the body's natural reaction to survive.

I wait as long as I can and open my mouth. A rush of water invades my throat. The frozen tendrils wrap around my lungs, suffocating me.

Drowning me.

I'm losing my energy, my strength, and darkness starts to creep around my vision. My arms stop flailing, and I'm about to give in to the peaceful depths sweeping inside me.

This is it. After everything, this is how I die.

But then...

The pressure of his hands is suddenly gone, and I'm lifted out of the water. I cough, spurting up water as I try to breathe.

"That's it, you're okay. You're fine." Pulse turns my head to the side as I continue to spit up.

"You son of a bitch!" I hear Amos yell.

Pulse lifts me into his arms, and my teeth chatter together from the cold. "Let's get you inside."

"N—no," I shiver. "I want to know who it is."

I need to know who almost killed me.

The stranger slams against Amos, but Amos is bigger. He doesn't move. He swings another punch, knocking the guy off his feet.

"You're my brother!" Amos screams, wrapping his arms around the guy. Carson, maybe? I didn't get a good look at him. Amos throws him on the ground and stands over him, getting prepared to deliver the final blow.

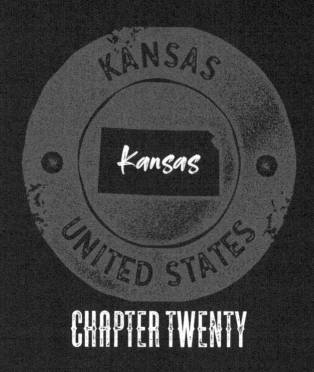

Kansas

UNITED STATES

CHAPTER TWENTY

W HEN I HEARD HER SCREAM FOR ME, I'VE NEVER MOVED SO FAST in my life.

By the time I got up, out the door, and ran to the end of the breezeway, she was underwater. She's been through too much to ever know fear again.

I kneel onto the sand and wrap my hands around his throat. This fucking hurts. It's a close second to what I felt when Violet was in her car accident.

"Why? Nigel, why would you do this to me?" The one person who I thought was my best friend, my brother before I knew I had any, has betrayed me. "I haven't seen you in years. This doesn't make sense."

He stops fighting me and his blue eyes collide with mine.

They are glassy, sad, but I don't see an ounce of regret in them. "You were mine," he says.

My brows shoot up to my hairline, hell past my hairline. I could not have heard him right.

"You were mine. We are meant to be together, Amos. It's been you and me from the start. I didn't know how to tell you, but I knew you felt the same. All those times growing up, all the time we spent together, all the looks we shared... I love you. I've loved you forever. I came back from my trip to see you, but saw you with her," he sneers.

I tighten my hand around his neck more and curl my lip. "I don't love you. I've never loved you like that, and I never will. I love her, and you were going to take her from me." I can't believe he is saying all this. I had no idea. He never made it seem he liked me in that way, and maybe that's because I'm straight, and I don't look at men, but for him to go to this extreme...

I can hardly comprehend it.

"I love you," he says again, a tear dripping from his eye as his hand falls to my cheek. "Can't you feel it?"

"No, Nigel. I—"

He smashes his lips against mine, and I rear back, but he clutches onto me. I'm not able to pull away. I do the only thing I can do.

I take the knife I always keep for backup in my cut pocket, flick it open, and slide it into his heart effortlessly. It's like butter as it enters, and he gasps, his hot breath against my lips. He looks down, then lifts his head to look up at me.

"I hate you," I sneer, slowly pushing the blade further into his chest, watching the blood drip from the wound. "She's my everything. She's mine. My love belongs to her. It has never, it will never, belong to you. You made a mistake going after her when you could have just talked to me."

He coughs clutching onto my shirt as he lies down against the sand, the frozen puffs of his breath are getting fewer and further between. His teeth are red, and he has the nerve to look betrayed by me.

"No one threatens her. No matter who it is—" my fingers press against his chest around the handle of the knife until it's flat against his chest, "—I will kill them. Always."

"Amos," he gasps.

"I really did love you, Nigel. I loved you like a brother," I admit to him as he struggles to breathe. "Now I hate you like the enemy." I yank the knife out, then slice it across his throat, watching waterfalls of blood cascade down his shirt.

He takes his last breath, a rush of air escaping him, and I'm left staring at the body of someone who used to be my best friend. I trusted him more than I've ever trusted anyone. I told him everything. Granted, the last few years we haven't talked as much due to what has been going on in my life, but that didn't make us distant.

We were the kind of friends that didn't have to talk every day. Life happened. Life got in the way. I never thought our friendship would come to an end like this. It's Nigel.

My best friend.

Who loved me.

Who was with me through thick and thin. Who helped me stand up to my dad. Who always knew how to make me laugh. How to cheer me up.

My brother.

I stand up and wipe the knife on my jeans before closing it and putting it in my pocket. Everyone's eyes are on me, but the only person I can look at is Violet. She's freezing as she holds onto Pulse.

She needs to be hanging onto me.

With a heavy heart, I drag my feet through the sand.

"What do you want me to do with him, Kansas?" Prez asks me as I stand in front of them.

"I got her," I say, not answering him just yet, and Pulse transfers her into my arms. She's freezing, and her teeth are clanking together like a broken engine. "You're okay. I'm never leaving your side again," I tell Violet, holding her so close, I know the pressure hurts. She doesn't complain. "And Prez?" I turn around before heading to my room. "I don't care what you do with his body. My care died when he tried to kill Violet. Feed him to the sharks."

"You got it, Kansas. Take a few days. You and Violet need to recuperate "

"Thanks, Prez. Let O'Crowely know that he's dead. The threat has been taken care of."

"You got it, Kansas," he nods.

I take five steps before he calls out my name again.

"Kansas?"

"Yeah?" I don't stop walking. Violet's cold, and the last thing I want to do is look back. Violet strokes my chest with her hand, trying to calm me. It isn't working. I feel like I'm about to burst out of my skin if I don't get inside and check her injuries.

"I'm sorry this happened. I know he was your friend."

"All friendships come to an end at some point, don't they?"

"No, not the good ones," he says.

"I'll come by later to check-in, but I don't think she'll be needing me. Her wounds are superficial," Pulse adds before I open my bedroom door.

Carson is standing there with his hands over his mouth. "Dude, I'm sorry. I had no idea. I got a text that told me you got a new number and didn't need me to watch her; I thought it was you. It won't happen again. I'm so fucking sorry."

"It's not your fault, but I do need to be alone with Violet. We will talk later, okay?"

"Violet, are you okay?" Carson steps forward and that's when I see that he has been crying. Fuck, he really does feel guilty.

"I'm fine. Just rea—really co-old," she trembles.

"Right, I'll go." He heads out the door, and right as he tries to shut it, I stop him.

"We will catch up later, Carson," I try to sound sure and that I want to see him later.

"Sure. Just rest. I'll take care of whatever Boomer wants me to." With that, he closes the door, finally leaving me and Violet alone.

"Springs," I choke, holding her close to my chest. I place her on the bed and start to undress her from her wet clothes. "I'm so sorry. I should have been here. I'm so fucking sorry." I strip off her pants and toss them on the floor, then rub my hands up her frozen flesh to check her wounds. I inspect her stitches, and while they seem red and irritated, they are okay.

"It isn't your fault. This would have happened anyway. He would have figured out a way."

I tug her shirt off next, and I don't see any new cuts or bruises, just the old ones from the car accident. The seatbelt line is still across her chest, finally fading from black and blue to gray and yellow. "What did he do to you in here? Did he—"

"—No, god no." She sits up and places her hand against my chest. "He tried to suffocate me with a pillow, but I smashed his head with a lamp. I tried to get to you."

I reach behind my head and yank my shirt off by the collar, then slip out of my sweatpants. I wrap my arms around her and pull her close. Her skin takes my breath away at first since it's so cold against mine, and I pinch my eyes shut, thinking how Nigel could have taken her from me.

Fucking Nigel.

I swing her into my arms and head toward the bathroom to get her in a nice hot shower.

"Are you okay? I know Nigel was your best friend, and he was in love with you."

I stare at her as I turn the shower on, and for some reason, I wait for her to laugh, but she doesn't. Her big violet eyes are tilted on the sides, concerned and full of sorrow for me.

"You're allowed to be sad. That was someone who you thought you could trust. You have years of memories."

I don't say a word. I think I'm still processing everything. I peel the shower curtain back and whisk her into my embrace again, then hold her tight against my chest under the steady flow of hot water.

She groans, tilting her head back into the stream. The tendons in her neck are protruding, and the divots of her collarbones seem so delicate at this angle.

"I don't want to think about him right now, because I don't know what to think," I finally say. "He was nothing like I thought he was. Just like my dad. He threatened to take everything from me, and I could never forgive that."

I lift her head up and hesitantly press our lips together.

I'm afraid I'll hurt her for some reason. That she will shatter in my arms, and what then? What would I do then?

"I just want to feel you," I whisper against her lips. I lift her injured leg over my hip so she isn't standing on it, my fingers digging into the side of her thigh, and her mouth drops open. "I need to feel you." I feel desperate, the urge to mark and claim, to make sure she is really here with me and is mine. I line my cock against her entrance and sink into her inch by inch, keeping my pace slow.

"Oh, Amos," she moans against my lips as I feel her.

I'm fucking trembling, from the outside in, my bones threaten to give out.

"I need to feel you," I say again, needing her to understand just how unhinged I am, how unstable seeing her in his hands made me.

I don't care about him like I should. I don't care that I killed him like I should. And I sure as fuck don't care that he said he loved me.

I want to erase his lips off mine and feel the ones that belong there instead.

Violet's tongue wraps around mine, and a whimper slips down my throat from her as I pull out to the tip. I thrust back in, flexing my hips and moaning from how good she fucking feels. I take my time, staying pushed to the hilt without moving. Stretching her, filling her, wanting to feel every goddamn second of her heat wrapped around me.

She's not shivering anymore.

As long as she has me, she'll never know anything but warmth.

"I fucking love you," I say almost painfully as I slide out again. I feel open, raw, and bare. I know she can see right through me, and yeah, I'm fucking scared.

I'll always be scared when it comes to her, because that's how this works. This is what love does. It fucks you up and puts you back together over and over again until the only thing that can hold your pieces, is the person that caused all the breakage.

She doesn't break me. I want to clarify.

The outside world threatens to break her, to break us, and that's what fucking hurts. The pain of living this life without her is unnatural now that I've had a taste of what the good life is.

"I love you too, Amos." Her hips rock against mine, and I take her slow like this, just like this, with the water dripping down our bodies and the steam in the air.

With broken, desperate breaths we cling onto one another as I fill the ache in my chest with her love, her touch, her presence.

She says everything is in Kansas, and she's wrong.

Violet is everything.

KANSAS

Kansas

UNITED STATES

EPILOGUE

"H EY, BROTHER," I GREET WOLF, WHO IS SITTING IN THE SAND staring out at the ocean. There's a nice fire going to keep us warm, and he has one of Arrow's juice boxes in his hand.

"Hey," he replies.

The greeting is short and dull. I don't plan on going anywhere. He hasn't talked to anyone, and I plan on him talking to me. It hurts like hell to see him like this. Out of everything, this might be the thing that fucking kills him.

Heartache.

It's a real bitch.

I peer over my shoulder to see my sister Stevie talking to Violet. They have plans to go get their nails done and whatever girly shit girls do. One-Eye and Carson will be going with them to keep an eye on them. Should be an easy enough job for the new prospect. All threats have been taken care of, so they should be okay.

I had to tell my Mom Nigel died in a hit-and-run accident overseas since Nigel always kept in touch with her by sending her postcards. She cried, but I didn't.

I knew his truth.

"Abigale would have loved it here," Wolf says out of the blue. "I sit out here, day after day, staring at the ocean, staring at the sunset, and I always go to reach for her hand," he scoffs at himself as if he is an idiot for doing that. "She's dead, and I still reach for her."

He shows me by picking up a clump of sand. "And all I'm left with is this. I tell myself she isn't here, but I swear to god, I feel her all around me, man," his voice breaks, and it has me getting a little choked up too. "She's here, and I can't see her. I can't touch her. I can't hear her voice. I'm just left with staring at the fucking waves she loved so much and the orange in the sky when the sun sets because it was her favorite color."

He turns his eyes to me, the whites of them brimming red with tears. "I love her, and I don't think I'll ever love like that again. I don't want to. She was beyond... everything."

"I'm so sorry, Wolf. Have you talked to Rayleen? Maybe talking to her will make things better."

"Nah, don't feel like talking to her. Don't feel like talking to anyone. I've been ignoring her calls."

"Don't do that. Don't push everyone away. We are here for you, Wolf. We aren't going anywhere."

"She wasn't supposed to go anywhere either, and now I'm left figuring out how to take my next breath." He stands up and throws the juice box into the fire pit. "I'm going to bed. I'll see you around, Kansas."

"I'm always here for you to talk, Wolf."

"I know." He shoves his hands in his pockets, hunches his shoulders, and vanishes to his room.

Stevie and Violet sit on either side of me. Violet holds my hand and leans against my shoulder. "How is he?" she asks.

"Not good. I'm worried about him," I admit, throwing a shell closer to where the waves crash onshore.

Violet is finally all healed up, and she's kept that side of her head shaved. She looks like a little badass. Until a bug flies around her, and then I'm there to save the day.

"We will keep an eye on him," Stevie says.

Falling into the big brother mode was easy when it came to my siblings. Once I let go of the anger, accepting them was one of the easiest things I ever did. They don't plan on going anywhere, even after Dad passes, which he will, because the bone marrow transplant didn't work. I'm still mad at him, and there is a part of me that will never forgive him, but it's been good talking to him in the last months of his life.

"Hey," Violet says, opening my arms wide while she wiggles between my legs. She rests the back of her head on my chest, and we stare out toward the sunset together. "Hold me?" she asks, reminding me of the first few encounters we had.

"You never have to ask, Springs." I wrap my arms around her and pull her close.

Holding is how it all started.

I fell in love with her with an embrace.

I'll make sure I die in one too.

KANSAS'S PLAYLIST

KANSAS CITY BY THE NEW BASEMENT TYPES

DUST IN THE WIND BY KANSAS

WICHITA FALLS BY HOUSTON MARCHMAN

OKLAHOMA SKY BY MIRANDA LAMBERT

TELL ME SOMETHING BAD ABOUT TULSA BY GEORGE STRAIT

HANG ME IN THE TULSA COUNTY STARS BY JOHN MORELAND

YOUR MAN BY JOSH TURNER

I WILL POSSESS YOUR HEART BY DEATH CAB FOR CUTIE

TAKE YOUR TIME BY SAM HUNT

CRY WOLF BY LUNA SHADOWS

ACKNOWLEDGEMENTS

Wow. It's been a year! Thank you to all the Ruthless Readers that have stuck by us on this crazy first run.

Give Me Books you've been with us since day 1. 365 days later and you're still there. We thank you for all you do.

To all the bloggers who reviewed and shared Kansas thank you.

I know I say it every time, but none of this would be possible without Wander and Andrey. Andrey and I shared a conversation where he said the universe would give back to us when we were discussing a donation we planned for Wander's birthday. What Andrey fails to see is, the universe gives back to us daily because we have them in our lives and that is right there is everything. Added bonus they share Donna and Jenny with us.

Donna you are the third in our threesome! Yes, there are four of us, but you get two for the price of one. #BOOMERISDONNAS

Stacey at Champagne Book Design you continue to one up yourself every time. We could not be happier the amazing job you do.

To my Instigator.............

Lynn, I know I've sucked these last two months, but thanks for having patience.

Carolina thank you for all your hard work.

The Harloe Rae I miss your face. Thanks for always being there for my thousand and one questions.

Mom #moretti.is.moms *Lynn here—Don't worry mom, Mateo and I will send you strawberries for your birthday.*

Jeff 5 LITTLE WORDS...*Still thinking of those sexy arms-The Instigator*

Austin as always y'all are such a blessing

Kay, where do we even start. You are a force to be reckoned with. Like, a category 5 hurricane, lmfao. We all drive each other crazy sometimes, but that is bound to happen with people that work as closely as we do. We still love you at the end of each and every single day. We wouldn't be where we are without you. Love you lots—Lynn and The Instigator

Viviana your squeeee moments are infectious. Thank you for being so extremely helpful and a great fit with our team.

Becca we're glad you took on a bigger role. You go the extra mile, and we appreciate it. It doesn't go unnoticed.

Bluenose we're so glad we were able to team up with you! You are awesome!

ALSO BY
K.L. SAVAGE

RUTHLESS KINGS MC™ LAS VEGAS

RUTHLESS KINGS MC™ ATLANTIC CITY

RUTHLESS KINGS MC™ BATON ROUGE

BOOK ONE — COWBOY

RUTHLESS KINGS MC™ NEW ORLEANS

BOOK ONE—POCUS

RUTHLESS HELLHOUNDS MC

BOOK ONE—MERCY

RUTHLESS ASYLUM

BOOK ONE—LUNATIC

BOOK TWO—CHAOTIC

BOOK THREE—EPATHIC

MORETTI SYNDICATE

BOOK ONE — MATEO

ROYAL BASTARDS MC PORTLAND OREGON

BOOK ONE —THRASHER

BOOK TWO —RAVEN

RUTHLESS INK

BOOK ONE—LUCIFER

RUTHLESS ASSASSINS

BOOK ONE—SAVAGE

RUTHLESS KINGS MC IS NOW ON AUDIBLE. ALREADY AN AUDIBLE SUBSCRIBER CLICK HERE TO LISTEN NOW. NON AUDIBLE SUBSCRIBERS CLICK HERE TO ENJOY A FREE MONTH NOW.

CLICK HERE TO JOIN RUTHLESS READERS AND GET THE LATEST UPDATES BEFORE ANYONE ELSE. OR SIMPLY SCAN THE QR CODE TO VISIT HTTPS:// AUTHORKLSAVAGE.COM OR STALK THEM AT THE LINKS BELOW.

FACEBOOK | INSTAGRAM | RUTHLESS READERS AMAZON | TWITTER | BOOKBUB | GOODREADS | PINTEREST | WEBSITE

Made in the USA
Columbia, SC
13 April 2021